WEST TOWARDS THE SUNSET

A Novel of the Pioneer Trail

By

Celia Hayes

Dedication and Appreciation

This fictional exploration of a wagon train journey from Ohio to California in the year 1846 is provided with affection and hope to young readers everywhere, in the hope that it may inspire them to read farther into our fascinating and unique American history.

It is dedicated also to my grandson, James Alexander-Page Hayden, in the hopes that he will grow to become all that is and was the best in my male characters.

I also extend my own thanks and appreciation to Allen Van Ness, to Chris, Denise and Lee for attentive beta reading of the initial draft and for their helpful suggestions.

Celia Hayes,
San Antonio, December 2024

Contents

Chapter 1 – My Name is Sarah

My name is Sarah Elizabeth Kettering, but most folk call me Sally. I was born in Mount Gilead, Marion County as it was then, in Ohio. Pa's family were English, from Kettering in Northampton, a long way back. Ma's folks were English, too – originally Quakers from the Welsh borderlands, long settled in Pennsylvania. We were distant kin through Ma's family to Mr. Webster the postmaster, who built the first cabin thereabouts. I had just turned twelve years old in the winter of 1845 when my father and mother decided that we should leave Ohio for California. Ma, Pa, my little brother Jonathan who was just six and I, all lived on our farm a piece distant from town, where my paternal grandfather, Reverend Josiah Kettering was the preacher at the Methodist church. We had other kinfolk living nearby; Aunt Rachel who was Pa's sister, and her husband Uncle Eb and their children, my cousins Matilda, David, and baby Ebenezer. Pa and Uncle Eb were farmers. The harvest was bad that year, and Pa said that being a farmer was almost like being a gambler, but more respectable, and maybe next year would be better.

But things didn't get better. A lot of people had got sick over that summer from the fevers, including my Grandmother Eliza Kettering, Pa's mother. Granny Eliza got sick, and just never got better. She went into a decline and died just as winter set in. This made our whole family particularly disheartened and sorrowful, especially since the harvest had been so bad. Many folk were taken sick that year from the ague and summer fevers, but most of them didn't die.

Granny Eliza had taught me to do fine embroidery, and I missed her something awful. She was about the only one who didn't get impatient with me for always asking questions about things. After the funeral, I couldn't stop crying over Granny Eliza being put in the cold ground, all lonely and cold herself, with the first winter snow coming down like feathers shaken out of the clouds and dusting all the Methodist burial grounds. Grandpa Reverend tried to comfort me.

"It's all right, Sarah Elizabeth," Grandpa Reverend stood tall, in his black coat, with newly fallen snow brushing his shoulders. He was the only one who ever called me by both my names. "She is now an angel in heaven. Your grandmother can look in on you any time she likes. Dry your eyes, child, and think of how happy she is now, being in Heaven."

What a thing to say, I thought – but I didn't say. Jon and I and our cousins didn't ever talk back to Grandpa Reverend, who was stern and tall and had huge knuckles and big ropey veins all over the back of his hands. When I was very little, I believed that Grandpa Reverend was a close friend of God, whom I pictured with a snowy-white beard and dressed in a long white robe, sitting in a golden throne on top of the hills behind Whetstone Creek. As I said, I was little when I believed that. What Grandpa Reverend told me didn't help none. I couldn't look in on Granny Eliza any time, or ask questions that she would patiently answer and so what was the use of saying that?

But things got even worse. Just before Christmas, my little cousin Matilda – we called her Matty -- she got real sick and in three days she was gone. Which shouldn't have surprised us, as she had been delicate from babyhood. Not like me; Pa always said that I was sturdy and stronger than I appeared, like one of those ponies they used to pull peddler's carts in that part of England where his family came from. But Matty was small for her age, with delicate bones and a complexion like a wax doll – she looked ever so much like a pretty doll in Mr. Trimble's general store, one of those with real hair and a ruffled silk dress. She looked like a doll, too, once Ma and Aunt Rachel's hired girl dressed Matty in her best dress and put her in her coffin.

Aunt Rachel cried and cried. She couldn't be comforted, until Uncle Eb went to Mr. Crane, who was the apothecary in Mount Gilead. Mr. Crane sent for a friend of his who kept a photographic studio in Marion, which was the next town over; this was a very newfangled invention at this time. Mr. Crane's friend brought his camera in a special wagon and set up to make a daguerreotype portrait of poor little Matty in her best dress, lying in her coffin with her eyes half open for her mother to treasure as a keepsake. They put off the funeral until this was done. Grandpa Reverend had some things to say about that, and the delay caused some talk, I tell you!

Aunt Rachel had that daguerreotype framed in a gold case with red velvet on the inside and treasured it more than anything else; she took to her room after Matty's funeral, and if it weren't for Ma and the hired girl, little David and baby Eb would have had a hard time of it for days.

I don't rightly know if it was Pa's notion to leave Ohio for California, or if it were Ma who first had the idea. All I do recollect was that one evening at supper, Pa sat back in his chair and said,

"Sue, you know I've been giving serious thought to selling up and going to California when the trail season opens this spring. Everyone says that California will fall into American hands soon anyways."

Ma looked at him with a thinking expression on her face; whether she agreed or not, she didn't want to be rushed altogether into saying anything impulsive. Finally, she answered,

"My cousin Angelina Morrison has letters from a friend who went there with her husband more than a year since – for her health. Cousin Angelina's friend is married to a doctor, and he would know. They say that the climate there is quite healthful. The weather is mild, and the soil is quite rich and suitable for almost every imaginable crop. I better like the thought of a place without summer agues and the winter grippe. Oregon territory would suit, almost as well, But the journey there is said to be very long and difficult, dangerous, even." Ma's father had been a doctor, too, Ma knew quite a lot about herbs, setting broken bones and curing sick folk. If she had been a boy, she might have been a doctor as well.

My brother Jon and I sat silent, but I had a thousand questions that I wanted to ask. Ma and Pa were sometimes indulgent about answering and explaining things to me – although never as patient as Granny Eliza had been. Grandpa Reverend had always insisted that children be seen and not heard ... and not seen much at that. Pa and Ma were not so strict with us as Grandpa was, but anyone could see that this was important, and a matter for the adults to talk over without children interrupting.

"We can't take much of this with us," Pa said, as if he were trying to break bad news gently. "There'll only be room in the wagon for necessary supplies."

Ma lifted her chin. "The children's lives are more important to me than earthly things, Elkanah – much more important. And ..." Ma looked even more determined. "I cannot abide the thought of a fair territory which our country might fall claim to, would be governed by a slave power."

You will gather from this that Ma was an abolitionist. All of us Ketterings were. Grandpa Reverend was particularly against slavery and often thundered so from the pulpit on a Sunday. There was considerable talk at the time of the danger of Ohio becoming a slave state, and most of our kin were powerfully set against that,

I can close my eyes and picture us all in our kitchen in the Ohio house, with the big patent cast iron stove, and red-checkered curtains over the glass window which looked out at Pa's big wheatfield beyond the farmyard, with the chicken house and the big barn, all covered with snow. Ma had blue and white china which had come all the way from England, and many pretty things in our household which she treasured. But I could see how Ma could be so settled in her mind regarding emigration, after so soon tending to little Matty, and recollecting how Aunt Rachel grieved so for her daughter. Ma would be imagining in her mind, if she lost me, or Jon to an untimely grave – and willing to risk that long, cruel, dangerous journey. It would take us far, as far as almost the other side of the world, away from everything comfortable and known, away from the dear and familiar.

But I was certain in my own mind that Ma already pictured a fine, healthy climate, free of pestilential fevers, even as Pa dreamed of rich soil, easy to plow and grow good crops. At that time, I was beginning to understand my parents' character: Pa so sociable and merry, a good friend to all; he was like the stream of water in the brook where it bubbled over rocks, the spray white and sparkling, with dragonflies with jewel-eyed and transparent wings flitting around the mist. Ma was quiet; grave and soft-spoken, with a tranquil reserve, flowing like deep water with barely a ripple on the surface to show how powerful the current was. In this, they were a perfect complement to each other.

I do not wish to be thought vain and boastful, but at that time Ma and Pa were said by all in Mount Gilead to be a handsome couple. Most folk spoke admiring of my Pa, Elkanah Kettering. He played the fiddle for country dances and did a bit of carpentering when he could spare the time from the farm. Ma was slender and dainty, with light yellow-brown hair the same color as beech leaves in fall. She wore her hair in the fashion of the time, a part down the center and combed back smoothly into a braided coil pinned into a knot on the back of her head. I often wished then that I looked like Ma, but I didn't; I resembled Pa, who was square and sturdy; rather short for a man, but with powerful shoulders. I had the same dark brown hair as Pa, but with auburn streaks in it, and blue eyes. It was my brother Jon who looked most like Ma, but when I lamented this once, Ma comforted me by saying that I would cut a fine figure as a woman when I was grown out of being childish and ungainly. She even said that I had beautiful hands, with long and slender fingers, and that anyway, noble character and a good mind were ornament enough for a woman, which made me feel somewhat better. Still, I did wish that I could have been pretty, like my cousin Matty. But then, Matty was dead, and I was alive.

Jon and I listened to Pa and Ma talk, as they discussed what was to be done; what could be sold or given away, and what we could take with us in a single wagon, which was what we had, then.

"Two more yoke of oxen," Pa ventured. "Perhaps three, in addition to Star and Brandy. We can better afford extra oxen than mules... they say that the wild Injuns out west are powerful fond of mules, and take every opportunity offered to make off with them." Star and Brandy were Pa's ox team, which he had trained from calves. They were as gentle and obedient as oxen could ever be.

Across the table from me, Jon's eyes got very big. It had been many years since Indians were a danger, here in Ohio. But he stayed quiet, until after Ma had sent us upstairs with a candle and a hot brick wrapped in an old sack to warm the bottom of the bed. We were to wash up and go to bed, in our little room tucked under the eaves, with a single dormer window already scribbled over with frost. The pale scribble of frost was outlined clear against the glow of moonlight behind the white clouds and the already-fallen snow blanketing everything.

I washed up as quick as I could. Leastways, I didn't have to break ice in the pitcher, but the water was cold and I could see my breath, before I blew out the candle and crawled into bed, under heavy quilts piled onto the little bed that we shared.

"Sally," my little brother ventured, as we cuddled together, pressing our feet against the hot brick. "Do you think Pa and Ma are really set on going to Californy?"

"I think Pa and Ma have already made up their minds," I answered, for I was certain in my own mind about this. The more that I thought on it, the better that I liked the idea. "I think it a fine idea, Jonny-cakes. *(Jonny-cakes was our pet-name for him, just as mine was Sugar-plum.)* And it will be an adventure, like one of Ma's novels. Besides." I added. "Ma and Pa will always look out for us."

That contended my brother; he was quiet then, and I think he soon fell asleep. I had my arms about him, and he curled close against me. I should say here that Jon and I were very close. When he was born, it was as if I had a real, living baby doll to care for. And of course, Ma being so busy with seeing to the care of the house, the gardens, and the chickens and all – I was the one who cared for Jon, although I was only six at that time. I held his hands and helped him to walk when he began toddling, sang to him, and comforted him when he was frightened and crying. When I grew up, and married, and had children myself – I always thought that Jon was almost my first baby. A stranger once asked Jon who his parents were – and he answered, "Ma-and-Pa-and-Sally!"

In any case I stayed awake, considering all the things that Pa and Ma had decided. Although I would be sad to leave Granny Eliza and Cousin Matty's graves, and all those places that we had come to love, dear and familiar. But I could see that the deaths that came from the summer fevers and the winter grippe gave so much sorrow and worry to Ma, and the bad harvests and the bank failures burdened Pa terribly. He was a good farmer; he took pride in plowing a straight furrow on land that he owned.

Pa's folk in the Old Country were tenant farmers. They hated that kind of servitude and had fought for Parliament back in the day. Grandpa Reverend's grandfather, Tobias

Kettering came away from Northamptonshire, serving an indenture for his passage to the Colonies. After he worked off his indenture, Great-great-grandfather Tobias swore on the family bible that he brought with him that he and his descendants would never again serve another man, lord, or king. So I knew at once that Pa was troubled in his mind at the prospect of being a landless man, even if that would only be for a time, until we could get to California and settle on fine land there.

Chapter 2 – Leaving Mount Gilead

Although Pa and Ma had high hopes for a better situation in California, it grieved me something sore when the last day came to leave the farm. I had lived there for all of my life, and Grandpa Reverend was one of the first settlers around Mount Gilead. The truth is that the prospect of taking to the trail did not seem quite real to Jon and I, until the very day that we finished packing the wagon with all of our traps and treasures, to stay at Grandpa Reverend's house for a week or so until we departed for Missouri and the beginning of the trail west. The new owner, a man named Roberts, wanted to move his own family into the place before he began spring ploughing. It was not quite time for us to head west, as snow was still on the ground and the weather still very cold. Pa said we would linger a week, maybe two, if it stormed bad. The journey from Ohio would take us at least six weeks to get to the jumping-off place, if the weather stayed fair and we didn't encounter any delays. We meant to go to Independence, on the great Missouri-Mississippi River, and join with other travelers to form a company to venture across what was then called the American desert.

"The grass has to have grown tall enough to feed the animals," Pa explained when I asked. To me, it made perfect sense. Our teams of oxen had to graze, all eight of them, and Daisy the milk cow which was to come with us on the journey. The snow wasn't anywhere near off the fields yet in Ohio, so it likely wasn't any better in Missouri – or across the river, where the trail led west.

Still, it was a wrench to leave the farm, and see our house emptied out of our things, the rooms echoing and comfortless, and to think that it was not ours any longer. All the furniture – and there wasn't much, as we were not rich folk – was sold or given away. Pa said cheerfully that he could always make more, as he was a fair hand at carpentering as long as there was good wood to be had. On the last afternoon, Pa found me in the barn, where our favorite barn cat, Cally *(for Calico)* had birthed another passel of kittens the week before. She had them in a nest of old horse blankets in the stall where we had kept harness and tack for the oxen.

They were beautiful kittens, and their eyes had just begun to open, all blue and wondering at that strange world around them. Cally was accustomed to Jon and I, so she let me hold the new kittens without raising a cat-ruckus. The largest was another calico, like their mother, but I liked best the orange kitten with four wee white paws and a white tip on a brief little snip of a tail. I thought that was the sweetest and best-tempered out of the litter. I was holding it in my lap, and letting it play with the end of a wheat-straw, when Pa found me. Boomer the hunting hound pattered after him, but he knew well enough not to pester Cally when she was nursing kittens. Boomer lay down on the old straw and rested his nose on his paws, while Pa asked Cally if she had caught any more mice that day, since mice were a plague in the wintertime, and came inside from the fields looking for warmth. Pa liked animals, and animals liked him, you see. There wasn't a better hand with oxen or horses in the whole of Marion County then.

"I should have asked for another dollar for the place, seeing that a new litter of barn cats are included in the sale," Pa said, finally.

"Pa, this one is so pretty," I held up the orange and white kitten. I was crying, all of a sudden, as if a ball of sadness suddenly unraveled inside me, like a skein of yarn. "Can't I keep just this one, and take it with us to California? Please, Pa?"

Pa heaved a sigh, shook his head, and sat down on the straw next to me, while Boomer pricked his ears up and looked back and forth between us, as if he were wondering about what we were saying. "We can't do that, Sugar-plum," he replied. "It's too little to be taken away from mama-cat. Besides, cats ain't really anything like dogs. See – cats; they're set on a place that they like. Oh, they'll tend to like the people in it, well enough – well, mostly. But it's the home-place they favor over anything. Not people so much. It's pert-near impossible to move a cat from a place that it's accustomed to. Now dogs," and Pa fondled Boomer's ears, "Dogs are different. Dogs favor the person they love over anything. Leave a house for someplace else, that dog will follow you to the end of creation. A cat will just yawn at you and wonder when that new person in the home place will give them some fresh milk. So, no, Sugar-plum. Leave the kitten with mama-cat. Besides,

I hear tell there's wolves out west, big hungry prairie wolves. A little kitten like this wouldn't last a minute, and you couldn't keep a cat in a cage all that way to California. Tell you what, though," and Pa ruffled Boomer's ears again. "I can promise you this; when we get to California, and get ourselves a nice farm there, and have a good house – then I'll get you a pretty orange kitten to keep for your very own. A pretty orange kitten with white feet, just like this one."

"Promise, Pa?" I had no notion of the likelihood of finding an orange kitten in California, or even if they had cats there at all. I knew practically nothing about the place, even from hearing Pa and Ma and our friends talking about it. But I had every reason to believe that Pa would find a way.

"Of course, Sugar-plum. Now, wipe your eyes and blow your nose. Don't I always keep my promises?" Pa fetched out a calico handkerchief from the front of his heavy roundabout jacket and handed it to me.

"You do, Pa," I gulped, still feeling tearful. Pa kissed my forehead and said,

"Now, say goodbye to Cally and her babies, and go find your Ma. She's packing up the last of those things that we're taking with us, and needs your help."

I walked through the house – from the kitchen, through the parlor, listening to the hollow sounds of my footsteps. I found Ma in the empty room where she and Pa had slept, folding the last of her good quilts into the small trunk. She stuffed a pair of good goose feather pillows into the top of the trunk. They didn't really fit, until she punched them down as if they were bread dough on the rise and looked up at the sound of my footsteps.

"Sally, come and sit on the lid, so that I can close this latch."

"Yes, Ma," I answered. I did so, and Ma snapped the latches closed.

"You look sad, like you've been crying," she said, and I nodded, still sitting on the trunk.

"It was ... I wanted to take one of Cally's kittens, and Pa told me why we couldn't and then I was so sad to think of leaving... I don't know why I felt like that, all of a sudden. It's such a long way, Ma. So far from Grandpa Reverend and Aunt Rachel ... even Granny Eliza in heaven, but her grave is here and..." I began to feel the tears coming on again, and Ma patted my cheek.

"It's all right, Sugar-plum," she said. "California is a very long way; indeed. So much farther than it was from Pennsylvania to here, when I was a little girl and my ma and pa decided to come to the Ohio country. I cried then too, about leaving my friends and all the kinfolk around Downingtown. Oh, it was a wild frontier when I was your age, even more than California might be. The wars with the Indians were just barely over, back then. But there was something new to see, every day. So many curious and marvelous sights, and so many strange people! My ma – your Granny Sarah that you are named for – she told me that I should always look ahead. I should think of it all as a wonderful adventure, like in the old storybooks. A new story, a new page, every single day."

"But what about Indians? And wild beasts – wolves and lions and such?" I asked. From what Jon and I had overheard the grownups talking, there were such dangerous things out along the long trail to California. Ma laughed.

"Oh, the stories that men do tell! I wouldn't pay them too much mind, Sally-child. Men will say such things to each other, boasting how brave they are for facing such perils! Besides," Ma added, "Your Pa will have his long hunting rifle, and I am certain that other men in our company will have such rifles and patent pistols as they have thought to bring with them. I am certain that they will be the equal of any wild beasts or Indians that we might encounter! Now, help me carry this out to the wagon. I do believe that Father Kettering will be expecting us in time for supper tonight at his house in town, and it has already gone past four..."

Ma and I carried the small trunk between us, until Pa came around from the barn with Jon, to help load it into the wagon, all hitched to three yoke of oxen, waiting in the farm yard. Daisy the milk cow and the two extra oxen had already gone to Uncle Eb's farm, to be pastured with his own cattle until the time came for us to depart. The sky was grey overhead, with a scent of snow in the cold air; spring seemed as if a faraway dream.

Pa lifted Jon up to the wagon seat, but I scrambled up by myself, up and over a wagon wheel nearly as tall as myself. Ma came up with a boost from Pa, and we all squeezed together on the wagon seat, huddled against the cold with a heavy blanket around our shoulders. Pa strode with his big stock whip in hand and gave a quiet command to the lead pair. The wagon lurched once, and then rolled steady, lurching as the wheels turned. Out of the farmyard, past the blank windows of our house, the house that wasn't ours any longer but belonged to Mr. Roberts, and onto the winter-rutted road that led to town.

I didn't look back. Ma had said, always to look ahead.

I should say something about our wagon, since it was to be a home for six months at least, as well as our means of traveling. Pa talked with such of his friends who knew of such matters. He exchanged our old light two-horse farm wagon and some other considerations for one which was slightly larger, with a back and front which sloped outwards like the prow of a boat in both directions. It sat high on the ground, on four heavy iron-bound wheels which were as tall as my chin when I had shoes on.

When Pa first brought that new wagon, telling us that it was the wagon that would take us all the way to California, he took Jon and I out to look at it, standing in the farmyard. He pointed out the wheels, the axles and running gear underneath the great square box of the body.

17

"Children – I thought this wagon was perfect for the journey – see the wheels, particularly? I thought them superior to every other wagon which I considered. The hubs are fine, well-seasoned elmwood and the spokes of good solid oak. The trail is long and very rough, in places, and the last thing we want is for our wagon to break down."

Eight beechwood hoops held up the wagon cover, which was sewn of heavy canvas made waterproof with linseed oil – the hoops on back and front flared out slightly. There was a seat on metal springs that sat on the front of the wagon, somewhat more comfortable to rest up on as the wheels bumped and jounced over ruts and stones in the road. The front and back of the wagon cover could be drawn tight, or loose, with an extra flap to cover up the round opening, keep out the dust or the rain.

The wagon itself had tall sides. Together with the hoops holding up the cover made it like a small room with an arched ceiling, nearly tall enough for Pa to stand in. But once the wagon was loaded with all that was said to be needful there was no room to stand. The one space which was not packed almost to the height of the cover was at the front, just behind the seat. A pair of big flat-topped trunks sat there, topped with some straw pallets and a featherbed. This was where Jon and I would sleep, once we set out. For themselves, Ma and Pa had a stout canvas wall tent to sleep in at night. We had a small patent tin stove, and a box full of tin plates and silverware, another box of Ma's kettles, a big frypan on legs and a covered iron Dutch oven. We had a fine maple rocking chair which Ma treasured since it had come with her family from Pennsylvania, and the parts to a cherrywood bedstead, stowed in the wagon. Ma also had her writing desk – an inlaid and brass-bound box of ebony-wood with a felt surface, and little spaces for paper, pens and ink bottles. Pa's precious patent steel-share plow was strapped to the back of the wagon, as he intended to take up farming again, when we reached California.

Most space in the wagon was taken up with supplies. There were but two or three places beyond Independence where one could buy more, but Pa had told us it would be better to bring everything we would need for ourselves to carry us through the journey, enough for six months or longer; so many barrels of flour and cornmeal, sugar, and a firkin of molasses, a box of coffee beans and a tin-lined box of China tea, another of hard tack, some fine smoked hams and cured sausages from our own smokehouse and another barrel of salt pork. A covered crock of fresh eggs packed in isinglass, a bushel bag of beans and another of rice. Pa said that he would rather purchase good quality from merchants which we knew and trusted, rather than strangers in Missouri. Of course, Ma had some crocks of pickles, jams, and dried fruit of her own preserving, all packed away in boxes or in crates padded with straw.

We had been all that late winter, packing and procuring those supplies we would need on the journey. We packed our few precious things as well – Pa's carpenter tools and his fiddle, Ma's sewing basket and the box of china dishes which had come from England. Jon had his wooden Noah's ark with the pairs of animals that Pa had whittled and painted in lifelike colors for him, all winter long when Jon was four years old, and I had my doll, Priscilla, with her rag body and china head, hands and feet. At the age of twelve, I wondered if I were almost too old to play with dolls, but I couldn't bear to think of leaving Priscilla behind, any more than Ma could countenance abandoning the maple rocking chair, or her fine English china dishes.

Grandpa Reverend came to meet us at the door of his house in town, just as the sun set.

"Welcome, Daughter Susan – I expected you some time past." He sounded disapproving; Grandpa Reverend was that way. I don't believe Ma sighed, but I think she wanted to.

"It took us a little longer than expected, to pack the last of our things, Father Kettering. I am sorry that we did not foresee this…"

Brief bands of yellow light lay across the thin snow, and then it was twilight. Pa unhitched the teams, and went away with the six oxen, leading them to one of Grandpa Reverend's neighbors, where they were going to be pastured for the time that we waited for the weather to lift.

Grandpa Reverend's house was a very fine one, but tall, joyless, and stern, much like Grandpa Reverend himself; a parlor and a dining room, many bedrooms upstairs, and a fine kitchen with a patent iron stove even larger and fancier than the one at the farm. There were lacy curtains at the tall windows, and stiff horsehair upholstered furniture in the parlor. Granny Eliza had kept a perfect house, but it now seemed emptier, desolate without her welcoming presence. Grandpa Reverend hired Widow Jesperson, a neighbor of his, to come in and clean and cook daily – but Widow Jesperson had her own house and children to care for, so it was not anything like the same as when Granny Eliza lived. The house still felt cold, and echoing, like a cave. My brother Jon and I felt Grandpa Reverend's dour judgement very heavily. He was a man with a countenance permanently set in lines of disapproval regarding any kind of light amusement or laughter. I had often wondered how Pa had come to be so different; cheery, generous, and kind-spoken to all. Perhaps it was Granny Eliza's influence, and now that she was gone, Grandpa Reverend's stern character had hardened.

The weather continued cold, dreary, and wretched. Our days only lightened in the evenings when Ma read to us by the light of the parlor fire. Grandpa Reverend usually withdrew to his own solitary room after supper, to write his sermon for the following Sunday. Jon and I were relieved of his forbidding presence and felt free to giggle and to ask questions of Ma and Pa, and for Pa to tell us again what he knew about California.

"There is never anything like winter that we know in Ohio," Pa said. It was Saturday. We had been at Grandpa Reverend's since Monday, and we were heartily tired of

Grandpa Reverend. It was not the same, a visit without Granny Eliza. "The winter there is soft and warm, and the grass is always green, or so write all those who have been there for certain. The Spanish friars established missions there and planted groves of orange and lemon trees."

Jon and I had never seen such a marvel as an orange tree then, although we knew of them – as we knew of other tropical fruits like pineapples. Indeed, the newel of the staircase in Grandpa Reverend's downstairs hall was carved in the shape of one. Ma said that in the English colony days, they were said to symbolize generous hospitality.

Jon's eyes got very big and round in the firelight, just as the tall-case clock in the parlor chimed out the hour of eight. "Pa," he asked, "Will we have oranges to eat every day in California?"

Pa laughed, and ruffled Jon's hair. "We might just do that, Jonny-Cakes," he replied. "We might at that ... but we must get there first. And it's bedtime for both you and Sugar-plum. And you both get a good night's rest, because the weather is clearing... clearing enough for us to leave the day after tomorrow."

I was glad hearing that. It seemed an interminable wait in Grandpa Reverend's house for those five days. I wanted to go, just go, since we had already left the farm, Cally, and her kittens, and said our goodbyes to everyone. Remaining in Mount Gilead now was just painful, as if everyone were just looking at us and thinking. '*Ain't you gone yet to California after talking so much about it? Why are you still hanging around?'*

Ma woke Jon and I early, that Monday morning – even earlier than we were accustomed to on the farm. It was still pitch dark outside, and we dressed hurriedly by light of a single candle, shivering in the cold room. We came downstairs to the kitchen, where Ma and Widow Jesperson had laid on a good hot breakfast; bacon and biscuits and porridge, scrambled eggs and ham chops, with plenty of fresh butter for the biscuits, honey and jam. The smell of fresh coffee filled the room. Jon and I each had a cup of fresh milk. Ma didn't hold with coffee for young-uns. Pa came into the kitchen, shaking rain off his hat, and saying,

"The storm is letting up and blowing east! The oxen are all hitched and ready – my, that smells good! Eat up, children – this may be the last meal cooked indoors that we may sit down at a table for, until we have a new house in California."

Pa looked happy, exuberant; I could tell somehow that he felt the same as I did. It was time for us to cut loose of Mount Gilead, get over the pain of leaving all that was dear and familiar. Ma seemed about as calm as always, and Jon looked as eager as did Pa, but Widow Jesperson sniffled and dabbed at her eyes with the corner of her apron.

"A turrible long way," she quavered. "And we won't never see you again, I'm bound! And all that dreadful desert and bandits and wild Indians! There ain't no good, Mr. Jesperson used to say, of going to all those foreign parts! Full of pirates and cannibals, an' all manner of heathens..."

"I'm certain that we will never be in any real danger, Mrs. Jesperson," Ma said, calmly. "Not with men like Mr. Kettering to protect us... and there will be other brave men with us, of course. I've been told that we will be part of a company of similar pilgrims. I cannot imagine that such men will allow any harm to come to us ... no, finish your breakfast, children – every bite."

"I'm finished, Ma." I finished the last bite of chop, as Jon swallowed his milk.

"Good," Ma sounded distracted. "Then run upstairs and wash your face ... your Pa will be champing at the bit to get started already. It's cold outside, and Father Kettering is waiting on us."

I didn't know what Grandpa Reverend could be waiting outside for unless it was to see the last of us as a disruptive influence in his cold and silent house. But Jon and I washed our faces and hands and put on our warmest winter things. Outside, Ma and Pa were waiting for us, the oxen stamping impatiently and breathing out clouds of mist into the cold spring air. It was just starting to be light in the east. To our surprise, there was a small crowd gathered around the wagon, dim-lit by hand-carried lanterns; Grandpa Reverend, Widow Jesperson, Aunt Rachel and Uncle Eb, a scattering of friends from Mount Gilead, to embrace and weep over all of us in turn, and finally Grandpa Reverend to raise his hands and bestow a benediction upon us, naming us all with our full names, which made me feel bashful and embarrassed. Finally, Grandpa Reverend intoned,

"May good fortune guide these, our precious children! May our Heavenly Father attend and bless their endeavor on this perilous journey. It is so written in the Good Book: '*For the Lord Thy God bringeth thee into a good land, a land of brooks of water. Of fountains and depths that spring out of the valleys and hills; a land of wheat, and barley and vines and fig trees and pomegranates; a land of olive oil and honey; a land wherein thou shalt eat bread without scarceness; thou shalt not lack anything in it.*'"

Well, that made California sound awful promising, although I had my doubts if they really had meant to be talking about California when I was pretty certain that the Bible folks meant the Promised Land of the Hebrews. But if it meant that Grandpa Reverend was done talking, this was all to the good. It seemed that he was; Grandpa Reverend gave Pa a hug, and Aunt Rachel began to cry over Ma, until Uncle Eb helped Ma climb up into the wagon and sit with Jon huddled between us. It was chilly, although the rain had blown off to the east, as Pa had said. Ma had thought to fill a brass foot warmer with hot coals and put it in the wagon. We were all bundled to our ears with mufflers, mittens, our thickest coats and Ma's heavy winter shawl wrapped around the three of us, so we were tolerably comfortable. Pa spoke to the lead team, the wagon lurched – and we were away, at last, with a bounce, creak and the wagon-top bellying like a sail, the oxen plodding steadily as if they had no particular interest and Boomer trotting at Pa's heels. The sky paled behind us in the east, and our friends and kin called a last farewell, as we turned our faces to the west.

Chapter 3 – Independence, Missouri

It was nearly a month of journeying, until we reached Independence, that town on the river that was the main jumping-off place for the trail to California and Oregon that year. Oh, my – what a wicked, wretched, muddy, and brawling place, full of loud voices and disreputable men, and even more disreputable women – women and men which Ma told Jon and me not to stare at. I had not realized until that day how Mount Gilead was such a quiet, solid place, as were all those many little towns that we had passed through on our way. Independence was as rowdy and noisy as a circus – only even rowdier because it was set in one place, so the wickedness congealed and turned solid. Gambling halls, and thirst parlors, merchants hawking their goods and auctioneers taking shouted bids for goods among the crowds in empty lots. Steamboats with slender chimneys leaking clouds of smoke from their fires crowded the landing places at the river's edge. The muddy streets were full of wagons and teams of critters, with herds of loose cattle, horses and mules roving everywhere, churning their dung into the mud, the smell of smoke and overflowing privies ... oh, it was strong enough to make your eyes water. Wagons of travelers like ours threaded through town, bound for a fitting camping place, someplace where there was grass, water, and space to park the wagon and set up a tent, with drovers shouting crossly at their teams.

Halfway into town, Pa finally said "Woah!" to the lead team, and whistled to Boomer, who was frisking back and forth, stiffing at every bit of garbage smeared into the mud. "Up into the wagon with you, dog!" Pa lifted Boomer up to the wagon box, where he sat warily at our feet, eyeing the crowd with ears pricked forward in curiosity. "I'm feared that he'll get lost or trampled on," Pa explained, and Ma nodded. Boomer was too well-trained to bark at other dogs, but Jon kept his hand through Boomer's collar, just in case.

There was so much to look at, as we picked our way slowly through town. It was midday. I had never seen a place so lively, not even on Election Day back in Mount Gilead. There were enormous wagons packed with goods pulled by four and five yoke, all bound for the Santa Fe trade, and strings of pack mules, strung with strings of jingling bells, and every kind of humanity there could be, save for maybe South Sea islanders wearing necklaces of shells and skirts woven of tropical leaves. The plank or brick-paved sidewalks – what there was of them – swarmed with all manner of folk; soldiers in Army blue, with tall, peaked caps and bright polished brass buttons, Mexicans in black velveteen suits with short jackets adorned with silver buttons, sober townsmen in plain suits and grizzled plainsmen wearing fringed buckskin like Indians, with caps of whole furred critters on their heads. Oh, and there were Indians, too – half-naked and bronzed brown from the sun, wrapped in red blankets, stalking through the streets, glancing warily from side to side. We couldn't help but stare at them; their heads shaved bald but for a top-knot adorned with beads and feathers hanging down.

"We can say for certain now that we have seen the elephant," Pa remarked, his hat at a jaunty angle as he smiled at us. "I can't think of anything much that we need to buy here ... let's go find us a place to wait until the grass has growed high enough and see if we can find some likely folk to travel along with."

So we did just that; there was another emigrant wagon that we followed out to the edge of Independence town. They seemed to know where they were bound. That wagon was driven by a tall man who somehow looked a bit foreign. A gangly fair-haired boy a little older than I walked with the tall man. We went to the north and east of town a little way, following the track along the river. We went a fair piece, before we came to a set of open meadows, dappled with trees just coming out in leaf, with wagons parked every which way, and tents set up between them, all among rough corrals made of rope tied to trees, or long poles set into the ground to contain oxen. A lot of oxen wandered free, though. It looked to me as if the ground had been pretty well trampled over.

"We'll look for a place farther out. Where there's plenty of fresh grazing," Pa called back to us, and Ma nodded. We had worked out setting up camp over the long weeks of traveling from Ohio. In a way, without the long hours of daily work of the farm, it was like a holiday, even for Pa. Not so much difference between walking alongside our lead ox team for long hours, and following a plow, hour after hour. At least this way, there was something different to see, around every bend of the road. I milked Daisy every morning, Jon gathered wood for Ma to set up a fire and cook a meal, Jon and I slept in the wagon every night, bundled against the late spring cold. Ma and Pa slept in the tent with Boomer guarding us all, sleeping underneath the wagon. That was the routine of our days. From what Pa had said, and Ma's friend Angeline Morrison had written about the experience of her friend on the trail, it would be pretty much the same, once we crossed the Missouri River. But there would not be other farms and villages; just empty wilderness, as far as the eye could see.

About late afternoon, Pa found us a good open space to set up camp. There were other wagons and critters grazing there, and Ma liked the look of the trees, all leafed out in fresh green. It was not crowded, but still near to other emigrant wagons and tents.

"I'll go around, and talk to other folk," Pa opined, once we had the oxen unhitched, and the tent set up. Boomer sat with his nose on his paw, watching us. He was a good guard dog; we never felt nervous, with Boomer guarding our camp. He followed us, though, when Jon and I went off to gather dry wood for a fire; dry sticks and lengths of wood that we could manage ourselves. I had a croker sack, and Jon a length of canvas, besides what I could gather up in my rough work apron. When Boomer suddenly growled at our backs, both Jon and I turned around to see.

"Allo," It was the boy from the other wagon that we had followed. He was taller than me, much taller, with a floppy foreign-looking peaked cap on his straw-fair head, and an empty sack of coarse-woven jute over his shoulder. "Are you for wood searching? I saw much, down closer to the river. The floods, I t'ink. My father said we should gather enough for several days." He hesitated, as if he was suddenly uncertain of himself. "My name is Heinrich. Henry. Henry Steitler."

"I'm Sally – Sarah Elizabeth Kettering," I said. "And this is my brother, Johanthan. And our dog, Boomer. He's friendly enough, if he sees that we like someone. We saw your wagon, in town. I guess you're emigrants, too."

"Indeed. Sally-Sarah," He took my hand, and bowed over it, in a very foreign way. I liked him right away. He had very blue eyes, the same as my poor dead Cousin Matty, back in Ohio. "My father and I, we are going to California."

"So are we," I replied. "Maybe we'll travel in the same company. Pa says," I confided, "That it's best to organize into companies and elect a leader. We haven't joined a company yet. Our Pa is going to talk to other emigrants, to see if there is one organized yet."

"An American custom," Henry observed. "That is a good thing, my father says."

"You talk funny," Jon remarked, "Are you from around here?" I was embarrassed, but Henry only laughed.

"My parents came from Dresden, in Saxony. It's a *köinig-reich*. A kingdom, you say. But the ruler is a grand duke. My father is an educated man and did not care for being ruled by a 'First' – by a noble. So my parents decided to leave Saxony and come to America. We lived in St. Louis, but my mama … she died of a fever." Henry looked momentarily sad, but he shrugged. "My father was then unhappy, and so he decided to try our fortunes in California. And you?"

"The same," I answered. "But it was my grandmother … and my cousin who died of fevers, back in Mount Gilead. That's in Ohio – we had a farm there. Ma and Pa decided that we could do better in California. You said there was more wood by the river? We may as well go there and gather it. I think we're going to be here for at least a couple of days. Until the grass grows tall enough, on the other side of the river."

So, we three, trailed by Boomer walked down to where the spring flood had thrown up all manner of wood; scraps and branches, some of it well above the water line and small enough for us to manage. Most of what we found was bleached and mostly dried enough to burn well. We could hardly see the far shore, the river was that wide, flat-flowing, and almost silver in the afternoon sun. We walked far along the bank, much excited at being able to gather so much wood. We stopped at one place where the river curved around a tall bank. We were nearly out of sight of the pale wagon-tops and the smudge of smoke from town. There were great shoals of broken bits of wood, cast up there – a wealth of firewood, free for the taking.

We set about gathering up the choicest, dryest pieces. While we did, a girl about my age, came along the riverbank mounted on a nimble and neat-footed pony. There was another much younger girl mounted double behind her. They both sat there on that pony, watching us for a few minutes, before the older girl slid out of the saddle, and tied the trailing reins to a handy branch, after lifting the younger girl down.

"You behave now, Billy!" she said to the pony, and then spoke to us. "Hi," she ventured, with a tentative smile. "Are you from the emigrant camp? So are we. That looks like a good lot of wood. I'll have to tell Baylis about it. That's our hired man. He's a bit lacking, I'm afraid – he couldn't find any wood worth burning this morning, when Father sent him to gather up enough. I'm Ginny. This is my little sister, Patty – and this is my horse, Billy."

Well, she seemed nice enough, even if she had something of a fine lady air about her: dark hair, piled in curls on her head, under her sunbonnet. Patty looked to be about Jon's age.

"Sally ... my brother Jon, and our friend Henry. Are your folks headed west, too?"

"That we are," Ginny replied. "Where are you from?"

That was something to talk about as we gathered wood. Ginny's folks were from Springfield in Illinois and were traveling with friends from there. They had brought their grandmother with them, as their father had fitted out a special wagon for the family to travel in, as well as purchasing the pony for Ginny to ride. She and Patty helped us gather so much wood that we could scarcely carry it all; we slung our sacks of wood over her pony's saddle and walked so that we girls could pick armfuls of purple bergamot, blue chicory, and wild yellow butterweed, which covered a whole meadow uphill from that place where we had gathered so much wood. I had never seen such flowers; white dogwood blooms on the bare branches of some trees, and shy purple violets growing in clumps where they were most sheltered from the sun. Henry and Jon exchanged expressions of mild exasperation yet waited patiently with Billy the pony while we gathered bouquets and bunches of fragrant blooms.

In all, it had been a very good day, we agreed. It turned out that our families were camped in the same general area, and Pa had been conferring with Henry's father, Mr. Manfred Steitler, and several other men, while we were out gathering firewood and flowers. Ginny said goodbye to us. She and her sister mounted double on Billy, and Henry went to their families, bearing the wealth of firewood and flowers with them.

We sat together at our own campfire, as the fire burned down to red coals, in a square hole that Pa had dug, so Ma could cook supper. This was how we set up our kitchen, all along the trail; Pa cleared out a square in the ground that Ma could set up the griddle, and tripod over. We could bake bread and biscuits in a covered iron Dutch oven set in the coals and simmer a stew in a pot hung from the tripod. The sun slid down in a smear of red in the western sky and turned the sliver of river that we could see to molten silver. Lanterns bloomed golden in the twilight, like the yellow butterweed flowers that we had gathered. Ma asked me to chop onions and potatoes for a stew. Boomer curled up under the wagon, and Pa lit his pipe from a twig held to the fire. Ma was slivering bits of salt bacon for the stew and adding them to a pot of broth already simmering.

"I had a good talk this afternoon ... a lot of fine, enterprising folk gathered here this season. Some bound for California, others for Oregon ... the usual traders for Santa Fe, too. They tell me that the trail is well-marked now, from previous seasons. No need to hire a guide."

"Still ... it would be better having the advice of someone who has been along the trail before," Ma observed, and Pa chuckled.

"Maybe ... having someone along to palaver with the Indians would be a handy thing, I suppose. But there's a fine trail guidebook put out just this last winter by a fellow named Hastings, who has made the journey and noted all needful. Mr. Steitler showed me his copy. Every crossing, landmark and camping place is listed along the way. Hastings has also found a fair way across the desert, so he says in his book, that will spare us considerable days on the journey. Most of the fellows I spoke with think there is no need for anything more."

"Still..." Ma didn't sound convinced, and Pa laughed comfortably. "Another day or two to rest the oxen and top up our supplies. That's all. The grass is well-enough grown to feed the critters; that's what the Santa Fe boys say. I think we should pull out soon. After all," he added with a more serious expression. "We must be over the mountains and into California by the time of the first snowfall, or risk being stuck in that last high pass. We can't lollygag around, Sue. We have to shift soon – get started on the trail. Root hog or die."

"Don't say that," Ma replied, and it was as if something made her shiver. Pa reached out and caught her hand in his.

"Don't fret, Sue – just an expression. Don't take any mind. But there is one thing that we need to remember always, once we cross the River. They tell me that the trail is perverse, in that the first thousand miles or so are easy. The country that we travel through at first is ... comfortable, level. Not a hill to be seen until we reach the coast of Nebraska. Oh, there are rivers to cross; no danger, with proper care taken and the water ain't running high. One might think the trail is a picnic that goes on for weeks and months under a summer sky. But just when we are most wearied and most worn from travel – that is when the country worsens. Desert, miles and miles of it. Far between clean water, grazing for the critters, our supplies decreasing by the day. Winter is drawing close. And then the mountains – steep and rocky. Hard. Rocky. Dangerous. Winter coming on, and all. Just when we need to take the most care, face up to the worst of the trail, is when we are the most wearied and desperate, near to the end of our rope." Pa looked around us, with a serious expression. "That's why I'd just as soon leave out early – by the end of this week. I'd sooner risk no good grazing for the critters for a few days and the rivers being high in the spring flow early in the trail, then deep snow in the mountains come autumn."

Ma looked down at her hands. "Elkanah, I do not like the thought of going against all the advice that we have heard," she said. "Everyone says that there is not grass enough ... not for another week at least."

Pa shook his head. "I'd rather take the risk now at the beginning, when we are well-rested and the oxen fat, then in six months when winter storms are brewing, and our supplies are low."

Ma was quiet for a long considering moment. Finally, she ventured, "Do you think that we made the right decision, even leaving Ohio?"

I held my breath, waiting for Pa's reply. For what if he agreed with Ma, and admitted that they had made the wrong choice? What would we do then? Turn back from the trail, and go back to Ohio? But we couldn't, of course. Pa had already sold the farm.

I needn't have worried; Pa answered firmly. "Of course we have, Sue. We're as good as already committed. Mr. Steitler and I have already agreed! There are some other wagon-owners who think the same. We'll cross over in four days and form up a company with anyone who wants to come along with us."

This is what we did – although I was sad enough to leave after making friends with Ginny and her little sister, and spending much of those three days with them. Their father was waiting on some other friends to join their party, friends who had not yet arrived in Independence. I had hoped that we could all travel together, but it was not to be. Or at least, not then. Ginny and I sewed a new little dress and petticoat for Patty's carved and jointed wooden doll from a lace-trimmed lawn handkerchief which had been stained beyond all a repair. Patty cherished that tiny doll, which she called Dolly.

"You couldn't think of a prettier name?" I asked Patty, and she shook her head, mulishly.

"No, she likes being called Dolly," Patty replied. "I tell her everything!"

Patty loved Dolly and took Dolly with her almost everywhere. I loved Jon very much, but I often envied Ginny for having a little sister like Patty. In the days that we camped outside of Independence, we became fast friends, spending every moment that we could in each other's company. Ginny was exactly my age, high-spirited and adventurous, eager for the adventure of the trail. Compared to her, other girls my age seemed tame and dull.

"She must be quite a handful for her poor mother!" Ma exclaimed, at least once. I think that she was; Ginny's mother suffered often from sick headaches, and her grandmother was all but blind. Ginny adored her father, even though he was really her stepfather.

"Papa married Ma about the time I grew out of being a lap-baby," Ginny explained. "I don't remember my own father – he died when I was born."

"That must have been sad for your ma," I said, and Ginny tossed her head, until her curls bounced.

"I guess it was – but Papa is the darlinginst father in the world, so it doesn't matter to me a bit."

It would have been very pleasant to have had her company along the way, since she had the pony, Billy, to ride. Her indulgent Papa intended to travel with several wagons, including one which was cunningly fitted out as a little house for them to travel in – with a tin stove in it and all, including a little staircase leading to a door along the side. Ginny's grandmother, Granny Keyes was traveling with their family. She was very old and blind, and the family wagon was for her comfort on the journey.

Before we departed Independence, Ma wrote letters to Grandpa Reverend, and to Aunt Rachel and all back in Mount Gilead to tell them that we had safely reached Missouri – and now we were embarked upon the long journey across the wild plains, desert and mountains. I bid a sad farewell to Ginny and her little sister Patty and promised that I would write to them when I could.

Mr. Steitler and Henry and their wagon, and Ma, Pa and Jon and I took ours, with our spare oxen and Daisy and Boomer, and bought deck passage on a steamboat headed to the other side of the river, around and down a long bend; a half-day of a journey on the river. It was the first time that we had ever been on a boat so big and powerful, on a river so wide and deep. The broad decks of the steamboat were packed tight with wagons, with their wagon tongues detached and stowed underneath the box. The wagons themselves lashed tight to the deck, and everything packed cheek by jowl. You couldn't have fit in another thing, there was such a crowd. The cattle were all led below; I do not think they liked it very much. Pa had to pay a more for passage than Mr. Steitler, as our wagon was bigger, and we had more oxen, and Daisy. The mighty steam engine made the wooden deck under our feet shake as if a mighty heart throbbed within the boat. The great paddle wheels turned and turned again, first slow as we pulled away from the landing, and then faster as it churned out into the middle of that great river, murky and brown from what had come down in the spring floods and spiked with dead branches and even entire whole trees. We stayed in our wagon, as the steamboat main deck was terribly crowded; no room for us to get down, with cargo and wagons packed onto the main deck, and anyway, we could see everything well enough from the wagon. We were away into the west, on the trail towards California at long last.

Chapter 4 – Into the Ocean of Grass

Even though Pa said that we were in advance of most of those wanting to take to the trail that spring, there were a fair number of wagons camped on the far side of the river. To be plain, the other side didn't look all that different from where we had camped outside Independence town. Just raw grassland prairie, broken with a few stands of trees, and a well-trampled trail, grooved with deep ruts where the trail to Santa Fe had been established so many years before. We had to go a long way out, before we found a good place to camp – so had all the other parties with wagons and oxen. It felt to Jon and I as if there was a whole village on the move, the white canvas wagon tops stark against the sky, glowing like Chinese lanterns after dark.

That first afternoon, after crossing the river, the men held a big meeting, about electing a captain, deciding on the rules for the company and setting watches for guarding the oxen at night. It was as big a to-do as Election Day had been, back in Mount Gilead. Ma and the other women were busy getting supper on, but Jon and Henry and I watched.

To our disappointment, Pa wasn't elected as captain, nor was Mr. Steitler, being a foreigner and all. That went to a big-talking man in a fine-cut blue cloth coat. He had a boney pink face and a puff of white hair like a hank of carded cotton scraped over his pink scalp and made the most long-winded speechifying that we had ever heard before. He talked about the dangers of the trail, and about how it was important that we be organized just like a militia company against those awful hazards ... and on, and on, and on, walloping us all with words and more words. He had a way of shouting, and then whispering which was really quite disconcerting. He gave out that he had been in the Army himself for a time, after graduating from Army cadet school at West Point. He was Major Persifore Clayton, from Kentucky.

For all his talk, he did sound like he knew about how to run things, so all the wagon owners – they were the ones who could vote in the company, being property owners, you see – voted him as company captain. Maybe it was just to make him stop talking, I think. One of the hired drovers standing at the back of the crowd with the women and children, and who couldn't vote because they didn't own a wagon, spat tobacco juice on the ground and remarked that Major Clayton was the biggest blowhard he had seen in a fair piece, and if words were hot air, the Major would just up and float away on the first brisk breeze.

Henry Steitler was standing with us, and he whispered, "What is blowhard, Sally-Sarah? I do not know that word."

"A big talker," I replied, and Henry nodded, in perfect comprehension.

"Ah. A *Sprücheklopfer* ... one who sells words by the yard."

That made me laugh, because I imagined Major Clayton measuring off yards and yards of important-sounding words, cutting a length with big steel shears, and folding them all up into a neat package, all the shouts and whispers packaged together. Because Major Clayton was getting up on a box and making another speech – mercifully a shorter one. It seems that they were going to elect some watch lieutenants and decide on the rules for the company ... and that was so boring that Jon and I gave up listening, and went to our wagon, where Ma was setting out the plates for our supper and looking impatiently towards where the men had gathered – still palavering. The sun was lowering down in the western sky, and it was time for supper. Ma had already lit the lantern which hung from the first wagon bow, the light of which would guide our steps after dark. We were hungry. So was Ma. I reckon everyone else was hungry as well. Knowing that we would start early in the morning was good enough reason for the meeting breaking up.

"Thank goodness," Ma said, when she spotted Pa walking towards our wagon, accompanied by Major Clayton. "Oh, for land sakes – the man is still talking! Well, I hope he will keep it brisk! The biscuits are already getting cold."

Pa was listening. I thought that he was trying to keep his face polite. I thought that I should tell him that supper was ready and we were hungry and when I went up to Pa to say politely that Ma was waiting on him to dish up supper, Pa gave me a conspirational look and said,

"Sally – this is Mr. Clayton, who is the captain of our traveling company now. This is my daughter, Sally." Major Clayton looked down at me.

"Pretty li'l gal, your daughter," he replied, and it looked as if his lips got sort of wet and slathery. "Pleased to meet you, Miss Sally," and he patted my cheek as if I was an infant. I stepped back, as I didn't like the familiarity. "I envy your family, seh. A nice-looking li'l gal, every bit a lady. You raised her right, Mr. Kettering. She'll be a fine wife for some fortunate fellow someday. Wisht it was me and I were a younger fellow…"

I did not relish that compliment – it seemed to me to be all wrong. Under the wagon, Boomer lifted his head, and I heard him growl softly. No, Boomer didn't like the man at all. Neither did I.

"Supper is on the table, Captain," Pa said. I had the feeling that Pa wasn't all that respectful of the company's leader. "And I wish you a good evening. We roll out at sunrise, which comes early enough."

"It sure does, Kettering," Major Clayton looked as if he would like to pat my cheek again, but that I had backed away a few steps. Instead, he looked down at Boomer, still under the wagon, warily watching us all and frowned. "Better do something 'bout that cur of yours. Undisciplined dogs are a dangerous quantity. I won't have that kind of trouble that those critters can create called down on this company."

I started to say that Boomer was a good dog, well-mannered and all, but Pa shot a warning look in my direction and nodded towards Major Clayton.

"I'll see that he behaves – good night, then."

Major Clayton looked towards our campfire, and Ma standing there with a stew ladle in one hand and a plate in the other. I wondered if he was hoping for an invitation to join us, but then he nodded and tipped his hat towards us and walked away.

I did see Ma pursing her lips. I don't think she liked Major Clayton any more than Boomer and I did, but I thought at the time it was just because he had made Pa late for supper, that first day out on the trail.

I think that if I live to be as old as Methuselah, I shall never forget that first day that we set out with the organized company, out in the wilderness west on the far side of the Mississippi. Now we were well and truly on our way, across the river and at the start of the trail – and such a clamor, such bustle and excitement there was on that morning! There were so many wagons in our company. Pa said there were a hundred and twenty-seven, although one of them wasn't a wagon at all, but a buggy drawn by a pair of fine Kentucky-bred mules for the wife of Mr. Jeptha Glennie who had two ordinary wagons besides the buggy. His wife was in a delicate condition. *(This meant that she would have a baby; that was the polite way to say so, Ma told me.)* Abigail Glennie couldn't endure the constant jolting of an ordinary wagon or be strong enough to walk as Ma and Jon and I expected to do, when the trail got rough.

"Lucky woman!" Ma exclaimed, when Pa told us this, and then she looked at Pa and added, "Oh, Elkanah – I meant no criticism of you! Only that she is fortunate indeed, not having to walk all the way to California!"

Pa grinned and held out his tin mug for Ma to fill it with coffee. We were having breakfast, seeing that we had time enough. We struck the tent and put almost everything back into the wagon even before breakfast was ready. Our own oxen were ready and yoked before sunrise, as they were all tame and well-trained. They were standing patiently, waiting for us to finish and stow away the last of our plates and kettles. From the sound of other voices in the dark, and the bellowing of unhappy oxen, others in the company were not so fortunate and timely that morning. "Don't fret yourself, Sue. I know I'm not a rich man. Our wagon and Shanks' mare are good enough for us. When we get to California and I become a rich man, I'll have you a buggy and a pair of matched bay horses to pull it, see if I don't!"

"Would you really, Pa!" Jon crowed and Pa tousled his head.

"I'm certain-sure I would. I've promised your sister a ginger kitten, and your Ma a fine buggy and team – so what would you like for yourself?"

Jon looked thoughtful. "I dunno, Pa – I'd have to think about it, some. Maybe by the time we get to California, I'd have thought on it some and made up my mind."

"You have a good long think, then, Jonny-cakes" Pa told him with a grin as from somewhere in camp, a bugle sounded, shrill and silvery. Pa took out his pocket watch and opened it to see the time. "Ten minutes, until we break camp, Sue. Cap'n Clayton wants to run this company right and tight, and just like the Army."

"Don't know why he must," Ma replied. "We aren't soldiers."

Pa put the watch away, gulped some coffee and poured the rest out into the fire, where it burnt and sizzled. "I reckon we can endure, if it gets us along the trail, all safe and sound. Finish your breakfast, children. We are about to really see the elephant!"

I reckon we did see the elephant that morning; and it was a more splendid and stirring sight than any traveling circus or patriotic parade imaginable! A clear silver bugle call rose in the morning air, and that was the signal for the start of the day's travel. A hundred and twenty-six – twenty-seven wagons, if you counted Mr. Jeptha Glennie's buggy for Mrs. Glennie – moving out from our campground, as the sun paled in the sky behind us, and then came over the horizon, sending our long shadows stretching through the grass before us. And such a beautiful grass that it was, bending and rippling in the light breeze, a grass as green as emerald satin! The loose cattle came behind the train, and such a cloud of dust rose up from our passing but the morning breeze blew the dust away. If I close my eyes, I can call up that memory, of the wagon-tops shaking like sails, as the wheels rolled over the rough trail. Each wagon had at least three yoke of oxen to pull them, while the drover walked by the leading team, commanding them by voice, or sometimes a tap of his whip-stock. Some wagons had four yoke hitched to them, if they were especially large and heavy-laden. This wasn't very much like most pictures you see, nowadays. In those days no one went overland with horse teams pulling a wagon. A good horse was expensive, and the trail so rough and broken and in many places no trail at all! Only oxen or maybe mules could hold up under the hardships of that journey. Teams of horses would shrivel up and die within days under such hard use for miles every day.

Ma and I rode in the wagon for a piece, while Jon walked by Pa and Boomer trailed them both. Jon was so excited and proud to be with Pa, as he drove our three yoke of oxen. Pa even let Jon carry his whip, while Boomer capered at their heels. The jolting of the wagon over last year's ruts and all those ruts left in the years before by the Santa Fe trains didn't bother us very much at first.

So many wagons! Major Clayton tried at first to have everyone travel in a straight line. He rode up and down along the line of wagons on a tall grey horse, like an impatient sheepdog pestering a flock of rebellious, wayward sheep. In spite of his efforts and his shouting, the wagons soon spread out to avoid the blowing dust from those ahead. It wasn't as if there were a known road; just wandering scars scored deeply into the grassy dips and hollows, straight tracks which pointed towards the west.

"In line, in line!" Major Clayton shouted at Mr. Steitler, whose wagon was next to ours, nearly side by side. Mr. Steitler merely shrugged and waved apologetically at Major Clayton and continued plodding by his team. I could see plain that Mr. Steitler didn't want to be breathing dust, or his oxen, either, not when there was no real reason to do so.

"I don't know why that man carries on so," Ma observed to me, after we had watched Major Clayton on his horse, trotting the length of our spread-out wagon. "I can't see that we're got to get there any sooner, whether the wagons are in a line or not."

"Maybe he's afraid someone will wander off and get lost," I ventured, and Ma laughed.

"No, I daresay he is a man who loves to show off his authority."

The sun rose higher and higher at our backs. In contravention of all that Major Clayton fumed and ordered, as he rode up and down, the wagons spread farther and farther out as the day wore on. Jon got tired and came back to ride in the wagon. Ma and I got tired of the constant jolting, and stiff from sitting on the hard wooden seat, so we climbed down to walk for a while. In the long weeks of traveling from Mount

Gilead, we had worked out the easiest means of getting up and down when the wagon was moving. We stepped onto the outside and top of a wheel-spoke as the wheel slowly turned and let it carry us up or down. Then we hopped down onto the ground or back into the wagon. It was a trick which had taken us a day or so to learn.

In the early afternoon, the company stopped in the journey for a brief cold meal and to allow the oxen and other team critters to rest in their yokes and harness. Major Clayton and the other men who had saddle horses staked them out on picket ropes. We were stopped by the side of a small creek, which soon became muddy and unwholesome from all the critters drinking and piddling. Before that happened, though, Ma had sent Jon and I to bring pails of fresh water.

When we returned with the full pails, Ma spread out a blanket on the new grass in the shade of our wagon. Over our heads, the sky was cloudless and such a pure blue as I had never seen, undimmed by wood smoke or clouds. We had cold cooked bacon left from breakfast and cold biscuits as well. But Ma unhooked the covered pail hanging from underneath the wagon tail next to the tar bucket, poured out fresh buttermilk for us and worked and washed the fresh-churned butter from the milking that I had done that very morning. We had that butter on the cold biscuits and lay on the blanket to rest in the shade for an hour and a bit.

"We have to make fifteen miles a day," Pa remarked, when Jon complained that he was so tired that his shins ached and his toes hurt. "Every day, no matter what the condition of the trail, if we want to be over the mountains into California by the time winter comes. This here is the easiest part, or so they tell me."

"What happens if we don't make fifteen miles," Jon asked, as if we hadn't heard Pa and the other men say this a hundred times already. "What if we make only seven or eight miles?"

Pa grinned. "Then the next day, we have to make up for it." His face sobered, and he added. "We must plan to travel that distance every single day. Like my great-grandfather used to say in his day – look after the pennies; then the shillings and pounds look after themselves."

"But we will rest for a day on Sunday," Ma observed. I think that she was as tired as Jon, but it was not Ma's way to complain. Pa chuckled.

"Aye, we did agree to all that, after much discussion – to rest one day, as the Lord commands. However, that depends on how we have made tracks the previous six days and if we have arrived at a camp in a hospitable place, with plenty of water and grass for the critters."

From the other side of the sprawling camp of wagons, the silver notes of Major Clayton's bugle winged five or six notes into the clear spring air, and Ma sighed.

"I do declare that I will get tired to death of the sound of that thing," she observed, as she climbed to her feet. "Shoo ... I need to fold up this blanket and put it back into the wagon. The man clings to that bugle like a baby with a favorite toy."

"We'll all likely to get tired of it, Sue," Pa agreed. "Before the end of the trail. But it contents the man to play with his toy, so I reckon that we can put up with it. Especially if he leads us to California without any mishaps."

Ma and I tidied up what little was left from our meal and readied ourselves for the rest of that days' journey, which was rather like the first half of that day, only that we were tired, even after the rest at noon. The sun slid down, lower and lower in the sky, shining into our eyes, reaching past the brim of my calico bonnet. Jon leaned against me at first, and then slumped down fast asleep with his head in my lap; he was that tired.

Late that afternoon, Major Clayton and the mounted outriders rode ahead, scouting for a place where the company could set up camp for the night; a place where there would be plenty of water and grass for the critters. And as Major Clayton told Pa as he passed by our wagon, and when he thought that Ma and Jon and I weren't listening – a place he told Pa that would be easily defensible against the Indians.

"Little do I think those wretched savages would dare attack so large a company or so close to civilization," Major Clayton added. I suppose he meant to sound reassuring. But he didn't look very pleased as he glanced at Boomer trailing at Pa's heels. "But good habits established at the start of a campaign will serve us all well, don't you agree, Kettering?"

"I agree," Pa nodded.

Major Clayton put spurs to his horse, adding over his shoulder as he trotted away, "Ensure that wretched cur doesn't pester the cattle tonight!"

I did note that Ma frowned after Major Clayton's blue-coated back as he rode away. Pa looked over his shoulder, smiling at us.

"Only a bit more, Sue! We've done well for today – a good start to a good journey!"

"Why did he say that about Boomer?" I asked, mildly indignant. Boomer was an obedient, well-trained dog. He had never even chased the chickens in our farmyard, back in Ohio, let alone harassed the oxen.

"I believe the silly man has a strong dislike of dogs," Ma replied with a disapproving sniff. "Which makes no sense to me at all. What do you think we would do without a good watchdog like Boomer? Especially all the way out here in the howling wilderness, with the Lord knows how many hostile Indians and dangerous critters out there, roaming about. We sleep safe in our beds at night because of Boomer!"

Of course, I agreed with Ma. Boomer had been with us since Jon was just out of swaddling clothes, staggering about the house on uncertain tender feet, and Boomer was just a half-grown puppy. Many was the time that I had found my little brother and Boomer curled up together, sleeping sound on the rag-rug before the stove in the parlor back in Mount Gilead, utterly exhausted after a morning of romping together.

Oh, but we were weary, that first day, as we set up camp! The last of the sun faded in a blaze of orange, among purple clouds edged in fleeting gold, before we finished setting up. Major Clayton and the outriders had found a good camping place for the night. They marked out a wide circle in the prairie with four long poles at each quadrant, to the end of which was tied a length of bright rag. All the wagons drew together in a loose circle, and the men unharnessed the oxen and mules. They chained each wagon tongue to the wagon ahead, to make a secure corral for horses and mules. Everyone said that Indians couldn't resist the temptation to steal those critters. Being valuable, our horses and mules were kept secure at night. Pa said it was right ungodly to put temptation in the way of men who couldn't resist the urge to sin. The oxen and milk cows were considered tame enough to graze on their own, although there would be a constant watch kept throughout the night.

Pa had slung a length of canvas under the wagon, into which he had told us to throw such lengths of dry wood as we had encountered as we walked beside the wagon all that day – so that we would have enough for an evening fire to light the night, and for Ma to cook supper for us. The other women, and the bachelor travelers did the same, I reckoned, or men went to cut firewood from such trees as there were close to that camp. Not many as one might have thought, for trees were few and scattered far between. I could see that might be a problem for us, eventually, with so many wagon parties following the trail in season and cutting wood as they went. We set our fires outside the circle of wagons, and Jon and I helped Pa set up the tent. Ma lit our kerosene lantern and hung it from the first wagon bow, and it shed a homelike yellow glow over us.

All around us was our camp; glowing lanterns and wagon-tops, and fires spitting golden sparks into the sky. The stars hung silver-white in the dark-velvet sky, the Milkey Way laying across it like a twisting pale scarf of fainter stars. The stars had never seemed to burn as brightly, or the sky so big, back in Ohio. I had never before seen the sky so huge overhead, so richly hung with stars. It made me feel tiny, a mere speck of human dust in a vast universe, sitting with my tin plate in my lap, leaning against the wheel of our wagon, listening to the tired voices within our camp, the noises that the horses and mules made, as they grazed and settled down for a restless night. Across our camp, someone was playing a concertina hand-organ – sounding so merry, and defiant against the darkness. There was the rattle of tin plates, as women of other families cooked supper, and the men and children ate with good appetite after the hard haul of that first day. A baby cried crossly for some few minutes, and a woman sang softly to it until the crying diminished. I looked up into the dark sky, sequin-sprinkled with stars, and they seemed to grow and twinkle every more brightly, until I felt as if I was falling into the sky, floating among their silver glow ... and then Ma was taking the plate from my hand and saying,

"Sugar-plum, you're falling asleep where you sit. Wash up, you and your brother, and get to bed. And make sure that Jon washes behind his ears ... if he doesn't take care, he can start growing radishes there in the dirt behind them."

"Yes ma'am," I said, even as I yawned. Jon and I washed briefly in a bucket of water that Pa had fetched from the creek, and I drew my nightgown on over my shift ... oh, I was tired to the bone, that first day. I do believe that Jon and I were asleep even before we drew up the quilt over ourselves, safe in our bed in the wagon. Maybe Ma climbed up to make certain that we were warm, curled together under the canvas wagon cover. I was briefly aware of the comforting sound of Ma and Pa talking to each other, but I was soon soundly asleep, wearied beyond all awareness. I do not think that anything short of the Second Coming, with thunderous trumpets, ringing bells and choruses of angels could have wakened either of us, that first night on the trail west.

That first day set the pattern for the days following; rising while the sky was still dark, save for a pale apricot flush in the east, a hasty breakfast over a fire newly refreshed, the smell of coffee drifting on the fitful morning breeze. Rounding up the team animals and harnessing them to the wagon, striking the tent and packing everything away, leaving just patches of flattened grass and piles of quenched black charcoal and burnt wood ends where the tents and our cookfires had been. Walking beside the wagon when the bumping and rattling got to be too much to endure, while the sun climbed slowly up towards noon in a faultlessly blue sky lightly spotted with clouds that floated, silver-edged like puffs of dandelion fluff. A stop at noon, or when the Major's bugle directed, for a cold meal and a rest ... then to move on, while the sun slid down in the west, before our eyes ... walking through knee-high rustling grass with my brother's hand in mine and Boomer trailing our footsteps, with grasshoppers and other flying insects starting up out of the grass, their wings gossamer-transparent and glittering in the sun. As evening dimmed the sky, the wagon company drew into the circle-corral for the night, and men shepherded the oxen to graze in that grass which seemed to grow as thick as plush velvet, whispering as the wind stirred through it ... oh, those were rare days, rare days indeed!

We made friends with a few other emigrants in the company as we journeyed farther and farther along the well-trodden trail. At first I could find no girls anywhere near close to my age in the company, as large as it was, and with as many wagons. There were just a handful of women and children among them; most were men and older boys. The company was so large at first that we did not know many well enough to talk to. I wish that Ginny's family had set out with our party, instead of waiting for their friends to join up. She would have been good company for me. As it was, the only other girl anywhere close to my age among the Clayton company travelers was a whole two years older; Shivaun McCarty. She was traveling with her married older sister and looking after her sister's three boys. Their name was Herlihy; Mr. Donal Herlihy was a blacksmith, a big red-headed Irishman, with the broadest shoulders that I ever saw on any man who wasn't a circus strong man. His wife, Shivaun's sister, was named Mayve. They traveled with a pair of smallish wagons; one for supplies and the other for Mr. Herlihy's forge tools. Mr. Herlihy's two unmarried younger brothers. Darragh and Seamus also traveled with them. Darragh and Seamus were smaller editions of their brother.

Jon and I saw them on the third or fourth day, walking by Mr. Herlihy's wagons; a tall girl holding the hands of two small boys, and a third boy about the age of Jon, frolicking with a pair of dogs. The dogs were larger than Boomer; big white hounds with black spots. All three boys had bright red hair, almost the color of a shiny new copper penny.

"You had best not let Major Clayton see those dogs running loose!" I said, as Jon and I caught up to the three boys and the taller girl. She turned around and smiled at me, as we matched our pace. She was pretty, in a way that I envied whole-heartedly; ink-black hair, and of so fair a complexion, it was as if she were a princess in one of the old tales. Her eyes were a deep, dark blue and alive with intelligence and good humor.

"Oh, that bitty wee man w' a big voice and a bigger opinion of himself? Och, we know well his like and kind – and he will have no' to say about Macha and Lugh! Herlihy himself has already sent him off with a flea in his ear, when he complained of them..."

"He didn't like our dog either," I said, feeling as if we had found a kindred spirit, even if she wasn't as instantly likable as Ginny Reed. "I'm Sally Kettering, and this is my brother Jon. Are you going to California, too?"

"Aye," she nodded at me, with a merry smile, as Jon and I fell into stride with her, and the boys. "I'm Shivaun McCarty, and these are my sister Mayve's lads; Wee Donal, Liam, and Rory. It's a powerful long way, is it not? They say it's all dangerous enough, but not after what we have already endured, on the way from Ireland! I do not think my sister and her man care any, for they say it is just idle chitter-chatter, of men boasting and hoping to impress each other with how brave they are."

"My father's a farmer," I said. "He says that the land in California is rich and temperate, and my mother likes what she has heard – that it is healthful, without summer fevers and all."

Shivaun hooted with laughter. "Himself – Mr. Herlihy, that is – he heard a tale of an old man living there who finally wished finally to die, so he left, and did indeed die ... but when his family returned him to bury there, he came back to life, again! He's a grand one for stories, Himself is. As it is, my sister thinks more of California for being respectful of the Church. She thinks the world of a place where the true faith is not something to creep about in the hedges."

Well, that took me back a bit, for Grandpa Reverend was given to denouncing Catholics something awful. Mariolatry, simony, the perversion of the true faith and something to do with an immoral woman of Babylon ... Honestly, sometimes Grandpa Reverend was hard to follow when he went off on one of his sermons. He had plenty to say about Mormons, too. But Ma had quietly told us that there were many paths towards God, and who were we to judge which was the right path for anyone else? What mattered was to walk the path of righteousness as we saw it and not to go about harming anyone else in doing so. *Ma would want us to be friendly to Shivaun and her family,* I decided.

Besides, it wasn't like I had anything like a choice. Shivaun seemed nice enough, and Jon and Wee Donal, the oldest Herlihy boy already looked to have made good friends with each other.

Another fast friend in the company was one that Pa had already made; Mr. Steitler and his son, Henry. I have already described Henry, but not said much about his father. Mr. Manfred Steitler was a tall and rather gangly man, already a little bit bald about his head, and sometimes I think a little absent-minded; a bookkeeper by trade, but well able to turn his hand to almost any task that needed doing. He had a box of books in his wagon, and he and Pa both loved music. Mr. Steitler played the flute, a pretty shiny-silver thing, although Mr. Steitler did laugh and confessed that he really played quite badly. It was more for the love of music that he played. He kept a little sketchbook with him; the pages filled with little drawings of flowers and trees and the like. The prettiest ones were done in watercolor.

Ma liked him because some of those books were about medicinal plants and things. It seemed that Mr. Steitler had been a scholar of botany and geology back in Germany. He knew a lot about plants and rocks and such, only that he had quit his course of studies partway through. He had once meant to become a professor of what he called 'natural science'. Pa once asked him why he did that, and Mr. Steitler just laughed and said that it was because he was opposed to the nobility and the rulers, and he preferred to come to America with his wife and baby son, since we were free of the 'firsts' and royalty. Only Mrs. Steitler died, and that was why he and Henry were taking to the trail.

I liked Mr. Steitler, myself. He spoke to me as if I were a grown-up, and not a silly girl-child. Eventually, he and Henry would put their wagon next to ours of an evening, and we would share the same cookfire. It saved on the gathering of wood … and other things, you see. Henry became one of Jon's favorite people, even a playmate, although he was so much older than my brother and had responsibilities of his own. Henry helped his father with their wagon and took his turn standing guard at night. Farther along the trail, Henry Steitler rode as an advance scout and helped to round up cattle which had strayed at night, since he was near enough grown to be trusted with the responsibility. But Henry also played boy-games with Jon and his friends, Wee Donal, Liam and Rory Herlihy, and soon began teaching Jon to whittle. I liked Henry nearly as much as I liked his father; he was a bit overgrown in height, and somewhat clumsy with it, but he was otherwise quite handsome, and I thought that he had a very nice smile.

There were some other Germans in the company, I should mention; five young men, the youngest no older than Henry Steitler. They were traveling in a body, all five. Hansel owned the wagon, Fritzi owned two of the three yoke of oxen who pulled it, Oscar owned the other yoke, and Rickard and Norbert had put up all their own savings to purchase supplies for the trail for them all. They were rowdy, and friendly, and among themselves often raised quarrelsome voices. Sometimes they appealed to Mr. Steitler to decide whatever dispute they had among themselves. Eventually, I could tell them apart and remember their names. As our journey progressed, all the German boys, the Pierson lads and the younger Taylor brothers made cow-eyes at Shivaun McCarty, as the only girl of marriageable age in the party.

Of course, Miss Pierson was also a spinster and unmarried, but the younger men probably didn't want to risk getting rapped on the knuckles, as Miss Pierson was a schoolteacher, back in Pennsylvania.

Chapter 5 – Breaking the Company

As it turned out, we had to endure Major Clayton and his bugle for the space of a single week. During that week Jon and I paid as little mind to it and his orders as company captain as we needed to ... which was, not at all. Pa had to pay attention, seeing that he was one of the elected lieutenants, and responsible for setting the watch at night over the cattle. This was almost the first matter considered at the organizing meeting, after electing a company captain. Pa took his turn at cattle-guarding in the night, but Major Clayton, his assistant captain, and the half-dozen other lieutenants had somehow gotten themselves exempted from the duty of standing regular watches at night. This was considerable cause for resentment among those so detailed. The other matter was traveling on a Sunday, which the Major insisted that we must do. Pa and Mr. Herlihy the blacksmith and several others objected to not having a day of rest. No, Major Clayton insisted that we travel on that day. As we approached the rough signpost on the trampled road which pointed one way towards the Santa Fe trail and the other direction towards the long, lonely trail towards California and Oregon, those resentments boiled over like a simmering kettle spitting hot water into the fire.

It was the matter of dogs in the company which set it off, only two days after everyone got over the upset about having to travel on Sunday. It was clear from the start that Major Clayton didn't like dogs, and grumped and grumbled at those of us who had brought them. Even the German boys had a half-grown pup of no particular breed, which they played with of an evening, after romping along after their wagon during the day. They treated it with indulgent affection. I think it had attached itself to them when they passed through Independence. Anyway, this happened on the sixth day after electing Major Clayton as captain and leader that the company first fractured. I have been told since then that as the Clayton company wagon train first organized for the trail to California, it was too large, too unwieldy. Too many people and wagons to camp comfortably at one place, too many cattle on the grazing ground eating the grass down to the roots, too many people cutting down the few trees ... and way too many opportunities for folk to quarrel.

Late in mid-morning that day, we heard an almighty ruckus some way ahead of us. It was almost time for the noon halt; Jon and I were beginning to wonder how much farther we would need go until then. We were walking with Ma, next to Pa and the oxen, with Boomer trailing at our heels as usual. The train spread out, from side to side, and from leaders a considerable distance in the lead, down to the last and slowest wagon, just ahead of the herd of loose cattle. Suddenly several men shouting angrily, a woman screaming, and several oxen bellowing in a way that didn't sound usual. The noise came from over the side of a slight grassy rise that kept the source of the ruckus hidden from us for some few minutes.

"Oh dear," Ma said, "That doesn't sound good. I hope that no one is hurt."

Mr. Steitler's wagon and Henry were some distance ahead of us, at the top of the hill. Pa called out to them.

"Steitler – do you see what has happened? Do any need our aid?"

Mr. Steitler, silhouetted dark against the bright blue sky, turned and called back in reply.

"Ach – it seems that something has happened to the wagon of the Martindale family. Something spooked one of their oxen, and in a panic, they broke the wagon-tongue, I think that one of their oxen is down."

Pa turned to us, saying, "Well, that's readily mended. Glad that no one is hurt bad. I 'spect we'll noon here, while Martindale fixes his wagon. Martindale – I b'lieve he also brought a spare yoke or two for their wagon. Lord knows that it's heavy enough."

(It was – and eventually the Martindales were forced to lighten it, a fair piece farther on the trail.)

Our wagon topped the rise in a short time, our oxen plodding obediently as they always did. Life must be very boring for an ox. Even the lead yoke had their eyes down as they bent into the yoke. All they must see was the trail in front of their noses, and the following yokes had nothing but the tails and rump of the yoke ahead of them. We could see ahead, to the Martindale wagon, standing all forlorn, with Mr. Martindale unhitching his teams, and his wife standing by, wringing her hands. Major Clayton was there as well, scowling down from the saddle of his tall leggy horse. He had such an expression of wrath and exasperation on his face. I was afreerd that we were about to get another long sermon about how we must not waste time on the daily trek, a sermon which would last for a good few hours of the day. The German boys were alongside with their own wagon. Two of them were helping Mr. Martindale with unyoking his ox teams and assessing the damage to the wagon tongue. One of Martindale's oxen had a bloodied leg, where it had injured itself against ... I couldn't make out what exactly had happened.

Pa came up with our own outfit, saying, "Woah!" to our leaders, and asking if there was anything that he could do to help. Mr. Martindale wiped a hand over his forehead, all grimy with dust and perspiration.

"No, Kettering – all in hand. Them Dutch boys are helping out. Gonna borrow a horse and go back and find a tree big enough to mend the falling tongue with."

"What happened, Mr. Martindale? Did something spook your critters?" That was Major Clayton, looming above like one of the avenging angels come to wield fire and brimstone.

"Them boys's dog flushed out a prairie chicken from the grass," Mr. Martindale explained, "And it ran right under my team's nose. Startled them out of a year's growth, I swear it did."

Major Clayton's lips thinned to an angry line under his moustache. "Those damned dogs ... sorry, ma'am," he added with a nod towards Ma and Mrs. Martindale, and he turned that glare onto Pa and snapped, "We must do something about those pests, Kettering! We'll noon here, while the Martindales fix their wagon, and I'm calling a general meeting, here and now. We can't abide any longer with the trouble those abominable curs create! I want the situation dealt with, before we go a mile farther!" He took out his bugle and blew a series of notes on it, signaling for the noon halt. We thought nothing much about it, as it was about time for that anyways. Pa and the other men stopped their teams, and the women began drawing out whatever we had meant to have for the noonday meal ... all very routine, as we had been a week out of Independence, becoming accustomed to the way of life on the trail.

What wasn't usual was the called-for meeting of all the wagon-owners in the train, as well as those men like Pa who were the elected officers.

Pa went off towards Major Clayton's wagon saying, "This shouldn't take long, Sue – I'll be back in twenty minutes."

Ma sighed. "You say that now, Elkanah, but I know better! That man purely loves the sound of his own voice. Another hour is more like it! If you aren't done with the trail business in twenty minutes, I come and drag you back myself, see if I won't!"

As Ma predicted, the meeting was not done in twenty minutes. Ma looked impatiently toward the Clayton wagon, and the gathering of men around it, and said,

"Go fetch your father, Jon. I'm about to feed his share of dinner to Boomer."

Jon went off at a run, as Ma finished filling Pa's plate with cold biscuits and some slices of ham from our stores, and a scoop of apple crumble that Ma had made from dried apples the night before. I was hungry, impatient to sit down and eat. But within a minute or two, Jon returned, breathless and tearful.

"Ma, Sally – come quick! They're talking about shooting all the dogs!"

"Oh, my dear Lord!" Ma exclaimed. She flung off her apron; we had already lost any appetite for food, after hearing this.

"Pa wouldn't let them shoot Boomer, would be?" Jon demanded tearfully and Ma replied,

"No more than he would let someone shoot one of you!" That seemed to comfort Jon at least a little, and he loved Boomer so very much. I recollected how Major Clayton disliked dogs. *He was the captain of the company, and would Pa have any voice in a decision that the men of the wagon company had voted on?*

It turned out that Pa had more voice than I had thought at first, as well as more respect among the men of the company generally. When Ma and Jon and I came running to where the men were at the meeting that Major Clayton had called, it had already gotten fractious and angry. Big Donal Herlihy was already shouting, so angry that his face was nearly as red as his hair and wiry beard, his powerful hands knotted into fists. His two brothers stood at his back, scowling – and ready for a fight.

"God blast you for a treacherous, murdering salpeen!" Mr. Herlihy bellowed into Major Clayton's face. "Murther me own dogs, you say! In hell you will be, before ye and your bully-boys harm a hair on the back of them!" And he went on, the Irish in him coming out so thick that we didn't rightly understand more than one word in five.

"I will not stand for being addressed in this disrespectful manner!" Major Clayton shouted back in reply when Mr. Herlihy had run out of breath and before anyone else could get in a word by turning it to the thin side and wedging it in.

"Then you had better sit down for it!" Mr. Herlihy roared, and the shouting from all the men present burst out like the whistle from a steamboat. In the meantime, Mrs. Glennie, the poor invalid woman had her little spotted spaniel in her arms, hugged to her as she wept torrents and her husband had her arm around her, trying to talk reason and not being heard by anyone. We stood next to Mr. Steitler and Henry, at the edge of the crowd. Ma asked Mr. Steitler what had happened to bring about all this ruckus.

"The lad's dog," Mr. Steitler replied. "Our commander of wagons has put it to a vote that all the dogs should be shot as a hazard to the company, since he blames the dog for panicking Herr Martindale's cattle and breaking the wagon-tongue. All those dogs are a danger, he claims. Putting the wagon-train at the risk of harm, he says."

"Surely the men have not approved this!" Ma replied, and Mr. Steitler shrugged.

"The majority voted so – that the dogs are a risk to all. I did not agree, but since I am a foreigner..."

This was appalling. We could not allow this, not Boomer. It would be like murder. *What would Pa do, now?* Ma assured us that Pa would as much countenance someone shooting Boomer as Jon or I ... but this was the company, and we were out on the wagon trail, a week-long journey from where there was any settled law.

Meanwhile, Mr. Herlihy had taken a breath and resumed shouting at Major Clayton. He had such a powerful bellow that he could be heard over the clamor.

"Before God, I swear I will leave the company and set off on me own, and what say ye to that, ye thrice-damned pismire! The de'il will make a ladder o' your spine, afore ye murder my dogs!"

"You'll be murdered yourself by the Indian savages before you get a day farther!" Major Clayton roared back, and suddenly, there was Pa, stepping up on the wheel of the Major's wagon, where he could be seen above the heads of the

men gathered. Pa put two fingers in his mouth and whistled –
a shrill blast that cut through the babble. Such was Pa's
manner of resolute command, after the anger in Mr. Herlihy
and the others, that there was a momentary silence – likely
out of sheer surprise – into which Pa said, calmly,

"And I'll take my own wagon and go with Herlihy, here.
We voted to form a company, boys; we can vote to un-make it.
Who's with us, then?"

"I am!" That was Mr. Jeptha Glennie, with his arm
around his distraught wife, still weeping over the little brown
and white spotted Spaniel puppy cradled in her arms. Mr.
Glennie looked around, as if he was looking for support in
indignation. Three of the five German boys chorused,

"*Ja! Ja* – yes, we go mit Herr Kettering! *Aber
naturlich*!" They were indignant over their dog being blamed
by the Major, in spite of them doing all that they could to
mend Mr. Martindale's wagon to make up for it. Mr. Steitler
also nodded, in vigorous agreement.

"*Mir auch*! We go, also *mit* Herr Kettering!"

At that, nearly a dozen other men called out their own
dissent with Major Clayton's captaincy; some had dogs, like
Mr. McNabb the Scotsman, others had not. I guess they all
had been unhappy with how the Major exempted himself and
his cronies from taking a turn at guard at night and for
insisting on traveling on Sunday, the Lord's Day. The Major
looked fit to be tied, almost white with rage at being defied.

"Then leave and be damned to you all!" He shouted. Some of those men and boys who had decided to break from his company jeered scornfully, calling him a tyrannical old windbag and other names that at the time I did not know the meaning of.

Pa, still perched above the crowd, put two fingers in his mouth and whistled again for attention.

"Lads – we'll move on in ten minutes, all of those who want to leave with me." He jumped down, and extended his hand to the Major, who refused it and glared. "No hard feelings, sir? We just can't countenance your latest order. Best that we go our own way, then."

Major Clayton looked as if he would spit on Pa. "You be damned, sir! You and all the rest of you vile, selfish ingrates!"

"I cannot say that it has been a pure pleasure traveling in your company and under your command," Pa replied. He seemed unruffled, although Big Donal Herlihy glowered, scowling as if he would like to strangle Major Clayton with his bare hands, once Major Clayton had taken a moment and untangled the real intent of what Pa had just told him. "Good day to you, sir." Pa looked past the Major, at the remaining crowd. "Any of the rest of you are welcome to join us and form a new company. Ten minutes, boys. We'll roll out in ten minutes."

And that was it; the breaking up of the company. Eleven wagons followed ours and Herlihy's two, away from that nooning place; the Piersons with their own two wagons, Mr.

McNabb, the widower Mr. Taylor and his brothers, young Mr. and Mrs. Shaw with their baby and some others that I didn't know at first. Mr. Martindale and his family followed a little later, rejoining us that evening, at the place where Pa and Mr. Steitler decided to camp, as the sun slid down into the west that evening.

"I knew you wouldn't let that awful man kill Boomer!" I said to Pa, as we walked back to our wagon together. Pa put his arm around me, and answered,

"You know I wouldn't, Sugar-plum. Not by the order of a fool like Major Clayton. I reckon we had our full measure of him, this past week."

"We're well rid of him," Ma put in, at Pa's other side. "I'm glad that I won't ever need hear that silly horn of his again, every blessed morning, noon and night."

Pa chuckled. "Me too, Sue. Me too." He sobered, and added, "Strikes me now that he really didn't know all that much more than any of us about the trail and he warn't no better as train-boss. Setting hisself above everyone else, on account of his fine coat and once being at West Point? It's a gift some men have, in getting people to do as you want them to do, and he sure as shooting didn't have a particle of that gift. At least we're shed of him before he could run us into real trouble."

"Will we run into real trouble, Pa?" Jon did sound anxious; as anxious as Ma probably felt, deep inside, at the thought of leaving the protection of the bigger company.

"There is a likelihood of that, Jonny-cake," Pa replied, as honest and sober as he always was, when Jon or I had hard questions. "Through no fault of our own. But in my mind, we'll have a better chance of being able to deal with it, if we don't have a fool like Major Clayton sticking his oar in and making it worse."

That comforted us both; even more now that we knew for sure that Pa wouldn't have allowed Major Clayton to have Boomer shot and having seen him standing tall and brave against the rest of the company. The dozen wagon-owners and the German boys held a brief meeting that evening, and elected Pa to be the company captain. That made us feel even safer. Because that was our Pa. If we were certain of anything in the world at all, we were positive that Pa wouldn't let harm come to anyone.

Jon and I went to our bed in the wagon that night, perfectly content and secure, although there were only fifteen wagons now, just enough to make a single small circle-corral for the evening camp.

Chapter 6 – Strange Encounters

We discovered a curious thing in the days that followed; our diminished wagon company moved at a much swifter pace, once Pa and Mr. Herlihy and Mr. Steitler and the others broke our wagons away from Major Clayton's large company. I think it was because those who came with Pa were a practical kind of folk, and much friendlier. They were not about to be patient with giving credence to pure nonsense, just because the man talking nonsense possessed a fine coat and the cast-iron conviction that because of having gotten a fancy education that everyone else ought to pay attention and obey. At any rate, there were enough grown men or older boys close enough to count as grown men, that we had no fear of being unable to defend ourselves against at attack by the wild Indians.

Our wagons rolled past the forlorn split in the wagon tracks; one set, grooved deep in the soil led towards Santa Fe – the other towards Oregon and California. The sky over our heads was blue, deep blue and unmarred by clouds, and the prairie rolled out in every direction, the grass grown to almost waist-high to my brother Jon. The grass was deep, lush and green, starred with brilliant wildflowers, stirring and rippling and waving in the wind like what I imagined the ocean to be like. A constant gentle motion, spread out in every direction as far as the eye could see. Butterflies and insects with glittery wings abounded, darting out before us – Jon, and I and

Shivaun and with Wee Donal, Liam and Rory Herlihy as we ran through the tall grass.

The only blot on our day was Ma's insistence on regular lessons, which was not a hardship for me, as I could read and write very well. Jon's lessons were very much a trial for him, although Ma did try to make him see that such book-learning was useful and interesting. Some days after our party split apart from Major Clayton, Ma turned to us both, saying,

"Now there is something you can do which will help your father. It will give you a reason to go around asking questions of all, Sally! You should make a count for him – a careful count of everyone else in the company. Every women, child and infant, hired drovers and girls, how many oxen and horses they have brought with them ... and dogs, too. There were so many before, I am certain that we did not even know of a portion of them."

"Cats?" I asked, wistfully. I was thinking of how big Cally's new kittens would have grown, since we left Ohio, and Ma smiled.

"Chickens, too – if any have brought them. Make a list for your father." Ma gave me a pencil, and the little bound memorandum book that she had used to keep track of the egg money.

All that morning, we went from wagon to wagon – not running, as we had no need for haste. The oxen plodded slowly enough, and we knew some of our company already. I told Jon to count, and I made tally-marks in the memorandum book.

Herlihy – 2 wagons, 10 oxen, 2 dogs
Family: Mr. and Mrs. Herlihy, brothers Seamus and Darragh, sister Shivaun, 3 little boys; Wee Donal, Liam and Rory.

Steitler – 1 wagon, 6 oxen, 1 pony
Family: Mr. Steitler, and son Henry

Glennie - 2 wagons, 1 buggy, 20 oxen, 1 horse, 4 mules, 1 dog - Family: Mr. & Mrs. Glennie, 2 hired drovers

German boys – 1 wagon, six oxen, 1 pony, 1 dog
Oscar Neuhaus, Hans Friedlander, Richart Bauer, Norbert Gruenwald, Fritz Eberhardt

Martindale – 1 wagon, 8 oxen, 1 milk cow
Mr. Mrs. Martindale, son Albert (4 yrs) daughter Meg
(6)

When Jon and I walked to the Pierson wagons, we were astonished to see a woman driving the second wagon. We had not noticed her before, when we first took to the trail, traveling with the Major's large company. We should have, for she was wearing a man's wide-brimmed felt hat instead of a sunbonnet, and a narrow dark calico skirt. The hem of that skirt only reached to the tops of her stout laced boots. She was about Ma's age, only not pretty, with shrewd gray eyes. I think something like her trail costume was called 'rational dress', made somewhat famous by Mrs. Amelia Bloomer a few years later. I didn't think that Ma would approve of a costume so unwomanly, but it certainly looked most practical, and the woman strode along beside the lead team quite capably.

"Good morning," I said most politely. "My brother and I are making a list of all the people and critters in the company. Ma says it will be a help to our Pa – Mr. Kettering, who is now our wagon company captain. Are you Mrs. Pierson?"

"<u>Miss</u> Pierson," the woman replied, with a smile. "I'm traveling with my brother's family. Your father is a vast improvement on that braggart little popinjay. You must be terribly proud of him."

"We are, ma'am," I replied. "Can you tell us how many people and critters there are with you?"

"Certainly." Miss Pierson replied. "My brother and his wife, their boys, Robert and Isiah, and as for critters – eight oxen, and Sister Judith's tame singing canary."

"Thank you, ma'am," I said, as polite as Ma would have wished. I wrote down what she told us in the book, and asked Jon, as we walked on, if he could add up in his head how many oxen there were so far.

He scowled at the page, nearly full of my neat notes.

"Thirty-seven?" he ventured after a moment.

"You're just guessing," I told him, with a sigh. "Fifty oxen, so far."

Pierson - 2 wagons, eight oxen, 1 pet bird
Family: Mr. and Mrs. Pierson, sister Miss Naomi Pierson, 2 older boys, Robert and Isiah

The next wagon that we approached was owned by Mr. McNabb; we knew him by sight, as his wagon was a small one but trim and well-maintained, painted light blue. Mr. McNabb was a dour-faced and gangly Scot, completely bald on the top of his head, but a fringe of dark hair all the way around. He was pleasant enough, generally. He had a hunting dog, a lean and well-mannered coal-black hound, with a fine red leather collar. This dog was the main reason that he had withdrawn from Major Clayton's party and cast in his lot with ours.

"Good morning, sir," I said, as we came close to speak. "I'm Sally Kettering, and my brother and I are making a list of everyone in the company, and their critters, too – to help our Pa."

"Aye?" Mr. McNabb replied. "It's just mysel' an' the dog."

"And how many oxen?" I asked, opening the notebook to a fresh page.

"Och, only the three yoke," Mr. McNabb replied, and Jon asked plaintively,

"Is there a Mrs. McNabb, then?"

Mr. McNabb shook his head, and it seemed to me that his gaze wandered in the direction of the wagons ahead. "No, laddie, 'tis just myself and Black Bogle here, but I have a wee dream of perhaps changing that condition, some day."

McNabb - 1 wagon, 6 oxen, 1 hunting dog.
Mr. McNabb (by himself)

By walking a little faster, we caught up to the next wagon ahead. This was one of the lighter wagons, with two yoke of oxen pulling it, a single unsaddled horse tethered to the rear of the wagon, and a large open crate tied to the back – a crate with several chickens in it. A young couple walked next to the lead yoke, hand in hand.

"John Simmons," the man replied, when we introduced ourselves and explained our errand. "And my wife, Nancy – we were only just married in March. I wanted to head for California, and settle a place there, and then come back to St. Louis for her..."

"Ohh, like I would let my darling Jo go alone, all the way to California or Oregon Territory," added Nancy Simmons with a teasing smile. She was very pretty, even prettier than Shivaun McCarty. "I told him that he could tell that notion to the cows ... I would not sit and wait for him for a year or more, fearing that he was facing all those wild Indians and critters and all. I'd sooner go with him and share the dangers together, than worry for months!"

"Aye, well, I was for Oregon at first, then there was so much said of California, so we got ourselves hitched and came away together," added John Summons with another affectionate glance at Nancy.

Simmons – 1 wagon, 4 oxen, 1 horse, 4 chickens
Family: Mr. and Mrs. Simmons

That left just three wagons ahead of us, wagons for which we had not yet taken a full accounting. The Clayton party had been so large that most of the other folk were ones which we had not made the acquaintances of before the company split. The first of the three was a heavy wagon, somewhat resembling ours, with the canvas top having the same slight cant forward and aft. There were three yoke pulling it; heavy, lumbering beasts. Three men walked by the lead yoke, striding confidently, the one with the staff to guide the oxen casually over his shoulder. He was the oldest, heavy-shouldered and with a dark beard already coming out on his jaw and cheeks. The other two were younger – a little older than Henry Steitler, I thought.

"Ruston Taylor," answered the bearded man. "Started out in Kentucky, moved to Missouri. Guess we got the itchy feet for certain … but the river fever done for too many of our kin. M' brothers, Mad – short for Madison, an' the baby, George."

"Hi-dy," The youngest Taylor brother allowed shyly and blushed so deeply red that I felt sorry for him. George Taylor was as tall as Mr. Herlihy the blacksmith but would have only made about a third of him for width. In the coming weeks, George Taylor made very wistful eyes at Shivaun McCarty, but I don't believe he ever worked up nerve enough to say more than two words to her.

Taylor – 1 wagon, 8 oxen, 1 horse.
Family – Ruston Taylor, brothers Madison and George.

Jon and I quickened our pace, as the next wagon was pretty far ahead; another wagon which looked as if it had done hard work on the farm, before being fitted out with hickory wood bows and a canvas cover waterproofed with yellow paint. Like our own wagon, there was a new patented plow secured to the back tailgate. Two yoke pulled it; the lead team older critters, the second looked fractious and jumpy, as if they had been bought from the outfitter's pens in Independence, and not entirely agreeable to their new expectations, or happy with them.

"Peter Shaw," their owner introduced himself. "Jenny ... that is, Mrs. Shaw – she's a cousin of Ada Pierson. We all came away together. I thought – whyever not? Best to travel with folk you know. Jake and Miss Naomi – we been friends and neighbors for years, back in Indiana."

Shaw – 1 wagon, 4 oxen, 1 milk cow
Family – Mr. and Mrs. Shaw, infant son Jimmy

That left only the one wagon in the lead. Pa had carried on the practice of rotation in order every day, so that every wagon driver could have a turn at not breathing in the dust kicked up by others. This last wagon was another one of the smaller wagons, light enough to be pulled at a good pace by only two yoke of oxen. The driver of it ambled alongside his lead ox with his hands stuck unto his jacket pockets and a straw hat tilted on the back of his head. He was a man a little younger than Pa, happy-go-lucky and as adventurous as a man without family responsibilities could be.

"Charley Jepson," he grinned at us, when I explained what we were doing for Pa. "Pike County is where I'm from. Say, this is prime country, isn't it? Why'd I decide to hit the trail? See, I'm a man who likes to fish – settle me down by the side of a river that jumps with fish, and I'm as happy as a pig in the mud. I heard that California is prime fishing country."

Jepson - 1 wagon, 4 oxen
Family – Mr. Charles Jepson (by himself)

Pa and Mr. Glennie, Mr. Herlihy and his brothers had a fine time. They were lucky in hunting now and again; prairie hens and rabbits, which made good eating roasted and stewed over a fire of an evening. Fresh meat made such a nice change from the salt-bacon that we had brought with us, you see. Mr. Steitler's copy of *Hastings' Emigrant Guide* which Pa and the other men studied said that buffalo could be hunted as we traveled.

Our company fell into a much more pleasant condition, after breaking from Major Clayton's party, which I have since thought made for a happier conclusion. There were no serious quarrels between members, nothing so bad as to fracture the company. Really, the only regular eruptions of temper came from the German boys, and they usually were soothed over without much fuss. Just as we shared our fire in the evenings with Mr. Steitler and Henry, others fell into doing the same: Mr. McNabb, the Scotsman, usually drew his wagon next to the Piersons, themselves related to newlywed Mr. and Mrs. Shaw. The other bachelor wagon-owner, Mr. Jepson, was from the same locality in Kentucky as Mr. Taylor and his brothers. In this, we were very fortunate that so many of our company were connected by ties of kin and long friendship, much more so than other companies on the trail that year.

In truth, we did not need or want to hunt the buffalo, even though some of the more reckless young men wanted to, very much. The buffalo came to us one day, but in such a very large herd that we did not dare. That day came about when we had been about three weeks on the trail; reaching the Platte River, and what some had begun to call the Coast of Nebraska, seeing that we had been as sailors crossing an ocean of grass.

The river itself was a broad, shallow muddy sweep, edged by low bluffs. There weren't any trees at all, save on low islands in the river, and the water wasn't fit to drink, even after letting all the mud in it settle out.

That morning, we broke camp, and moved on, at a steady but not at too fast a pace, as we had become accustomed to since the first days. Mr. Glennie owned a fine riding horse, in addition to his two wagons and buggy, with two hired men to drive the wagons. He was most always charged to ride a little way ahead and scout the trail for us. Mr. Glennie was accounted to be the wealthiest in our company, but he was agreeable to this task, which kept him in the saddle for much of the day. He would ride out ahead of our wagons with Henry Steitler and Oscar, one of the German boys. Oscar splurged at the Kansas River crossing by purchasing a half-broken spotted mustang pony from the tame Indians who ran the river ferry there. He got it for cheap, since that pony was still mostly wild, barely broke for the saddle. Oscar amused his friends by falling off the pony many times, while accustoming himself to riding and the pony to being ridden. Mr. Steitler had also purchased a pony from the Kansas Indians, a pony for Henry to ride. Henry Steitler's pony was better trained and mannered; I do not think Henry fell off his pony nearly as often as Oscar did. Henry and Oscar and Mr. Glennie were our outriders, mounted trail scouts and helped in the early mornings by searching for oxen who had strayed far in the night.

On that day, Mr. Glennie and Oscar came galloping back, from where they had ridden ahead to find a place to spend the noon rest. Oscar was out of breath, from trying to hold his seat on his fractious pony and recall the English words for what was over the ridge ahead of us.

"*Herr-kapitan* Kettering, there is a *gwaltig* ... a most ... huge ... *herde von* ... *buffel*... the wild..." he gasped, and the half-tame paint pony pranced in a nervous circle.

 Mr. Glennie reined in and walked his horse calmly next to Pa. "Biggest damn herd of buffalo-critters that I ever thought possible. They're moving slowly towards us, and there's too many of them for us to go around. Thousands – like fleas, crawling over the land in our direction. What do you think we ought to do, Kettering?"

Pa pushed his hat back on his head. "I reckon we try not to make 'em mad. Too many to just go around?"

Mr. Glennie shook his head, quietly astonished at what he had spotted, and which we would soon encounter. "Thousands of the critters, far as they eye can see ... just moving slowly, grazing as they go. Might take days if we want to fort up and wait them out."

"Can't do that," Pa replied. "We might lose too much time ... time that we might never be able to make up when the trail gets rough. Reckon it might just be best to keep on moving slow and careful-like. Like as not to panic them. All they are is big, woolly wild cows. We all got plenty of experience with the tame kind. Tell everyone to draw the wagons close, though. Pass the word for anyone on foot to ride in their wagon for a while ... until the buffalo are gone."

That is what we did; Jon and I, and all the other women and children. We climbed up into the wagons and watched. Pa even lifted Boomer into the wagon with us, where he sat with Jon's hand on his neck, gentling him into still and calm. Mr. Herlihy's pair of black and white spotted carriage hounds slunk underneath his wagons at a command from him. They were well-trained dogs and obeyed instantly. Pa and the other drovers walked close to their teams, closer than ever, as if they sheltered against the safe bulk of their tame oxen. Mr. Glennie, Oscar and Henry reined in their own horses close to the wagons, as we watched the first of the buffalo meander over the brow of the ridge. And then more, and more of them, until it seemed as if the waving green grass was slowly blotted over with a floodtide of dark brown buffalo. They came down from the ridge, meandering at an unhurried pace which would take them across the direction of our wagon train. The drovers closed up what would normally be the wide gaps between us. Mr. Glennie's buggy and wagons were next to ours, with Mr. Herlihy's two wagons on the other side,

"Do nothing to send them into a panic!" Pa commanded, as the leading edge of the buffalo herd wandered close, so close that we all got a good close look. Great woolly humpbacked beasts, broader across the forehead than our oxen, or our milk cow, with wickedly curved horns. Thick, shaggy brown fur covered their heads and shoulders, matted across their foreheads with dried mud.

"They look like lions," I murmured to Ma, "As if a cow had wanted to be a lion ... and covered himself with a bearskin rug."

Ma only nodded, and reached down to pet Boomer, who seemed terribly puzzled by the strange creatures – but too obedient to do more than whine a little, deep in his throat.

It seemed to take forever for our party of wagons to pass through the slow-moving, incurious buffalo. Pa later said he was ever so grateful that they were in a placid mood, interested in nothing much but an occasional mouthful of grass, torn from a clump at their feet ... thousands of hooved feet, which raised dust in their wake that made me sneeze.

Looking at them as they passed before and around us, I saw that some were smaller, not as massive. There were many even smaller ones, small and without the great shaggy manes. Calves, of course. It was late spring, the time for cows to bring calves. I reckon that the buffalo were the same in that regard as our tame cattle. Pa and the other wagons forged steadily ahead through the flowing river of buffalo, buffalo which spread to one side or another as we came upon them. Like a river of brown woolly backs, they went on plodding steadily towards wherever they were going. I think that it took several hours to make our way clear of the vast herd – such as sight as I was glad to have seen, once it was well over. The last of the stragglers vanished over the grassy horizon to the south of the trail, and Pa called to Mr. Glennie.

"Find us a good nooning place, Glennie – one far ahead enough that those woolly-backs haven't pissed and shat all over the grass!"

Mr. Glennie, laughing, doffed his wide-brimmed hat in a brief salute. "I'll see what I can do, Cap'n – but make no promises."

Pa, also laughing, touched his ox-goad to the brim of his own hat. When Mr. Glennie and Oscar had ridden off, raising a new cloud of dust from where the buffalo had trampled the grass, Pa turned towards us. "What a sight, Sue! I had read of such herds but I thought such were exaggerations, intended to entice the curious into purchasing them. Instead ... I hold that my father and our friends back in Ohio would scarce believe what we have just had pass before our eyes!"

It turned out that within a few more days of travel, we would have to give thanks of a kind for the presence of so many buffalo. The rolling grasslands that we traveled through were devoid of trees, any sort of trees. Which put the women of the train in a quandary, with nothing to build a fire with, and no means of cooking. On the second woodless day, Pa and the other men called a meeting during our noontime rest to discuss what might be done, and to explain to us all the alternative to the lack of wood along this part of the trail.

"Well, you see ... the solution as it has been described in *Hasting's Emigrant's Guide* is ... to burn the dried buffalo scat," Pa announced, and the women immediately chorused their disbelief and disgust at cooking meals over what came out of the north end of a south-bound buffalo. I admit that my own stomach felt a bit rebellious at the very thought. Pa continued, trying to sound as reasonable as he did when Ma had objections to a proposal of his. "It is what Mr. Hastings wrote, due to the lack of wood along this stretch. Dried buffalo excrement. As a solution to a clear lack of wood. There just isn't any." Pa looked around at the gathering. "Not without going miles out of our way, seeking trees, and wasting days that we can't spare. You see, the stuff burns well, hot enough to boil water over. Steitler here has agreed to set up a demonstration to prove it."

Mr. Steitler, holding a small burlap croker sack, nodded to Pa and stepped to the front of the gathered crowd. He smiled genially and emptied out the contents of that sack – yes, odd-shaped chunks of buffalo scat made a haphazard pile at his feet.

"You will note at once that the material is well-dried," Mr. Steitler explained, with something of the air of a traveling lecturer. "Composed entirely of waste grass stems and other fibers indigestible to the creature, compacted tightly together through the digestive process. There is no perceptible unpleasant odor ... Heinrich, will you attend with the flame, *bitte? Danke...*"

Henry Steitler leaned close over the heap, with a small branch of smoldering wood, and touched the tiny flame of it to the pile of buffalo droppings. The flame took at once, and in less time than it took to tell, dancing yellow flames took over the whole pile. There was no more smoke rising from it than from an ordinary wood fire, and Mr. Steitler smiled, triumphantly. "Such a fire as this burns very hot, and quite rapidly. But with a sufficient supply of such fuel ... and there is indeed sufficient..."

Mr. Herlihy cleared his throat.

"Sufficient, indade ... after the other day, 'tis a marvel that this part of the desert is not paved several times over with the muck from those creatures! Ah, well; needs must when the de'il drives. In our old home in Ireland, we burned dried peat, ye'll know. Dug from the bog, it was. And my father said that the fire in his fathers' cottage had never once gone out in four hundred years."

There was a chorus of agreement from those attending the meeting, although I do not think any were enthusiastic regarding using the buffalo chips to cook over, as much as Mr. Herlihy and Mr. Steitler and Pa tried to make it a reasonable solution. I already knew that just as Jon and I and the other children had been sent to gather wood, or to collect it as the wagon train moved, we would be gathering buffalo chips, every single day.

That is exactly what happened. The chore was not nearly as unpleasant as it sounded as long as the droppings were well-dried. Those peeled up readily from the grounds where the great beasts had grazed. The only unpleasant aspect was that there were sometimes snakes resting nearby. For some reason, those large and nasty rattlesnakes favored resting in those same sheltered patches warmed by the sun which the buffalo had also favored as a privy. On most days, buffalo chips were plentiful. It was a simple matter to collect up a satisfactory number, filling several sacks full to the top and carrying them back to the wagons – although Jon usually had to drag his full sack. They were lighter than firewood but burned faster, so we needed much, much more. I tried my best not to think about where the chips came out of, as Ma cooked supper over them.

I think it must have been two weeks after leaving the big company that Jon and I became lost on the prairie late one afternoon. We were gathering buffalo chips, while Pa and the other men made camp. Ma and the other women sorted out what they were going to cook for supper, especially if the menfolk had managed to hunt some fresh meat, as soon as we brought more chips – and wood for the fire, assuming that we were able to bring enough back to camp.

Jon and I walked away from camp that afternoon, each of us with an empty pair of big croker sacks. We were with some of the others at first; Wee Donal and Liam Herlihy and Shivaun. It was one of those days with a clear blue sky arching overhead, spotted only with little shreds of cloud, like bits of rag and clumps of lint torn or scraped from some larger fabric.

The rolling prairie stretched out all around, almost completely featureless, save for the distant thread of the Platte River and the range of low bluffs that ringed it. The trail at this point meandered along parallel to the river, but not really close to it. It seemed hardly any time at all before we had wandered farther and farther from camp, deeper and deeper into the grasslands. I can't recall why; only that the air seemed clear and fresh, the wind stirring the grass at the tops of the low rise, and I wanted to see what I could beyond. Then there was a good, well-dried spread of buffalo chips, and another higher hill that promised a better view, the grass waving in the light breeze as the sun slid father down in the west ... and Jon suddenly looked around and said, tremulously,

"Sally ... where's the camp?"

We were well out of sight of the wagons, I realized with a horrible sinking feeling in my stomach. That feeling sank even farther when I realized that I didn't know which direction to go. I could not hear – as hard as I listened – the clamor of our company setting up camp. The clank of harness chains, the men calling to each other, Boomer and the other dogs barking, the cattle lowing to each other as they grazed ... nothing, only the whispering rustle of the wind in the tall grass.

But I knew better than to panic. I couldn't let it show that I was nearly frightened to death, all alone on the wild and trackless prairie with my little brother.

"We have to sit down and think," I said finally. "And not run as if we were being chased by wolves..."

"Are there wolves here, Sally?" Jon's lips trembled. I was afraid that he was going to cry; I wished that I hadn't mentioned wolves.

"There are, I think. But they only hunt at night ... and it's still daylight," I said. That was the first thing that gave me a notion. "See ... there is the sun, in the west. If we keep it to our left as we walk... then we aren't going in a circle. If we walk in a straight line, Jon, I think that we'll come to the river. But before then, we should see the trail."

"All right," Jon answered. He already sounded reassured. I didn't tell him that when we found the trail, we should have to examine it very carefully, to see if our party had passed over it, or were the tracks from one ahead of us? Would we walk to the west ... or back along the tracks and hope to find our company, before it got dark. If night came ... I didn't want to think about that. I hoped that Pa, or Mr. Glennie and Oscar would be sent out on horseback to find us, but as Grandpa Reverend always said, '*God helps those who help themselves.*' I couldn't build a plan on hoping that someone would find us. I had gotten us lost; it was up to me to get us un-lost. I also hoped that we could find our camp before Ma would begin to fear that she would lose us the way that Aunt Rachel had lost our Cousin Matty. I took Jon's hand, hoisted our two sacks of buffalo chips in my other hand, and we set out walking. I tried to set our path in as straight a way as was possible, hoping that every moment we would see the thread of smoke from our campfires rising into the air, and then the pale canvas wagon covers.

Straight as a rule, we walked, although it did take us a tiresome way, up the side of a low hill, and down the other. I didn't see anything but more of the same rolling prairie grasses, but reassuringly, the line of bluffs, far and away on the far side of the river. At least, we were walking in the right direction.

How had we managed to wander so far? It was as if everything had been swallowed up by the sheer vastness of it all. Jon and I toiled up another rise, down the far side, up another. Then I was reassured of the value of my own good sense. We finally came upon the trampled tracks of a cattle herd, scored briefly here and there by the deep ruts of wagon wheels – a track that went towards the setting sun.

"Look here, Jon," I said to my brother. "I think this must be the trail. Whether it was made by our company or another ... I can't really tell. Look around – and do you think we came this way, today?"

Jon frowned and shook his head. "It all looks the same to me, Sally. The same hills and grass. Nothing – all the same. It's not like back in Ohio, with different trees, different hills."

I sighed. "Let me think, Jon – about whether to go east or west. There might be a party ahead of us. I just can't tell how old the marks are. I think ... I hope that we have crossed our own track, and everyone is towards the west of us. I just don't know..."

It was at that moment that I nearly jumped out of my own skin. A party of Indians appeared, as if out of the very air – not a sound, not a warning. At least a dozen of them, all men mounted on horses with unshod hoofs. They didn't make a sound on the battered grass where a big wagon party had passed with a passel of loose cattle. The Indians were just suddenly there. Jon didn't make a sound, for which I was grateful, but he pressed close against me, and I put my arm around his shoulders.

"Hello," I said, although I was quite certain that they wouldn't understand me, but it was polite to say, and Ma always insisted on good manners to strangers, even Red Indians.

That was the curious part; the two who stood closest to us, after they all slid down from their ponies – were really red. Half of their faces, anyway; painted with red paint. They had also shaved their eyebrows and the hair on their heads nearly bald, save for a scalp-lock at the top. One had adorned the top of his head with a crest of stiff horsehair, dyed red and yellow. That one Indian man, who seemed like he was the leader, stepped closer to me and held up his hand. He said something that I couldn't understand, guttural and harsh sounding, and waggled his fingers.

I said 'Hello," again, as politely as I could.

I was glad that my voice didn't shake. We were mortal afraid of Indians, then; especially being alone as Jon and I were. Although the Indians that we had seen in Independence, and those who ran the ferry over the Kansas River crossing hadn't seemed that much off from the ordinary. They were just people, although considerably more browned from the sun and much more skimpily dressed than most.

I saw then that half of the Indian party were really boys. Boys of about my age, and perhaps a bit younger – skinny, half-naked and ... really not all that dangerous-looking. *Were Jon and I supposed to be mortally afraid of boys hardly as old as I was?* They seemed as curious about us as I would have been – that is, if Pa and Mr. Herlihy or Mr. Glennie had been with us. Indeed, one of the boys came up really close to us, as the older ones talked among themselves over our heads. That one boy reached out and touched Jon's hair, feeling it with his fingers in one hand as he reached for the little wood-hilted knife hanging from the string that held the little flap of cloth around his middle to hide his male parts. It was as if that Indian boy were considering a bit of scalp-taking, and Jon flinched.

That was it, for me. *No one had the right to scare my little brother out of his skin!* I was so angry that I shoved that Indian boy so hard; so hard that he fell backwards on his behind.

"You let my brother alone!" I yelled at him, as fierce as if I were chasing off Aunt Rachel's bully goose, who used to chase Jon and the other little children something fierce. The boy glared at me, but he didn't dare come any closer. He scrambled away rapidly, before he got to his feet again. I was a bit taller than he was, and I must have been at least as strong. All the grown-up Indian men laughed. They said things to the boy that sounded as if they were making fun of him; he looked abashed and embarrassed. I put my arm around Jon and pulled him even closer to me.

"Don't worry, Jon," I whispered. "We'll be all right. We're close to camp, and they don't really seem to want to hurt us."

Jon's lips wobbled. "Is Pa gonna come for us soon?"

"I hope so," I whispered back. I had just about decided that I should chance our luck. The Indians didn't seem all that inclined to take us prisoner, before or after scalping both of us. I thought I should just say goodbye and stride off confidently in the direction that I thought that our camp should be in. After all, they hadn't tried to hurt us or take us officially captive. I reasoned if they hadn't yet done Jon or I any harm, maybe they would allow us to just go our way.

Whichever way that might be – which I didn't know, but no one had to really know <u>that</u>, least of all these Indians.

Just as I had made up my mind to do this, I heard the jingling of harness, and the steady dull clip-clopping of shod hooves. The Indians – they all turned, alert in every bone. Half of them slid from their horses and vanished. It was like a trick from a traveling magician; one minute they were there, and the next they were gone, melting into the remains of tall grass, or shallow hollows in the ground.

"Well, well ... what do we have here, Deacon?" drawled the man holding the reins of a wagon drawn by half a dozen mules, hitched two and two and two. He was a dark man, with grizzled hair, dressed almost like an Indian himself. He halted the mules and regarded us all – Jon and I, and the remaining visible Indians with great interest.

The other man stood up in the wagon, with a big black book clutched to his chest. He was older. I mean, I think both of these men in the mule wagon were about the same age as Grandpa Reverend, but the dark man driving the wagon looked somehow fitter. Spry. He was dressed in a fringed leather hunting coat and fringed leggings that looked somewhat like the Indians wore, and a long knife hung at his belt. The man called Deacon just looked old, with white hair down to his shoulders, like the picture of a prophet in the Old Testament – but he looked happy, not thunderously angry, as Grandpa Reverend always allowed that the prophets were, given that they were sent to chastise sinners.

"Children, Mr. Bayless – white children, and the heathen that I was sent to redeem!" Deacon exclaimed, waving his free hand, and the other man – Mr. Bayless heaved a great sigh and seemed to roll his eyes in exasperation. "It is a heavenly sign, indeed! Tell them that I mean no harm! I have come to bring them the good news!" his eye finally fell upon Jon and I. "Children ... are you of the Kettering party? I was told that such a company was on the trail, and we were desirous of joining such a godly company!"

99

Meanwhile, Mr. Bayless was making peculiar sweeping gestures with his hands. Sign-talk, I think they called it. A simple manner to speak with another tribe if there was no language in common. It was a curious matter: the Indian tribes in the wild lands beyond the Mississippi River had no single language between them, other than this signing-talk. Then the dark man ventured some words, and then more of them; words which the red-painted Indian with the horsehair crest to his scalp-lock and the others seemed to understand – from the rapt manner in which they all paid mind. The Indian leader then responded with similar.

The other Indians, the ones who had hidden, emerged silently from wherever they had concealed themselves. They stood around, listening to Mr. Bayless and the horse-hair-crested Indian leader as they talked, and chattering among each other. I replied,

"I'm Sally – Sarah Elizabeth Kettering, and this is my brother Jon. Mr. Kettering is our pa. We were out finding chips, but then we got turned around. You haven't seen our camp, have you?" I tried not to sound pathetic.

The man addressed as Deacon smiled at me, a brave and sunny smile. I was cheered to see him, although I secretly wondered if he was as addled as a loon.

"Oh, children – you have strayed, but been found! No, we have not seen your camp, but they are ahead of us, we are assured. The Lord has directed us! Mr. Bayless and I are on our way to join your godly company of pilgrims. I am Deacon

Absolom Zollicoffer, late of St. Louis, but called by God and ordained by my congregation to minister to the red heathen, and Mr. Bayless is my guide and a notable frontiersman! We will find your camp; I can assure you! Come up into the wagon, Sarah ... Jon – you are safe with us, now."

Mr. Bayless had finished talking to the Indians; apparently explaining who we were, and that. Deacon Zollicoffer leaned down to help Jon up into the wagon. I handed up our sacks of chips, feeling much relived at our rescue, but before I could scramble up into the mule wagon, the big Indian with the horsehair crest boldly put his hand on the front of my dress, where I would have had breasts, when I was grown up. The big Indian with the horsehair crest said something to the others, and they all chuckled. The boy that I had pushed away from Jon scowled like a thundercloud. Deacon Zollicoffer looked indignant – I think he was about to say something but for a warning look that Mr. Bayless shot in his direction.

But it didn't matter to me; we were safe now. On our way to our camp, without the trouble of Pa and the others searching for us. I had that feeling of safety from Deacon Zollicoffer and Mr. Bayless too, as Mr. Bayless chirruped to his mule team. The wagon lurched away from where the Indians had found us.

As we did, Jon asked, "What was that – that they said at last, that made them all laugh?"

Mr. Bayless looked down at his reins; we were all squished together on the wagon seat between him and Deacon Zollicoffer, with our bags of buffalo chips piled awkwardly at our feet. Then he looked sideways at me and chuckled.

"They were joshing with that one Pawnee boy," he replied. "The one that your sister pushed so hard that he fell onto his be-hind. Their chief told him, *'Nah, she isn't grown enough yet that he can take her to be a wife to him.'* That's what they all were laughing about, Li'l Miss Sally. Now, if'n I was a betting man, I'd say that Pawnee boy might have been sweet on you!"

I was indignant. "I thought he was going to hurt my brother!" I replied, for I think I was still getting over the alarm of being lost and the scare that those Indians had put into us. "I'd never be sweet on a boy like that!"

"No 'counting for taste," Mr. Bayless chuckled some more, and Deacon Zollicoffer protested,

"You shouldn't make a jest like that, Bayless! I'd think Miss Sally and her brother were put through an awful fright! But they're safe now. As soon as we catch up to the Kettering company, these dear children will be as safe as they can be."

I think that was when I began to like and trust Deacon Zollicoffer; because he was so kind, a much kinder man than Grandpa Reverend, although they were about the same age and of the same devout inclination. He sensed from the first moment without any words being said, how deeply frightened I was, and how very glad that he and Mr. Bayless had come along at that exact moment. Yet the Deacon was tactful enough not to mention it. Jon felt a bit of that too, although I thought he was more entranced by Mr. Bayless, with his fringed hunting coat, and the big knife at his belt, hanging in a sheath decorated with Indian beadwork. Jon had been fascinated by the Indians that we saw in Independence, and those running the ferry over the Kansas. He wanted to see real wild Indians, right up until the very moment that we did.

"How did you know those Indians were Pawnee, Mr. Bayless?" Jon asked, eaten up with curiosity.

Mr. Bayless grunted, "Just call me 'Choctaw Joe', boy – I'm not a high-falooting hoss like the Deacon here. As for your question – it'll be too hard for me to explain, boy. How do you tell an Irishman from a Dutchman? After a time, you just do. 'Sides, this is their hunting-grounds. The Lakota Sioux are a mite farther west and powerful enemies of the Pawnee, any roads. That's what they were doing, 'case you were wondering – coming back from a hunt with the young 'uns. In the main, the Pawnee are mighty well disposed towards whites."

"I'm very pleased to make your acquaintance, Mr. Choctaw," I said, as Ma would have insisted that I be polite and not call a grown-up by their first name. "And real grateful for having come along, you and Deacon Zollicoffer. I'm afraid we really were lost. I hadn't quite decided what direction our camp was in. Pa ... and Ma will be grateful, too. They must really have been worried when we didn't come back to camp right away."

"And I'm happy that we were able to be of service to so charming and responsible a young lady," Deacon Zollicoffer closed his arms around the thick leatherbound book in his lap. I could see that it was a Bible, like Reverend Grandfather's pulpit Bible. Holy Bible was written out in flaking gold letters along the worn spine. It closed with a metal clasp, like something precious. "Truly, we were guided by His Divine Providence..."

"More like a trail that a blind mule could follow," Choctaw Joe Bayless replied. Deacon Zollicoffer didn't sound annoyed or insulted in the least. He looked sideways at me and smiled.

"Mr. Bayless is every bit as much of a heathen as those poor souls that you encountered just there," he said. "But I have hopes of bringing him into the Light of our Savior's love..."

Choctaw Joe Bayless had an expression on his brown face which suggested that he might have said something rude but for the presence of Jon and I. Just at that moment we came around a rise in the land and saw a wagon encampment a little way distant. It was our company, which I saw at once and with considerable feelings of relief. There was Mrs. Glennie's buggy, Mr. McNabb's blue wagon, and the yellow-tinted canvas covers on the Herlihy's two wagons, all visible at some distance. And Ma, looking towards the Deacon's mule wagon with her hand shading her eyes...

"I am never going to let the two of you out of my sight again!" Ma exclaimed, when she got her breath back, after running up to Deacon's wagon and sweeping both of us into her arms. Ma sounded as if she were that close to crying. There was considerable of a crowd gathering around us. It was right embarrassing, so much notice being taken. I tried to explain how it happened that Jon and I did not notice how far we had wandered, while Deacon Zollicoffer and Choctaw Joe Bayless explained themselves over our heads. There was considerable excitement that evening. Even if Jon and I were the approximate cause of it all, we didn't get to see much more of it than that.

Pa and the other men held a confabulation with the Deacon and Choctaw Joe, which Jon and I couldn't listen to, as Ma hustled us away to our wagon, lecturing and chiding us all the while about how careless we had been, in wandering so far as to get lost. It was near to sunset anyway, and supper was delayed in all the fuss. It wasn't until we were in bed in the wagon that evening that I listened to Ma and Pa talking as they settled down to rest for the night. I liked hearing Ma and Pa talk, as I drifted off into slumber; it was comforting, being half-asleep and hearing them talk, even if it was usually conversations that I didn't quite comprehend, and I would often have fallen asleep between one word and the next.

They had pitched the tent just by the wagon, not three or four feet distant from our bed, and separated only by two stretches of canvas. Our camp had quieted down for the evening. I also liked the sound of our camp, as everyone prepared for a night of rest, after a hard haul on the trail all day. Somewhere opposite our wagon, Daragh Herlihy played Irish tunes on a penny whistle, Mr. McNabb had his hurdy-gurdy, or the German boys and Mr. Steitler and Henry sang German songs together for a while – and quiet talk and tired laughter from around other campfires. The half-dozen horses and mules corralled in between the wagons cropped and crunched grass, and sometimes rattled their picket chains. Outside the wagon circle, the oxen grazed as well, sometimes lowing to each other. *Telling each other ox-gossip, I used to tell Jon. Oxen, I said, were awful ones for spreading scandalous tales about other oxen.*

Ma said, "So you all voted to accept the pair of them into the company?"

Pa replied, "Well, it seemed like a sensible thing to do, Sue. 'Specially Mr. Bayless. Back in Independence, before we started out, we didn't think that we needed to hire a guide ... but it turns out that he was in the fur trade, back in the earlies with the Astor enterprise. Knows the trapping country out in the West better than he knows the back of his hand, so he claims. I'm inclined to believe him on that account, and how Sally said about how he talked to those Pawnee hunters. Mr. Bayless knows the trails, the shortcuts and the best camping places. He knows the wilderness. Best yet, he also knows the Indians and their palaver; I'd value his advice over any that *Hasting's Emigrant Guide* could give, even if it's been fifteen years or more since Mr. Bayless last trapped beaver in the Rocky Mountains. He says that he and his employer will hew with us until Fort Hall, at least. Maybe farther than that if Deacon Zollicoffer receives new orders from the Lord regarding his mission."

"And the Deacon?" Ma sounded as if she were trying not to laugh.

Pa sighed. "Sue, I can't decide if the man is a lunatic or a saint!"

"Probably a bit of both," Ma replied. Now she was laughing. "I'm mortal certain that every saint in the Bible must have struck their close friends as being a trifle touched in the head – even Martha and Mary, the sisters of Lazarus! Not comfortable people to be around. What is Deacon Zollicoffer's story? Who is he, really? Why is he haring off to convert the heathen Indians of the West, in company with an old fur trapper?"

"Deacon Zollicoffer," Now Pa sounded amused; amused and exasperated. "Is a well-respected and very rich merchant in St. Louis, who never before in his life gave evidence of eccentricity until a year or so ago, after his wife died of the summer fever. He suddenly confessed to a vision in which he received a direct commission from God to go forth immediately into the West and preach the Word to the heathen Indians. He turned control of all his business interests and his holdings over to his grown sons. To do them credit, they tried to talk him out of such a mad scheme. After appeals to reason failed, his sons prayed together and consulted with a respectable clergyman of their own congregation. Then they did the next-best thing; they hired Mr. Bayless and charged him with assisting and protecting their father to the best of his abilities, which Mr. Bayless assured them were considerable. So here we have them both in our company, and I am glad of that! Deacon Zollicoffer had a heap to say about Major Clayton's company, by the way."

"Nothing good, I take it," Ma said, rather crisply. Pa laughed.

"Nothing like a woman for tallying up the measure of a man or what a man lacks! The Deacon and Mr. Bayless overtook what's left of Clayton's wagon party about a week ago … already much diminished, to hear them tell it."

"And what did they say of Clayton and his party, Elkanah?" Ma asked. She had not liked the Major from the start, not one single bit.

"For one, the Deacon did not approve of Major Clayton's continued insistence on traveling on Sunday. Mr. Bayless agreed, for a wonder. In his experience, he says that it does a company particular good to stop and rest at regular intervals over a long journey such as ours. Clayton's party is reduced to a mere thirty wagons, or so. I understand …" and I could clearly hear the laughter in Pa's voice, "…that his group is now so reduced in numbers that his lordly self must take a turn at night guard with the rest of the lesser mortals in his party."

"The hardship will do him good," Ma observed. She and Pa chuckled together. If they talked any more after that, I do not know, for I was fast asleep after that eventful day.

As it came about, we made the practice of resting on a Sunday, as near as we could to a pleasant place to camp. Mr. McNabb accompanied the hymn-singing on his hurdy-gurdy, while Deacon Zollicoffer conducted a brief service, which everyone but the Herlihys attended. The church service had to be brief, of course – for there was usually too much else to attend to. Ma had lessons for Jon and I, sometimes we had laundry to wash and spread to dry on the sweet green grass, and Pa and the other men usually wanted to go hunting, if there was anything in the locality worth the shot and powder.

Chapter 7 – Too Thick to Drink, Too Thin to Plow

Deacon Zollicoffer and Choctaw Joe Bayless joined Pa's wagon company the day that Jon and I got lost and encountered the Pawnee hunters. Of course, Shivaun and the Herlihy boys wanted to hear all about that, but I was too embarrassed with how we had gotten lost in the first place to embroider our account with overmuch detail. Especially how the Pawnee leader had made a jest of me, telling everyone that I was not well grown enough to be taken as a wife. I thought that I was perfectly well grown, save that I didn't have much in the way of a figure yet, but I could cook, and mend, make soap, cheese and candles, take care of babies and milk a cow. I was ready to be a wife if I wanted to be one. If someone like Henry Steitler looked on me with favor, I would certainly consider accepting a proposal.

Only all the other young men in our wagon company – the German boys, the Taylor brothers and the Pierson boys all looked at Shivaun McCarty, who was pretty and two years older than me, and flirted with all those young sparks something shameful to see. Why none of them even owned their own wagon! Only shares in one, or they were hired teamsters, anyway. It weighed on my mind, wondering if I had no better prospects than Shivaun McCarty. Perhaps I would turn out to be a spinster schoolteacher, like Miss Pierson, but I didn't want that life at all!

Several mornings after Deacon Zollicoffer and Choctaw Joe had joined the company, I was alone with Ma and could ask about it without being overheard. I felt certain that the boys and even Pa might make fun of me for wondering. Each of us carried a pair of buckets filled with water from the little trickling spring on the rise above our campground which had not gone entirely dry or been spoiled and dirtied by critters trampling. The water was good and clear, fresh-tasting and no trace of wigglers or mud, like that from the river. We had set up camp in meadows along the riverbank. The night before, we had watched the sun set, reflecting on the river like an endless sheet of quicksilver.

"Ma," I ventured. "Do you think I am grown enough to be married?"

"Certainly not," Ma replied, without hesitation. "You've only just started your woman-courses. Your father and I wouldn't consent to you marrying, before you are sixteen, at the very earliest."

"Sixteen is an old maid!" I replied, but I was secretly comforted.

"No, it is just barely old enough to know your own mind, Sugar-plum." Ma sent me a sideways smile. "I wed your father when I was seventeen and a half. My parents only approved because they thought your Pa was of sound character, owned a prosperous farm and would be able to support a wife and family." Ma chuckled, adding, "Now, if Mr. Astor's son, or the Prince of Wales tendered an offer of marriage to you this very moment, your Pa and I might consider approving. Assuming that either of those young men were acceptable to you."

"Ma, the Prince of Wales is only the age of Jon!" I protested. "Practically a baby, still!"

"Well, you see!" Ma was still chuckling. "There's time enough for you both to finish growing up, before you even consider getting married!"

I was vaguely comforted, although it meant that Ma and that painted Pawnee Indian did agree; I was not yet well grown enough to be a wife. It still made me envious of Shivaun McCarty, who was old enough and pretty enough to have her pick of any man, anywhere.

We had reached our camp at that moment, and the fire to cook breakfast over was ready; we had found quantities of wood this time, and the fire was a bed of glowing coals gleaming like rubies. It wouldn't take but a few minutes for the biscuits that Ma had set to bake in the iron Dutch oven to be hot and ready. Water for coffee was already burbling in the kettle. Pa was already there, leading the last of our oxen from where they had been grazing, putting them under yoke and fastening the last set of chains that harnessed them to our wagon.

All four of our yoke were good oxen, so tame that they obeyed every command, even from Jon, when Pa let him help drive. Pa generally had not nearly as much trouble setting our oxen to yoke than folk who had purchased barely new-broke teams in the trail market in Independence. Even a month on the trail hadn't entirely tamed some of them.

"Breakfast nearly ready?" Pa asked. Not only had Pa needed to deal with our own teams, but as captain of the train, to help with those in the party whose oxen weren't nearly as biddable. He looked tired, already, and the sun had barely risen; an oyster-shell pale glow on the eastern horizon.

"As soon as the bacon finishes crisping," Ma replied. She left me to empty our buckets into the big barrel, while she bent over the fire and turned the slices of fat bacon frying for breakfast.

I was already hungry – my mouth watering from the smell of bacon cooking, and Ma's lovely saleratus biscuits baking. Pa sighed.

"It will be a long day today, Sue. We'll be fording the River."

"Do you fear there will be difficulties?" Ma's voice sounded calm, but the expression on her face was a worried one. We had heard all the stories about how the Platte River crossing was especially dangerous. Although shallow and muddy, the riverbed was very wide; almost a mile and a half when in full flood and full of deep tracts of quicksand. Once in the river, the teams and wagons must keep going; to pause or hesitate even if just for a moment meant being sucked down and drowned. That was what everyone said about it, anyway.

Pa shook his head and sounded as if he were making himself sound deliberately cheerful. "We'll take every caution that we can, Sue. Mr. Bayless says most of the talk about the quicksand is much overblown. It's just that the Platte is so very muddy and much of that mud is in the riverbed itself. There are much more dangerous crossings, to hear him tell it ... But just in case, we've agreed to double-team every wagon, and cross just half the wagons at a time. It might very well take us all day."

"Haste makes waste," Ma agreed, although she still looked a bit worried. Pa leaned down and dropped a brief kiss on her cheek as she stood up from turning the bacon over.

"We'll be careful, Sue," he assured her. "No need to worry, over much. Glennie and Oscar are going to ride across first thing as soon as it is light and mark the best path across with willow stakes driven into the bottom. Mr. Bayless' suggestion. The spring flood has gone down from full.He says he can tell from the lines of wrack along the bank."

"We are fortunate to have Mr. Bayless with our company," Ma said. "I would rather have him and his wise counsel than any page of *Hasting's Emigrant's Guide* that you could name."

"Because he is with us now, and Hastings is ... wherever he is, that he promised to guide across his new cutoff." Pa agreed, sounding all jaunty and cheerful. "Still – here we are. And today we cross the river!"

I trusted what Pa had said, over breakfast but I was still apprehensive about fording the river. Pa and Mr. Herlihy hitched three of Mr. Herlihy's yoke to our wagon – an endless train of backs in front of us.

"You sit tight, and ride easy!" Mr. Herlihy called to us, as the doubled teams drew our wagon first to the river edge. Pa had said that we would go first, as a good example, and to show everyone else that it was perfectly safe. Ma and I sat on the wagon seat, with Jon between us and Boomer at our feet. I trusted Pa, of course. And Mr. Glennie, Oscar, and Choctaw Joe – who had all ridden ahead into the river that very morning, as we watched from the bank. Choctaw Joe mounted up on one of the Deacon's mules, his legs sticking out every which way, from a flimsy Indian saddle. Each of the three rode with a bundle of long, trimmed willow stakes tied to their saddles, each stake tied with a rag of bright cloth. We watched them ride into the water, out into it farther and farther, the two horses and the mule up to their bellies in muddy water, flowing around them with barely a shallow ripple. When they reached the far bank. the three and their mounts seemed as small as a set of toy cavalry soldiers, mere dark specks against the pale water.

"The river doesn't seem all that deep," Ma remarked. She sounded relieved. We had crossed over the Mississippi on a steamboat – a river at least as wide as the one that lay before us that morning. Pa looked back us and tipped his hat so that we could see him smiling.

"We'll start across as soon as Glennie and the others return from marking the safest path through," he promised. In a few minutes more, the three outriders came up out of the river, their garments and their mount's coats dripping water. Mr. Glennie drew rein, and slid down from his saddle.

"We've marked it, all the way across," he told Pa, sounding cheery and relieved. "The current is strongest along about the middle, but not powerful enough to tip a full-loaded wagon off the wheels, and the water isn't high enough to float it. Oscar and Joe will ride alongside, upstream – just in case you wind up needing help, I'll stick on the downstream side, in case anyone loses their footing."

"Any quicksand bogs?" Pa asked, and Mr. Glennie shook his head.

"No, just that the bottom is thick with mud and muck, as near as I can tell. Go careful, but keep moving, is what Joe says."

"Good," Pa replied, and it seemed like he squared his shoulders. "Pass the word to the others. We'll start in, now."

Mr. Glennie touched the brim of his hat to Ma and I and rode on. Our wagon lurched once, twice ... and then Pa and our lead yoke waded into the river's edge. I put my arm around Jon, as we watched the water get deeper and deeper, until the nearest ox-team was up to their bellies in it, and Pa was up to his waist, and clinging to the neck of Brandy, our lead near ox. *(Brandy was as tame a critter as there ever was; so affectionate and biddable that he would allow Jon to harness and drive him; Jon, who barely came up to Brandy's nose.)* We could feel that the wheels were clogging with mud as they rolled slowly. Once or twice, it seemed like the wheels drifted free and our wagon floated, pushed by an especially strong current. The wagon dipped and swayed then, especially as we reached the middle reaches of the wide river. We could look back and see a little behind us when we turned, as the way through the water worked this way and that, marked by the little calico rag flags on willow branches thrust into the riverbed. Half of our wagons followed us, double-teamed, while the remainder waited on the bank, waiting for the oxen to be returned from the far side, once the first half of the company had been brought over safely. I did see Mrs. Glennie at the reins of her light buggy, following after the Herlihy's family wagon, which was not as heavy as the wagon bearing Mr. Herlihy's forge tools and the bulk of their supplies.

It seemed that it took an age, crossing over – until the far bank gradually drew closer and closer, the bank and the scruffy brush lining it grew distinct and individual. Our lead yoke shouldered up onto the bank, water streaming from their hides. In a moment, the wheels crunched on the gravelly bank – and we were over the river!

Ma commented, raising her voice so that Pa could hear,

"Well, that's done – over and safe. It wasn't near as perilous as everyone made it out to be."

Pa looked back towards us and grinned, although he was soaked from the shoulders down. "Never take counsel of your fears, Sue. It was easy enough, although I thought sure that I'd be baptized entire all over again! Good old Brandy! When the current got too powerful, I just hung on to Brandy, and he pulled us through! Best ol' ox in the world, that's Brandy! Now ... we set up our wagon, unhook the critters and go back and bring over the rest of the company!"

Pa seemed so cheerful; triumphant and even happy at having brought us and the wagon safely across the Platte, which was claimed to be a very hazardous crossing. As he was the company captain, he would feel a terrible responsibility ... the same responsibility that I felt about seeing after Jon. Only Jon was just one small boy for me to look after; Pa had been elected by all the men in the company. It was his duty now, to bring us all safe to California. I knew very well that the trail would be long and dangerous. Even if some of the dangers were considerably overblown. It was all unknown, or at best, not very well known. There was plenty of danger lurking, even if everything went well for us all from now on.

As Pa predicted that morning, it took the best part of the day to bring all the wagons and the herd of loose cattle to the northern bank. We camped there for the night, as the men were all uniformly exhausted, wet and muddy. The German boys wagon box wasn't entirely waterproofed, as they discovered to their chagrin, when they set up camp. All their bedding was soaked through. Ma, Mrs. Herlihy and Shivaun helped them spread out their quilts and blankets and all, on the grassy bank above camp, to dry as well as it might.

"About another two weeks to Fort Laramie," Choctaw Joe Bayless told the gathering that evening, as the first stars began twinkling in the eastern sky. "Prolly a lot of Sioux camping thereabouts, to trade. If any of you folks are getting low on supplies, you might try trading with them for dried meat, pemmican and suchlike. Don't bother offering them cash money, though. They ain't got any use for such."

"What would they want, then?" Mr. Herlihy asked, and Choctaw Joe chuckled. 'Waaall, they might hanker after some of our rifles, but I think we put too much value on the ones that we have. Better offer other goods that they can't make theyselves. Fancy glass beads is always a hit with the squaws, o' course. Steel needles. Blankets. Tobaccy. Hatchet and knife blades – really, anything of forged metal, even bitty little scraps that they can make arrowheads out of. Never know what might take their fancy, most ways. Anything you don't want to carry any farther – throw it onto the blanket and see what you can get for it. Besides," Choctaw Joe added with another chuckle. "It gets powerful boring over the winter in them teepees."

Chapter 8 – Castles of Stone

It was already well into summer, after we crossed the Platte; the land was drier and the grass had already begun to turn brown. We saw buffalo on most days, but scattered in the dozens and two-dozens, not anything like that vast herd that had crossed our trail earlier. The lay of the land was hillier, and in the early mornings and evenings at sunset there was a blue line of hills, or even what I thought might be mountains on the distant horizon. The hills became a little more distinct, and eventually visible as the trail meandered closer and closer. I had nearly forgotten what hills looked like, by then, as we had spent so many weeks crossing that gentle-rolling sea of the prairie.

Those monumental hills, which eventually came into clear sight, looming over the trail, were the most fantastic which we had ever seen; tall and square, seemingly set with elaborate pillars, arches and vast window bays and galleries, as if constructed by a mighty architect. Some in the company said that the largest of those heights looked like the county courthouse, and I said so to Ma, one morning as Jon and I walked with her. We preferred walking, in preference to jolting along in the wagon, unless we were very, very tired. The wagons had spread out a little to one way and the other, to avoid the dust churned up by so many wheels and hooves going over the same track.

"No," Ma replied, thoughtfully. She surveyed the distant buff under the brim of her calico sunbonnet. "I don't think that it looks like a courthouse – but rather what I always imagined the Hanging Gardens of Babylon would have looked like."

"What are those. Ma?" I asked. I had heard mention of Babylon in Reverend Grandpa's sermons and read in the Bible about the Babylonian exile of the Hebrews, but I had never heard that gardens were involved. Only the Garden of Eden.

"A scenic wonder of the ancient world," Ma smiled. She very clever, Ma was – she had been educated in books, and might have been a teacher, but for marrying Pa. "According to Greek historians and travelers. But are no more. They tell of a grand terraced garden, built by one of their kings next to his palace. He had married a princess from a mountain kingdom, and the land around Babylon was all as flat as an iron griddle – his wife was homesick for her country. He was a rich and powerful king, and he could have anything that he wanted. So he had his architects build a splendid terraced garden, piling terrace on top of terraces, and having them bring in soil to plant trees and flowerbeds. He had them create waterfalls and ponds ... I imagine that those ponds were filled with water lilies and fish with fins and scales like jewels. They would have had tame nightingales and peacocks. A most beautiful garden, for his wife to walk in and not feel so homesick for the mountains of the country that she came from." Ma gave a little sigh, and I looked at her, under the brim of my own bonnet.

Ma was remembering her own little garden of flowers back in Ohio, I was certain. I looked at the galleried bluff, and tried to imagine it, terraced and planted with trees, and fitted out with waterfalls and ponds of fish … No, I couldn't see it, at all. On Ma's other side, Jon spoke up.

"We'll have a garden jus' like that in California, Ma – just you wait and see!"

Ma smiled down at him, and when she replied,

"Oh, yes, Jonny-cakes, we will indeed," her voice sounded as if she were forcing it to be cheerful.

We were still a long way from California. And I just couldn't see the gardens that Ma dreamed of in that big bluff, crannied as it was with gullies and terraces.

Several days later, the company passed near to another strange bluff, this one very unlike the one that Ma fancied as the terraced gardens and wonder of the ancient world. This bluff was shaped like an enormous upside-down funnel. We could see it on the horizon for some days, the slender part of it sticking up like a shot tower or an enormous chimney. Choctaw Joe Bayless told Pa and the other men that the Indians had a very rude name for that rock, a name that made Mr. Herlihy laugh immoderately, but Pa wouldn't tell us what it was.

"The fur-trading mountain men call it Chimney Rock," was all that Pa would tell us. "And Choctaw Joe says that the first time that he came this way it was even taller."

That Chimney Rock could be seen for three or four days on the journey, every day looming closer and closer, until by nooning on the fourth day, it seemed as if we were just a stone-throw distant. When we stopped for the noonday rest on that day, Mr. Glennie and his wagons were next to us, on the other side of Mr. Steitler and Henry's single wagon. The tall rock looked over us; seemingly so close that it was almost like you could reach out and touch it. Ma spread a length of heavy canvas on the ground, and we sat down on it to eat our cold dinner. Everyone in the company was doing likewise, although when Mr. Glennie came over to our wagon to talk to Pa about where we were to camp that evening, he cast a look at that tall rock and observed,

"We're so close to that big ol' tower! I have it in mind to ride over and take a look. Oscar and Mr. Steitler's boy, they want to have a look, too – let their horses stretch out a bit. Bet we can be there and back before we get started again."

"Be my guest," Pa replied, grinning. Jon, with an eager expression on his face cried out,

"Oh, Pa! Can I go with them? Please? I want to write my name on it! Ma has been teaching us all this way, and I want to write my name on something like that!"

Pa looked amused at this. "All right, Jonny-cake! But you stick close to Mr. Glennie and the boys. Don't you go wandering away from them, you might run into more unfriendly Indians than you did last time."

Ma looked concerned, and whispered so that only Pa and I could hear, "Elkanah ... do you think that is wise? Jon is only..."

"As safe as anything," Pa replied, confidently. "You go with the boys, Jonny-cake! Be certain that you spell your whole name right; Jonathon Mathew Kettering!"

"Sure, Pa!" Jon sprang up from where he had been setting on the canvas. Mr. Glennie leaned down and lifted him up by one arm, as if he was Cally, lifting one of her kittens by the scruff of it's neck and settled Jon on the saddle in front of him.

"We'll be back before we roll out, depend on it!" Mr. Glennie assured us, and Pa just chuckled to himself as Mr. Glennie rode away, followed by Oscar and Henry on their paint-ponies bought from the Indians. I did note that Henry rode more assuredly than Oscar, as if he had sat on a saddled horse as often as did Mr. Glennie; back straight as a rule in the rough saddle, with his elbows tight to his sides, while Oscar's elbows flopped all over the place, like he was trying to scare chickens.

"Don't you think ..." Ma began to say, and Pa laughed outright.

"Don't worry about it, Sue," he answered. "They'll be back in two shakes of a lamb's tail! See that ol' rock that looks so close? It's actually near on to forty miles from our trail, even though it looks close enough to spit at."

"How did you know that!" Ma exclaimed, much indignant and ruffled like one of her angry hens back in Ohio. "And you didn't tell them!"

"I did," Pa replied, shaking his head with regret. "Last night, when we talked about it, estimating how far we had come that day. He told us that we weren't more than five miles from that chimney rock, and that he was going to ride up to it today and carve his name on it. Choctaw Joe said, no, it was near onto fifty miles away. Choctaw Joe and Jeptha Glennie near as came to blows over it, until I said that tomorrow would settle the question." Pa shook his head "I purely didn't want them to argue any more over such a trivial matter. Better they find out for themselves, than I count coup unnecessarily by leaning on my authority as captain. Choctaw Joe has been telling me about how the air is so clear out in the west. Without anything near to give a sense of distance, folk make mistakes all the time. I'd rather they work it out for themselves. It spares Jeptha Glennie looking like a fool in front of everyone."

Ma looked as if she wanted to say more but on second thought, considered it best not to. Because Pa was right. Just as Pa got up from the rest that he was taking in the narrow shade cast by the wagon, with Boomer curled up at his side, Mr. Glennie and the boys returned. They all looked tired – even their horses looked tired, and Mr. Glennie looked chastened. Jon scrambled down from behind Mr. Glennie. He looked as if he had been promised a great treat and then had it snatched away from him.

"Well, did you spell your name right, when you painted it on the chimney rock?" Pa asked, and Jon shook his head, downcast with disappointment.

"That ol' rock wasn't close at all!"

"Turned out that crazy old coot was right about it being forty miles from here, or thereabouts," Mr. Glennie admitted. He looked about as sad and regretful as Jon and the German boys did. "We rode until we were certain that damned rock – sorry, Miz Kettering – was just about as far away as it was when we set out! Serves me right, Captain Kettering, for being so damn cock-sure of myself, when Choctaw Joe has been out this way time without number. Sure as shooting; I won't soon disregard his opinion again."

"Neither should we," Pa replied warmly. "For we are new to the trail, and he isn't ... but for sure, I would myself have taken a bet that the Chimney Rock wasn't more than a mile or two from this very spot. Don't beat yourself up over the way that the clear air out here can fool a man, Jeptha."

"I surely won't," Mr. Glennie tipped his hat toward Pa, nodded courteously toward Ma, and rode away toward his own wagon.

Pa looked at Ma and winked. "What did I tell you, Sue?"

The other interesting thing that occurred was one evening, when we had set up camp for the night and Choctaw

Joe had come to our fire, as was his usual habit, Miss Pierson and Mr. McNabb came over from the Pierson campfire. It was curious; they were holding hands. Pa greeted them, assuming that their visit was something to do with trail business. People were accustomed to visit our fire to speak with Pa about such matters. I know that this bothered Ma sometimes, as it meant that Pa and the rest of us really couldn't settle to our evening meal.

But Choctaw Joe was good company, and so was Mr. Steitler and Henry. Choctaw Joe had entertaining yarns about his days in the mountains, and his travels with the Indians, and Mr. Steitler had his flute and his music, and his talks about botany and geology and all that so we relished their company of an evening.

The curious thing was that Miss Pierson and Mr. McNabb hadn't really come to consult with Pa. They were looking for Deacon Zollicoffer.

"The Deacon is at his devotions of an evening," Choctaw Joe drawled. "Communing with his guiding Spirit, I'd say. Is there a message you would have me pass to him once that he is done?"

"Indade," Mr. McNabb's bearded chin jutted aggressively. "We would like for him to read the banns over us … every Sunday until we reach … what is it, Naomi? Yes, Independence Rock – in three weeks or so. And then, if he would be so kind as to perform the service of marriage for us…

we … that is Miss Naomi Pierson and I would like to be married."

There was a long and astonished silence from us all when Mr. McNabb said that, but none of us were so rude or untactful to make a remark. Pa only set aside his plate, stood up and made as if to shake Mr. McNabb's hand.

"You do, then? Well, we should congratulate you, Ewan – and you too, Miss Pierson. Here's hoping for every blessing and life-long happiness for the both of you."

"I'm certain the Deacon will be happy to read the banns and to hear your marriage vows," Ma added, softly. "And that will be time enough for us to plan a proper wedding feast for afterwards. We're all very happy for you, Naomi … just a mite surprised, is all."

"I expect so," Miss Pierson agreed. "But it just seemed to us to be the proper thing to do, as we have become so very fond of each other, during these days of travel."

"Aye," Mr. McNabb agreed. *Was that an affectionate look towards Miss Pierson?* "Better to marry than to burn! Well, when you see Deacon Zollicoffer, tell him that I would speak to him in this matter."

Both Miss Pierson and Mr. McNabb said their good-nights and took their departure. I noticed that they were still holding hands, and that their heads inclined toward each other. When they were out of hearing, Choctaw Joe chuckled softly and commented,

"Well, for every sweet flower in the field there is a venturesome bee!"

"Don't you be sounding as if it is so comic!" Ma flared up, as Pa laughed, too. "I think it is sweet! "

"So it is, Sue," Pa replied. He took up his plate again and began cutting up his serving of pan-fried salt-beef for himself. "But if I were a betting man, I would have said that would be more likely that Miss Shivaun McCarty and any of those brave young hosses in the company would get hitched, long before a sobersides like McNabb and a spinster such as Miss Pierson!"

"Although," Ma added thoughtfully, "I can't think there is anyone among the company who would bring up an objection to their marriage. We're out here in the wilderness; who among us would know of any impediment!"

"It's a custom," Pa explained, mostly for the benefit of Choctaw Joe, "In most denominations, to read out an intention for marriage three times, each Sunday. You know – in case anyone knows of a reason why the couple ought not to marry. Previous marriage not annulled properly, religious vows, party promised to marry another... that kind of matter."

"Seems kind of pointless, doing so out here," Choctaw Joe agreed. "Still, I will acquaint the Deacon with what Mr. McNabb and Miss Pierson want, once that he finishes confabulating with the Lord God Almighty. I'm certain he will have no objection, being a man of God and all."

That marriage was the talk of the company for days among the women; at least as much for astonishment, as it was something new. News of it flew faster than the migrating birds overhead the ones that were seen as small dark 'v's in the sky, arrowing towards the south. Shivaun McCarty and the little Herlihy boys came to walk with us, upwind of the wagons and the blowing dust that their wheels raised in dun-colored clouds of grit.

"Sally, I have heard it from Oscar the German laddie! He says that he has heard a rumor that Miss Pierson is to be married to Mr. McNabb! Is that not the most incredible, ridiculous thing imaginable?"

"It is not!" I answered, "For it is true! Mr. McNabb and Miss Pierson came to our campfire, asking after the Deacon, saying that they wished him to say the banns for them during the Sunday meeting, the next three weeks! Pa calculates that we will be at Independence Rock by then and the wedding will be there!"

"Holy Mother Mary!" Shivaun exclaimed, and made the sign of the cross, after the Papist fashion. "So it is true, then! Mayve will be astounded, indade!" She lowered her voice, and murmured, "There she is, then – an' why does she wish to marry, now? What does she see in him? For he is not one of those men who are the gift of God for handsomeness, nor is he one for gab and charm ... Miss Pierson!" Shivaun called, for we had come up to the Pierson wagons, and Miss Pierson herself was walking by herself, that man's wide-brimmed hat that she was accustomed to wear for every day set square on her head. "Miss Pierson – 'tis said that you are to marry soon, and I did not believe it at first, but Sally says that it is true! Yourself and Mr. McNabb! Is this true?"

Miss Pierson looked around, seemingly a bit astonished to be asked such a personal question in such a hectoring tone.

"Why yes, it is, Shivaun. Mr. McNabb has done the honor of asking me to marry him, and I have said 'yes'. I know this company is like a small village, with nothing much to divert the gossips but I cannot see why this simple social transaction would excite such a degree of disbelief."

Shivaun seemed baffled for a moment. I suppose that Miss Pierson had used words which Shivaun didn't fully grasp their meaning at first. Finally, Shivaun replied, sounding slightly chastened, "He isn't all that handsome, for a gentleman of property. I cannot see why any woman would think him a catch."

"No, my intended is hardly the beaux ideal as sentimental novels have it," Miss Pierson replied. She sounded amused, rather than offended. "But as he is, he suits me very well. He has a good trade, he is musical, and we have similar tastes and interests in common. And besides," she added with a sharp sideways look at the two of us, "We are old enough not to have inflated expectations of enduring romance. We like each other very well and think that we can jog on happily in harness together. I think we shall do very well. Was there anything else that you wished to ask me?"

"Nooo ..." Shivaun admitted, sounding rather abashed. "I will tell my sister that you are planning to be wed. I do not know what we may be able to give you as a bride-gift. But we will come to the wedding, doubtless."

"And welcome you shall be," Miss Pierson favored us with an unexpectedly sweet smile. "I daresay that our nuptials will be the reason for much jollification. Other than the passing scenery, wandering buffalo herds, and visiting Indians, there is so little else to divert the gossips!" and she nodded and then walked a little faster, to keep up with their wagons, while Shivaun and I looked at each other, and I said,

"I told you so."

I did ask Ma later; what was it that Mr. McNabb meant, when he said that it was better to marry than to burn.

Ma replied, "He meant that it was better to marry and live with someone that you loved, than to live an immoral life, and then face eternal judgement for it."

I thought about that for a moment, and asked, "What kind of immoral life do you mean, then?"

Ma sighed. "You'll understand when you are a bit older, Sugar-plum."

I did, eventually – but that was because of where we lived in the gold camps in California, some years later. But at the time, I just shrugged and figured that Ma was right; I'd understand when I was a bit older.

I also had almost forgotten what a proper town might look like, but Fort Laramie was nothing at all like that anyways. It was a regular square fortress compound, white-washed and with walls standing twice the height of a man, with a pair of gates on either side, gates guarded by taller towers built over top of them. Pa later pointed out to Jon and me that the guard towers had narrow slits in the walls for firing rifles out of them. That was not so odd. What struck us all as curious and somewhat alarming was there were all the triangular Indian tents scattered around – as if a whole city of Indians had taken it in mind to come and set up their homes in the river meadows surrounding the fort. Tents and what Choctaw Joe told us were brush wikiups, and their horses roaming here and there, while boys in hardly anything but a string around their waist and a flap hanging down before and aft playing raucous boy-games.

"I have never seen so many Indians in a single place before," Ma remarked, as we set up camp that evening. Pa and Choctaw Joe had sent word to the commander of the fort, notifying them of our intention to rest several days, and to trade at the fort and with the Indians, if that was acceptable to them. Choctaw Joe had come to confer with Pa, complaining that Deacon Zollicoffer was already planning a foray into the Indian camps to preach the Gospel to them.

'Gives me the yips, hearing him go on," Choctaw Joe explained. "And on, and on. Wonder if the Deacon bothers the Almighty as much as he bothers me. I always calculated the

Almighty had so much else to worry about in the world that He'd be right relieved not to have to hear from me. I figger on spending time with you to better effect, Cap'n Kettering."

"Always a pleasure and an education," Pa replied with a smile. Everyone in the train liked Choctaw Joe, although I think he baffled many of the older folk. Jon and I took him at face value, his dark complexion, his Indian clothing, and his odd manner of sometimes listening to things which ordinary folk couldn't quite hear or comprehend.

Now, Choctaw Joe was helping Pa tighten the ropes which held the tent poles upright while he and Pa conferred. Pa thanked him for the assistance and added. "Stay and take supper with us? No...? I mean to ask – these Indians seem quite different from those that ran the river ferry on the Kansas. Can you tell me much about the tribes around here?"

"O' course," Choctaw Joe nodded. He seemed right pleased that Pa was interested. "They're Sioux – Lakotah, mostly. Call themselves 'the Seven Council Fires People'. The Lakotah are the westernmost of the seven councils. Used to be woods Indians east of the Mississippi River but ..." Joe shrugged. "... lost a fight with the Ojibweh years ago and moved out of the woods and into the open plains."

"I wouldn't have thought they warred so energetically among their own kind," Pa said, and Choctaw Joe began to laugh so hard that he began to cough.

"Lor' bless you, Cap'n!" He exclaimed when he could speak again. "Them tribes all live for making war 'gainst each other! It's their whole life – hunting fer buffalo, making war and stealing each other's women and scalps! Don't let anyone ever tell you different! See here," And Choctaw Joe's brown face got sober and serious. "Them tribes ... you jus' might see them as all Indians and all the same, but they are as different between them as an Irishman is from a Dutchman, and different again from an Eye-talian. Telling you the truth now, Cap'n. Them Lakota are the nobs and nobility ... 'especially compared to them trashy Comanche, down towards Texas-way. The Lakota, they got some high-class ways to them, like those noble lords you read about in books by that Scott fellow. In the main, though," and Choctaw Joe chuckled again. "They're jolly company. Good fellows. Nothing so entertaining as spending a winter evening in the lodges with them, telling jokes, spinning yarns about war, hunting and wimmen ... lies, mostly, but purely entertaining lies! Give me a choice of company that I want to get snowed in with for a winter, given a good fire and plenty of fat buffalo to eat ... I'll chose that company over any tavern in civilized country east of the Mississippi that you might name."

"What about these Lakotah, then," Pa persisted. "How do you advise that we treat with them?"

"As proud men among equals," Choctaw Joe replied at once. "As tender of their honor as any of them knights of the olden days, or a Southren gentleman with a reputation for dueling when anything of his'n been slighted. Tread careful-like, Cap'n. Tell the other men to do the same. I'll be around their camps, like as not. Deacon Zollicoffer plans to preach the Word to them, every day that we are here."

"I wonder how he can feel safe among them, if they are as quick to take offense as you say," Pa ventured.

Choctaw Joe chuckled in rich amusement. "Wal, the thing is among Injuns generally, it's considered heap bad medicine to harm someone touched in their upper works."

"You don't say!" Pa began to laugh, right along with Choctaw Joe. "Your considered opinion is that since they consider the Deacon to be as crazy as a coot, he will be safe among them?"

"That be 'bout the size of it, Cap'n." Choctaw Joe agreed, and Pa shook his head.

"The Lord works in mysterious ways, his wonders to perform! Well, I'll tell the other men to put on their best manners among the Sioux, should they come visiting tomorrow."

"Oh, they well, Cap'n." Choctaw Joe assured him. "Like I said – it gets powerful boring in those long winters up here." And he added, "They will come calling, o' course. Only without cards and expecting to set in the parlor for fifteen minutes. They'll be looking to trade for goods that they can't get otherwise."

"What kind of goods?" Pa asked. "And what can they offer us that you think of any value?"

"Dried meat," Choctaw Joe replied, instanter. "Pemmican, if they have any to spare against their own long winters. Likely to offer you cured skins, buffalo robes ... that kind of thing, in trade for anything from the East that you might be able to spare an' which takes their fancy. But then, you never know what might take their fancy."

Choctaw Joe was quiet for a moment, before he continued. "You have your women and children along with you, so they'll be ate up with curiosity, being that most white men they have ever seen were folk like me ... trappers and traders and that." It seemed as if Choctaw Joe thought a bit more, considering what else he would say, before adding. "It's a good thing in the main, Cap'n – that you-all brung your wives and children. Means that you-all are peaceful-like, and don't intend to borrow trouble."

"We don't," Pa agreed. "And we do intend to be peaceable ... and moving on to California in as many days."

Pa and the other men had decided that since the company had made such good time on the trail that we could spend three or four days resting at Fort Laramie. Mrs. Glennie's mule-drawn buggy and Deacon Zollicoffer's mule teams set a cracking pace for the ox teams, as they drifted to leading the train within an hour of setting out every morning. It probably tried the oxen sorely, keeping up to the two of them, but as Pa said, it was an ill wind that blew no one any good, and he was glad of it. We had made excellent time on that portion of our long trail. Choctaw Joe even said so.

"Oh, wonderful!" Ma exclaimed. "We can do our laundry, since there will be time enough for it all to dry! The bedding, even!"

It had bothered Ma and the other women something fierce, how dirty our clothes and linen had gotten, with never a chance to wash them thoroughly and allow to dry, spread out on the grass or draped over bushes. This would be almost the first time on the trail that they had a chance to wash, and freshen all of our bedding, since we would have four or five days camped at Fort Laramie. I was a bit downcast, because that would mean something akin to tedious hours over the wash-tub, rubbing soap into the dirty clothes and sheets, not to mention boiling water for the washing, wringing out the soppy-wet sheets and spreading them to dry...

But it would be nice to have clean everything again – smelling sweet from the open air, instead of stale and vaguely musty. I decided that I wouldn't mind having to help Ma. As long as Jon and I could see the Indians and the fort, with Pa and the other men close at hand.

It was a lot of work, though; hauling bundles of bedding and our spare change of clothes and Pa's calico shirts a short way from our wagons, down to where the water in the branch of the Platte which came down from the mountains ran fairly clean. Mrs. Herlihy and Shivaun brought their own washing, and presently Mrs. Glennie joined us, although she confessed that she wasn't up to laundering much more than her own shifts.

"I cannot think how women with children manage!" she exclaimed. Poor Mrs. Glennie! She was pale and fragile, slender as a white lily in Ma's garden back in Ohio. She had only begun to let her corset out, over the small bulge of her stomach made by the baby that she was going to have.

"Ah, but you see – you have the children to train up to work on the farm or in the house," Ma replied, crisply. Mrs. Herlihy snorted with laughter. Shivaun only rolled her eyes. Seamus and Darragh Herlihy had carried down the heavy washtubs for us, and some big kettles to heat water over a fire that Mr. Herlihy had built, before he, Mr. Glennie and Mr. Steitler went off in the direction of the fort. Very obligingly, the little Herlihy boys, Wee Donal, Liam and Rory dipped up buckets from the river and carried them to fill up the kettles, but then they vanished as well, leaving Ma, Mrs. Glennie, and Mrs. Herlihy with just Shivaun and I to help.

Still, it was not all that awful, out in the fresh open air, under a sky as blue as the little blue stones in a brooch in the shape of a bird that Mrs. Glennie had at the collar of her dress. She told me that they were turquoise and set in gold, and the bird's eyes were two tiny red rubies, and not chips of red glass as I had first assumed. I guessed since Mr. Glennie was rich and had purchased a carriage and a team of fine mules to pull it, that he could afford to buy his wife a brooch with real rubies set in it.

"And after all, we need not be moving on, in an hour or a day!" Mrs. Herlihy wrung the water out of her husband's long shirts with hands that looked as powerful as his. She tossed the shirt to Shivaun, who caught it deftly in a basket already full of wrung-out garments. I had a basket similarly full, and we went with them to where we could spread them out on the clean, untrampled grass, and over the branches of a clump of sweet-smelling sage, there being no trees large enough to string a clothesline from.

"Cut for fires, long since," Shivaun guessed, when I wondered aloud about this. "Close to the fort, since it is." She set down the basket of wet clothes and looked back towards the fort. "I'd reckon that they now must go a long way to cut firewood."

"Better than burning buffalo chips," I replied, as Shivaun shaded her eyes with her hand.

"Look, you," she said. "There come some of those Indians ... and Mr. Bayless hisself with them! I wonder what they are wanting, now?"

"Mr. Bayless said that they might want to trade a mite with us," I replied. "For whatever pretties that they might like. Hurry with these clothes, Shivaun! I want to see them, up close."

"Surprised that you would want to do that," Shivaun replied, as we set to spreading out the damp clothes and sheets wherever we could find a clear space for them. "After the scare you and your brother had from them Pawnee hunters…"

"I wasn't scared," I retorted. "Not a bit of it. They were mostly boys, and I'm not scared of a bunch of boys!"

Shivaun only laughed and looked at me sideways, as if she knew a secret that I didn't. In a very few minutes, we had spread out all the damp laundry over the grass and the mountain sage bushes; the day was so warm and the mountain air so thin and arid that I thought it would not take very long for even the heaviest flannel to dry thoroughly. Ma and Mrs. Glennie and Mrs. Herlihy had already hurried from our collection of tubs, the fire and kettles – back to our wagon camp, to meet Choctaw Joe and the small party of Sioux women wading through the grass towards us.

There were three of them, the youngest of about Shivaun's age. She was leading a pony by a bridle, the pony drawing a sort of frame – two long poles crossed over it's back, with the ends trailing on the ground, and a large bundle tied to a woven panel of cane and leather bands lashed between the trailing ends of those poles. Much later, I learned that the contraption of poles and cane was called a travois. The Indians commonly didn't take to making wheels and using carts; they carried everything with them on packs and travois, and could go places where our wheels couldn't travel. The other women were older than the girl and their leather dresses appeared to be more elaborately trimmed. I envied those Sioux women on account of their hair, which was long and dark, bound up into braids as thick as my wrist. Such long braids, whereas my own hair made a pair of measly little plaits, which barely came to my shoulders.

As we came, panting from the effort of running in the thin mountain air, Choctaw Joe was saying, by way of introduction,

"This is Han-tay-wi, her sister, Kimmi-Mila, and daughter Eh-hawee. They have come to offer goods to trade."

"Tell the ladies that we are most pleased to make their acquaintance," That was Mrs. Glennie, most regally formal, as if she were receiving them in her own parlor, and not in the space of trampled grass between our wagon, and Glennie's wagons and tent. "I do not know if we have any such goods as might please them, and that we can spare..."

"You'd be surprised," Choctaw Joe replied. Meanwhile, the younger woman was untying the cords which bound together the big bundle and spreading out the contents; three or four enormous robes of buffalo hide, with the thick wooly brown fur still on, a stack of painted hide boxes full of some crumbly brown stuff – pemmican, and six pair of moccasins, all trimmed with fancy colored stuff, and elaborate fringe. It wasn't beadwork, I learned much later, but flattened and dyed porcupine quills. Two of them were large to fit a man, but the others were smaller. There were some other things; pouches and sheaths for knives, all made of leather and trimmed with fringe, beadwork, feathers and porcupine quills.

"Oh, my!" Ma whispered, upon seeing the buffalo robes and the moccasins. Although it was only June and at the height of summer, we had felt the cold as we traveled higher into the mountains. "Those things certainly look as if they would be warm at night!"

"Yes, ma'am," Choctaw Joe looked as if he were hiding a grin, even as he cast an assessing eye over the robes. "Nothing better, softer or warmer to sleep on than a prime buffler robe. These are tanned and softened up real nice, too. You can't go wrong with one of them, Miz Kettering."

"Then let me look in the wagon, for what we can spare," Ma had a determined look on her face. Mrs. Glennie and Mrs. Herlihy were also eyeing the robes, with an acquisitive expression on their faces. I was looking at the next-to-smallest pair of moccasins, thinking that they would just about fit me, and the smallest would be perfect for Jon.

But that was a frivolous thing, and up to Ma to decide, anyway. I think the oldest Indian woman saw me looking at the moccasins, though, with longing for them all over my face. So did Choctaw Joe.

Ma emerged from our wagon, with a bundle in her hand – one of our store-bought blankets that came from the east, and some other things – a campfire turning fork with a busted tine, her needlework basket and a small iron kettle which we had hardly ever used on the journey so far.

"These," she announced calmly. "And three good steel needles and a paper of new pins. For two of those robes."

"I want one of those robes, too," Mrs. Glennie looked enviously at Ma, as Choctaw Joe relayed Ma's offer to the three Sioux women in their language.

Choctaw Joe listened to the response that the oldest woman made to him, and grinned. "A generous bid indeed, Miz Kettering. Very generous. For that, Han-tay-wi will add in a *parfleche* of good pemmican, and two pair of moccasins – she is an honorable woman and does not want the white folks to think she is taking unfair advantage."

"I appreciate Mrs. Han-tay-wi's sense of honor and generosity," Ma replied, as Choctaw Joe looked in my direction and winked. I was thrilled beyond words. My own pair of fancy moccasins, and another for Jon, too!

Although the pemmican looked perfectly disgusting. Choctaw Joe later explained how it had been made from buffalo meat, dried and then pounded to powder, then mixed with dried berries and made into bricks with the addition of melted bear fat. It was what sustained the wild Indians during winters, when they couldn't hunt. I don't know how anyone could relish eating it. I said so to Pa; Pa laughed and told us about scrapple that the Dutch folk made, back in the east.

"If you're hungry enough, Sugar-plum, just about anything that won't bite you back tastes good."

Mrs. Glennie emerged from the Glennie's tent with a blanket and a shawl hanging over her arm – the shawl was a pretty printed challis one, with a long silk fringe. She wanted a buffalo robe in exchange for the shawl and the blanket, two more pair of the moccasins, and one of the fancy leather pouches with beadwork on it. I could see Han-tay-wi's eyes light up, when Mrs. Glennie spread it out for them to examine closer. The three Indian women bent over the shawl, talking to each other as they stroked the fringe.

"Yessirree bob, you've got them something rare, there," Choctaw Joe murmured. Mrs. Glennie came close to laughing. "I have never favored that shawl! It was a gift from Mr. Glennie's sister Althea Murchison, and dear Althea deliberately chose it in colors which I find to be quite repulsive – and she knew that very well! But it was so very expensive that I had to thank her for her generosity and exquisite taste every time we encountered her ..."

"You don't care for your sister-in-law then," Mrs. Herlihy ventured, knowingly.

"She is a woman of many extremely dislikable virtues," Mrs. Glennie replied, and I could see that Ma was trying to hold back laughter.

Mrs. Glennie did get her buffalo robe, and some other interesting Sioux pretties. I wondered if the Sioux women spent their parlor hours, just as Ma and Aunt Rachel and their other woman friends back in Ohio; fancy work to keep their hands busy and to show off to their friends., knitting and crocheting, making embroidered and Berlin wool-work and tatted lace. Mrs. Herlihy had nothing much to offer, but some fine steel needles, and a box of odd bits of scrap metal from

Mr. Herlihy's forge works, but she got the last buffalo robe in exchange for it, as well as three or four of the hide boxes of pemmican.

"They'll make arrow heads from it," Choctaw Joe commented, knowledgeably. "Better than from obsidian – don't break and shatter so bad. And you'll be right glad of that there pemmican, Miz Herlihy, if we come to camping cold in the mountains with our supplies running low."

"Oh, it won't come to that, I'm certain," Mrs. Herlihy chuckled comfortably. "Himself says that we're moving briskly enough that we should be well over the mountains and into California before the first snow falls. As for the pemmy-whatever, Seamus and Darragh eat as if starving at every single meal. I could stand by the fire and put food into them with Himself's forge shovel, they eat so much and never bother to taste before swallowing it ... the great hungry lumps that they are!"

The three Sioux women seemed very pleased with their takings from the session of trade, but not half as pleased as Jon and I were, that night, with that heavy buffalo robe drawn over us, against the chill of the night ... or I was, later on when I grew out of my shoes. They rubbed such blisters on my feet that Ma said I could wear my Indian moccasins instead, lest the blisters turn purulent and poison my blood.

All that came much later, when we were crossing the great barren desert.

Chapter 9 – A Fateful Meeting

We departed from Fort Laramie after breaking our journey there for some days – nearly a week, as I recall it. Another large wagon party was coming up from the ford across the South Platte. Pa and the other men decided that the meadows where we had set up camp were too small to accommodate the two wagon companies and all the Lakota Sioux at once. We set out on the trail again, after having rested the critters, traded with the Indians and at the Fort, where there was not much to be had and that was expensive.

Ma wrote letters to Aunt Rachel and Grandpa Reverend, as there was rumor among the folk at the Fort of parties coming from the Oregon Territory and from California also; parties who would be agreeable to carrying mail back to Council Bluffs or Independence. I recollect that Ma was then worried about the war with Mexico, which had broken out that year. But Pa told her that we were a considerable distance from where the war was then going on, and California was so far distant as well … and from what he had heard, the few folk – the Americans and Mexicans both which were already settled in California were restive under what little power that Mexico could bring to bear on them.

Anyway, we were still hundreds and hundreds of miles away from California although Choctaw Joe assured us that we were about a third of the way there. Ma was very happy with how he had assisted her, and Mrs. Glennie and Mrs.

Herlihy in trading with the Sioux women. Because Pa was now captain of the company, and Choctaw Joe being familiar with the trail and the wild lands of the west, he was often at our campfire in the evenings, when it came time for supper. Ma took to inviting him to share our evening meal every night, as Deacon Zollicoffer meditated most evenings on his call from the Lord and ate very sparingly anyway on most nights.

Pa usually wanted to consult Choctaw Joe about what might be encountered on the next day of traveling. Mr. Steitler and Henry were already sharing our fire of an evening. Henry on his Indian pony was one of the outriders, so it made good sense that he was there as well.

One evening that I recall most particularly, I was finally overcome by curiosity. I asked Choctaw Joe straight out if he had run away from a slave condition. Ma's kin were abolitionists and Ma was very strong in that conviction. I had overheard her and Pa talking about Choctaw Joe and wondering if he were an escaped slave. Now Ma looked horrified, and started to chide me for asking impertinent questions, but Choctaw Joe only laughed.

"No, Sally-girl! I was born a free man of color! Never a slave, not even for a single day! My father was a rich white man, Josiah Bayless. My mother was a free woman; his housekeeper. They couldn't marry because of the laws in Maryland, but they were as good as wedded, for all their lives, and everyone respected my father. He apprenticed me to a tailor in Baltimore when I was grown enough. Fourteen, I was, then. He wanted me to have a good trade, had seen to my schooling so I could read and write, but I just didn't take to the trade. One thing and another, I hired on to Astor's fur brigade!" Choctaw Joe grinned, in memory. "Told everyone I was part Kanaka from the Hawaiian Islands; that I was the son of one of their big chiefs. Out beyond the frontier, no one cared if I was black or white, or a blue-painted cannibal, to tell the truth. It was just – how many pelts did you come back with and were you still alive, after two or three seasons in the mountains. It was a fine life, Sally-girl, Miz Kettering," Choctaw Joe sighed. "But I was young, then and trade in beaver pelts was all the crack. I did very well out of it until the fur market caved in after all those years ... enough to retire on my trade earnings and buy a little house in St. Louis in the colored quarter. My father was a good man of business, so I reckon I inherited that much of sense from him. I could sit in my garden and tell yarns to the young 'uns. But my heart was always ... out there. Mountains!" His voice was full of longing. "I have a wish in my heart to go to the mountains one more time, Miz Kettering. For the sight of them, tall and violet against the sky, in garments of snow, or clean green pine, golden in the autumn with aspens. It was providential that Deacon Zollicoffer's boys offered me a prime salary to take care of the crazy old cuss, but I think that I would have set out on my own, soon enough. I gotta see those mountains one more time, 'afore I leave this world."

The trail turned harder after we left Fort Laramie; no more the easy meandering across the open sea of grass that it had been in the first weeks. But rough hauling over rockier ground slowed us down. The oxen had to pull much harder, and sometimes there was danger for them from pools of bad water – alkali water, Choctaw Joe told us. Warned about this, we tried to keep the oxen from drinking at those springs, because such was pure poison. One of Mr. Herlihy's oxen got sick from it, but Pa and Mr. Herlihy doctored that ox by forcing it to swallow a big wad of salt pork. I didn't know why it should be such a cure, but Ma explained that likely the fat bacon coated every one of its four stomachs, and let the poison slide all the way through.

Ma also collected up some of the white alkali powder from a poison spring that had dried, up saving it in an empty tin against the day when we ran out of soda. Choctaw Joe told her that it was as good as saleratus for making biscuits, although we were at first in two minds about eating them! But Ma's biscuits tasted as good as they always did. Ma and I also discovered a patch of pea vines growing in abundance near a natural spring of sweet water. We picked a good apron-full of fresh wild peas; when we stopped to make camp for the night, Ma and I would shell them for supper. We so missed green garden vegetables! Gleaning wild fruit and greens from beside the trail hardly made up for it.

The very day that Ma and I found the wild pea patch, we met a small party of travelers coming east. Mr. Glennie and

Oscar encountered them first, as they were scouting ahead of the party, looking for a spot with sweet water, plenty of wood and pasturing for the oxen. Jon and I were walking along with Pa. Jon was holding Pa's ox whip and trying out his command of the team, for all that he barely came up to Star's nose.

"They're camped about three miles ahead," Mr. Glennie reported to Pa. "I know we wanted to make another five miles today, but I believe that we would find it to our advantage to consult with the gentlemen; a Mr. Clyman and Mr. Greenwood – both old hands as regarding the trail. They have come from the Sacramento settlements in California, returning east by way of Fort Hall with a mule pack train and a couple of wagons, intending to visit kin and friends back in the States. And ..." Mr. Glennie added, with a significant look. "They have come from Sutter's Fort in company with Mr. Lansford Hastings, assaying the difficulty of his recommended shortcut from the established trail. Mr. Hastings has come east, expecting to personally guide any companies willing to travel by his new route."

"Indeed," Pa replied, "Indeed, I would very much like to hear what these folk have to say. Not only about the situation in California, but what advice they have to offer us regarding the trail."

Mr. Glennie nodded, his expression one of relieved agreement. "I judge it would be worth a couple of miles, listening to what Mr. Clyman has to tell us. Not only has he come across from California just this season, but he has spent many years in the mountains."

"Joe Bayless may vouch for him, in that case," Pa's own expression brightened. "Any friend of Choctaw Joe is already a good friend of ours."

"We certainly can spare the time to consult with Mr. Clyman and Mr. Greenwood," Mr. Glennie agreed. "Mr. Clyman told me there are only three companies on the trail in advance of us. Less'n they have taken another trail." Mr. Glennie hesitated before he added. "He is making a count of all the travelers on the trail this year, as a matter of natural curiosity, I suppose. But Mr. Clyman is also well acquainted with Captain Sutter – a Dutchman long-settled in California. Captain Sutter encourages all men with an urge to prosper, especially if they are of good character and stable profession, to come and settle in the valley of the Sacramento. He has asked Mr. Clyman to encourage any Oregon-bound parties which he might encounter along the way, to come to California instead and paid him a small retainer to do so."

"Sounds like a man hoping to be the big man in those parts," Pa scratched his jaw. I think that he forgot that Jon and I were there and listening to this exchange, as quiet as mice. "Well, I'll talk with both gentlemen tonight. Thank'ee kindly, Glennie. If I hear anything of substance, you and the other men will know of if it within the hour."

"Good," Mr. Glennie saluted Pa with a touch to the brim of his hat and rode off. In the meantime, a thought occurred to me.

"Pa," I asked, and Pa seemed a bit startled out of his thought. "Do you suppose I could ask Mr. Clyman for a favor? As he is traveling east on the trail?"

"Depends on the favor, Sugar-plum. What favor would you ask of him?"

"Would he carry a letter for me to my friend Ginny? She and her family are traveling with a company somewhere behind us on the trail. I'm certain that if Mr. Clyman can take my letter with him, he will encounter Ginny's family! Their home wagon was biggest that I had ever seen; it took six yokes to draw it, Ginny told me! I do not think anyone could miss that wagon. They intended to travel to California, also. They could not be more than two or three weeks behind us."

"Sure, Sugar-plum! Write your letter and ask Mr. Clyman. I am certain he will oblige. A letter doesn't weigh very much, and if he is making a count of all the companies along the way he will have good reason to look for them."

I was heartened by the thought of writing to Ginny; we had only been together as friends for those few days at Independence. I really did miss having a friend of my own age in the wagon company most awfully. Shivaun McCarty was almost grown and had almost nothing in common with me. The other children in our party were either boys or very much younger, hardly older than babies.

"Of course you should write a letter," Ma said, warmly, when I asked her, as we set up camp early that day. "It will be excellent penmanship practice for you." Her writing desk was wrapped in a heavy quilt underneath the wagon seat. Ma had written letters at Fort Laramie and intended to write more when we reached Fort Hall, so had kept her paper and ink handy. I would have time to write, since we had stopped so early in the afternoon, Ma would not need my help in fixing supper for some hours.

Dear Ginny; Pa says that Mr. Clyman will carry my letter to you. We are almost at Independence Rock, which Mr. Bayless, our guide, tells us is a notable monument, where all who pass by write their names. My brother and I will write ours, so Mr. Bayless promises. I hope that this finds you and Patty in good health, just as we are.

There has been much to see along the way. We did part from Major Clayton's party, just before we crossed the Kansas River. They wished to shoot all the dogs and to travel on Sundays, and of course many in the company objected. So we separated from that company, and our Pa was elected captain. Since when we have gotten on tolerably well. Henry S. and his father are still with our company. You will recall Henry from that day of gathering wood by the river.

There are many interesting sights to be seen along the trail. Chimney Rock is to be seen for many days but do be warned that it is not as close to the trail as you might think. Mr. Bayless said that it was once much taller. We also saw an enormous gathering of buffalo. They passed among our wagons for many hours, one day – buffalo by the hundreds of thousands. Ma traded with some Sioux women at Laramie Fort for a pair of buffalo robes. They are so comfortable and warm to sleep under, since it is now quite cold at night. Mr. Bayless says this is because we are higher into the mountains, and there it is cold, even at midsummer. There is even snow still to be seen on the highest peaks!

We are to have a wedding when we reach Independence Rock. Miss Pierson, who is a very eccentric older lady traveling with her brother's family, is to marry Mr. McNabb! He is traveling alone with his dog. It is very curious, such a romance. Neither of them strikes me as being in the least romantic. I had often seen that Miss Pierson and Mr. McNabb walked together, during a day of travel, and he was accustomed to take meals with her brother's family – but never a hint that they held each other in special regard!

I wish that you were with us; I have missed your company all these weeks. I hope that we can meet again in California.

All my best wishes to you and Patty and your family.
Yours in affection,
Sarah Elizabeth Kettering

It was a short letter, only the back and front of a single page of Ma's fine letter paper, but I was proud of it – in my neatest handwriting and with no words misspelled and having to be crossed out and written again. I felt very grownup, as I folded it into a neat oblong, and addressed the envelope.

While I had been writing it, Ma had been teaching Jon. We most always had our school lessons on Sundays; this was an extra lesson for Jon and he was not happy about it. When Ma said that she was finished with quizzing him about the geography of France, and it was time for her to start supper, Jon ran away at once to play with the Wee Donal, Liam and Rory Herlihy. Ma watched him trot towards the Herlihy wagon, with a smile on her face.

"Your father went hunting with Mr. Bayless and Mr. Steitler," she said, "So it will be fresh meat for supper tonight! Although I don't know what form it will take," she added. "Flesh or fowl, or good red herring ... that's an old saying, Sally – it doesn't mean we will have herring." Ma stopped as if in thought. "I don't think I have ever eaten herring, come to think on it! But we gathered all those ripe green peas this morning, and I will bake cornbread. A providential feast! And a dried-apple pie for a sweet! I expect that your father will bring guests for supper, since he will want to consult with someone who has been so recently on the trail."

Pa did bring guests to our campfire; the travelers which Mr. Glennie had noted. Pa and Mr. Steitler and Choctaw Joe returned from hunting with a fine brace of wild prairie chickens. Mr. Steitler shot an antelope; which was about the size of a well-grown goat, but which would provide enough meat to share out with Henry and the German boys. Even

Choctaw Joe was impressed with Mr. Steitler's marksmanship. Mr. Steitler was particularly pleased with his hunting prowess. Henry was so proud of his father, for having bagged a fleet antelope with such a long shot.

(I recall that most particularly because of what happened a few days later.)

Anway, Pa plucked and gutted the chickens and went to bury the guts where they wouldn't attract wild critters and flies, while Ma made biscuits and a pie, and I shelled the peas. Choctaw Joe very kindly brought us some more wood, and remained by the fire, smoking his pipe and diverting Jon by listening to my little brother telling us all about the new words that he had learned to spell. Choctaw Joe often came to smoke by our fire when he consulted about the trail with Pa, as Deacon Zollicoffer was powerfully against smoking or chewing – and teetotal, as well. Anyway, Choctaw Joe looked up when two men came to our camp; one very old man with long white hair done up in Indian braids, the other somewhat older than Pa, long and lean and weathered; he had a long-jawed face and a fringe of chin-whiskers. The white-haired old man wore a fringed leather coat, and leggings like what Choctaw Joe and the Indians wore. He had very blue eyes, though – even bluer than Henry Steitler.

"Mr. Greenwood, Mr. Clyman," Pa replied. "Good of you to visit. I hope that you can settle our minds regarding certain matters of the trail."

157

"My pleasure," the younger man replied. That was Mr. Clyman. The old man with long white braids was Mr. Greenwood. I didn't know it then, but they were both renowned explorers, mountain men and trail guides. Mr. Clyman nodded courteously to Ma, who wiped her hands on her apron and made them welcome to share supper with us.

"Thank'ee kindly, Ma'am." Mr. Greenwood replied, "We have our own vittles – and don't want to put you to a difficulty on our account."

"It is no difficulty at all," Ma protested. "We have plenty to share!"

"I wouldn't say no to a cup of coffee, if you insist," the chin-whiskered Mr. Clyman replied. He looked across the fire at Choctaw Joe, seeming to recognize him for the first time. "Evening, Joe. Been a long time."

Choctaw Joe took the pipe from his mouth and nodded. "Jim. Caleb. On the Upper Green by Horse Creek, the rondy-voo in '35 – been ten year and more. How you been doing, since?"

"A bit of this and that," Mr. Clyman replied. "Settled down for a bit in Wisconsin Territory, but it didn't take. Got itchy feet and a bad cough and went out to the mountains for my health."

"For myself, I found retirement tedious dull," Mr. Greenwood replied. "Did a turn as trail guide, some years back. After which, my lads and I settled on a fair piece o' land in California. Jim and I are just headed back east to visit kinfolk."

They talked with Pa a bit more. I couldn't listen much, as Ma and I were busy, seeing to supper, but I had a sense that Pa and Mr. Clyman and Mr. Greenwood were taking a measure of each other, while they and Choctaw Joe exchanged yarns about their fur-trapping days.

They stayed for supper; I expect that the fresh prairie hen and Ma's cooking was too much to resist. The talk over supper was of a general and social matter, rather than the serious questions that Pa and the others in our party needed answers for. Those questions were held until supper was done, and Ma was slicing up the dried-apple pie, dripping with sweet syrup and the scent of cinnamon and nutmeg. Mr. Clyman thanked her for the coffee, saying that it was the best and only coffee that he had tasted in months. Apparently, such a luxury was not available in California.

Pa finally broached the topic. "We've heard much about Mr. Lansford Hastings and that new short-cut that he recommends in his guide, going directly west around the edge of the great Salt Lake. Have you gentlemen any notion if his new route is practical for a wagon company such as ours? And what of the passage over the mountains into California?"

I saw Mr. Greenwood and Mr. Clyman exchange a long look, before Mr. Greenwood replied,

"It's rough through the Sierra Nevada, but doable for wagons, long as you don't leave crossing the mountains too

159

late in the year. Snow gets deep, too deep for any critter that can't fly. Best be over the high pass by early November or risk getting stranded. I took a company up and over that way two seasons ago. Made it by the skin of our teeth. Stick to the regular path, don't dawdle and get over that final mountain range as early as you can."

"And Mr. Hastings' recommended cut-off?" Pa looked as if he had expected this reply, an expert confirming the conclusion already voiced by so many others. "What do you think of it? Would it save any days of travel for my company? Now Mr. Clyman exchanged another glance with Mr. Greenwood. He shook his head.

"No siree, not with wagons. It's real broken-up country, rough and rocky, pert-near impassible as it is. You'd be wasting too many days making a road for your wagons. Only possible on horseback, and a packtrain of mules."

Mr. Greenwood grunted. "Jim and Mr. Hastings traveled over that cut-off, back to front for the very first time this trip. Hastings insists that it would save days. Jim says no. Now, I ain't been over that trail myself, but I'd trust Jim any day and twice on Sunday over a big-talking greenhorn who calls hisself an expert guide after only a single journey. Jim here knows the country. If he says it ain't possible for wagons without a big parcel of roadbuilding to clear the way, then I'd be inclined to take him serious."

"So, you advise that we ignore Hasting's guide, then?" Pa asked, gently, as if he wished the two mountain men to make it clear.

"If you value your own skin, I would," Mr. Clyman replied, as blunt as a blow from Mr. Herlihy's hammer. "And the lives of your women and children as well. Take my word on it, Kettering: Don't take any cut-offs after Fort Hall that ain't been tried, true and vouched for by at least two other parties with experience. It ain't worth the grief. You and your company are as far along as can be this season. There are but three parties ahead of you. Two is bound for the Willamette Valley and the third is a passel of young bucks with a mule packtrain. You shouldn't have need of Hasting's cut-off."

"Save your strength for the Truckee River pass," Mr. Greenwood added. "And your supplies."

"Hastings is planning on meeting any emigrant companies at Bridger's fort, on the way to Fort Hall, and personally guiding them over his shortcut," Mr. Clyman continued. "At least he is putting his own skin at risk! But the road through the mountains is barely passable on horseback. Following on that, it's eighty or a hundred miles of hard pulling on the salt flats with not a drop of water in sight. Stick to the main trail, Kettering. That's my final word."

It looked as if they were making ready to take their leave – and I should take my opportunity now. I went to Mr. Clyman with my letter in hand.

"Mr. Clyman," I said, "My Pa told me that you might do me the favor of taking a letter to a friend that I have, in another company. Farther down the trail, since they were waiting for friends to join them before departing. The address is written on the envelope. Virginia Reed; her pa is James Reed, from Springfield in Illinois. You might know them from their wagon – it was very large; a cottage on wheels. It took six yoke to draw – and it had a wee stove inside, with a chimney coming out the top. Will you carry this letter for me? They were bound for California as well, so I think that you should find them easily as you travel."

"James Reed? Of Springfield?" Mr. Clyman's face brightened. "If your friend's father is the same man whom I recall – then, of course I know him! Know him well, since we served in the same militia company in the Blackhawk campaign! Of course I will search out his party. I doubt that I will miss a wagon of such comfort and good size," he added with a wry grin. He had very good teeth, white and even. "I didn't even think James Reed had such a taste for luxury!"

"It wasn't for himself," I explained. "But for Ginny's Granny Keyes. She is very old and blind, but she wanted to come with them all, and not stay behind, since they were going so far. I wish that my Granny Eliza could have come with us," I added. I still felt a tinge of sorrow at the thought of Granny Eliza. It was not even a year since she died at the very start of last winter. I still missed her.

"I will take care to seek out the Reeds," Mr. Clyman put away my letter in the front of his jacket. "Be assured, Miss Kettering; I will certainly not mistake James Reed and his palace wagon."

"They were waiting on some friends of theirs," I said. "Another family from Springfield – the Donners."

"I will find them, and deliver your letter," Mr. Clyman nodded. "Have no fear that it will go astray."

I did feel a little less lonely, knowing that Ginny would receive my letter – but there would be no way for her to send a reply.

Perhaps I would see her in California.

Ma and I saw to the washing-up, after supper, while Pa and Choctaw Joe went to confer with Mr. Glennie and the other men about the discouraging word they had been given regarding the short-cut in the trail. Because of having to help Ma and because I was very tired, I did not hear anything that was said, until I listened to Pa and Ma talking after Jon and I went to bed. Jon was very tired, and went to sleep almost at once. I remained awake for a little while, after the red sunset in the west paled to a pale smear on the horizon, and then to nothing but black, while the bright stars scattered themselves like silver sparks on the dark velvet sky.

"How did they take the news?" I heard Ma ask, and Pa sighed wearily – as if he had expected bad news and had not been disappointed.

"Glennie took it hard. He and his missus wanted to be safe in California before their baby is born. He put a lot of trust in Hasting's guidebook and expected that his cutoff would be a direct way and save weeks of travel. *Why would it all be in a book, if it weren't true,* he wanted to know. It didn't make sense, not to him."

Ma was quiet for some moments. "Jeptha Glennie is a trusting man," she replied at last. "Too trusting. Just because something is printed in a book does not make it true. Mr. Hastings has his own reasons – for glory or love of country … or just seeming to be Moses or Joshua, leading his people into the land of milk and honey."

"And his reasons aren't ours, Sue," Pa replied. "After talking to Clyman and Old Man Greenwood, I'd sooner take their word for it, based on their experiences. We're in good time; we're doing better than fifteen miles a day on most days. We have no need to gamble on Hastings' rough shortcut. I just hope that I was able to convince the others."

"You have, Elkanah," Ma assured him. "They elected you – and you've brought us all safely this far."

Chapter 10 – The Accident

We passed into the mountain country, after parting with Mr. Clyman and his small company. I believe that most of our fellows took his advice to heart; I know that Pa did. But Mr. Glennie was still in favor of the Hastings short-cut, and it was a matter that the men kept on discussing, in a casual kind of way for a time after that meeting. Mr. Hasting was a published expert, with an important guidebook to the trail, and Mr. Clyman and Mr. Greenwood were only a pair of ragged and disreputable mountain men.

"But they have been in the wilderness for years," Pa said, when he talked this over late at night with Ma. "In the case of Old Man Greenwood, for longer than I have been alive. Just two years past, he guided the party that found a pass over the mountains from the Humbolt – a pass that no one but the wild Indians had ever seen." But as Pa also added, philosophically, "Sufficient to the day are the evils thereof."

I think eventually that Pa was able to talk even Mr. Glennie around. Pa must have said quite a lot, about the hard work of making a new road for our wagons. We had quite enough in the way of daily toil; I believe that the men of our company did not wish for any more to be added to their portion of it. But Mr. Glennie and some of the other wagon owners were afire with impatience for California. That flame was kindled again when we got to Independence Rock and found a letter from Mr. Hastings posted on a board and addressed to any emigrants desirous of taking his shortcut. I will put more on that later in my story, as other things happened which first took a greater part of my attention.

We camped below the great grey dome monument of Independence Rock, although it was not yet the 4th of July. It was a Sunday, though, so we took a day of rest there. The most important thing was that Mr. McNabb and Miss Pierson were married.

This was a cause for much excitement among us, although honestly, I thought the happy couple were the calmest of all. We unpacked our best clothes for the brief ceremony; Pa and the other men trimmed their beards or shaved them off, put on their best white shirts with cravats and their best town suits. Ma let me put up my hair and wear the dress that we saved for Sunday best – my grey flannel with a full skirt, ruching on the front and white undersleeves trimmed with lace.

Miss Pierson wore her own best dress, and a bonnet adorned with lilac-colored roses and ribbons. Shivaun and I gathered a bouquet of wildflowers for her to carry, and Mr. McNabb put a sprig of them in his coat buttonhole. Her cheeks were very pink, and I thought she looked very nearly pretty. They stood up before Deacon Zollicoffer, under a canvas canopy stretched between two wagons and trimmed with more wildflowers. The Deacon read out the service for marriage from his prayer-book. It was all very solemn, although the German boys and Henry Steitler all stood together and whispered amongst each other. It sounded to me as if they were amused and mystified.

Afterwards, we had a festive picnic supper, all spread out on blankets in the grass. Mrs. Glennie and Ma had baked cake and decorated it with a bit of whipped sugar frosting and more wildflowers.

Pa whispered to Ma, "The condemned man ate a hearty meal!" I guessed that he meant Mr. McNabb, who looked quite proud, if a little bit like a man who had been pole-axed, every time he looked across at Miss Pierson. Ma slapped his shoulder and told him to behave, while Jon and I giggled.

I think Pa leaned on his authority as captain when he told the younger men that they were absolutely not to make a rude shivaree around Mr. McNabb's tent that night; a tent that Miss Pierson would be sharing with him for the first time. Although they did gather at a distance from the McNabb wagon and serenade the newly-weds with a few choruses of *Come to the Bower.*

I was so very puzzled about Miss Pierson and Mr. McNabb marrying. They were both so much older than the marrying sort, and already seemed settled in their ways. Why should they bother to be changing all that?

The second most momentous thing after the wedding came on the following day. Pa and Choctaw Joe, Mr. Herlihy and the German boys took all of us children a pretty steep scramble up the rock, so that Mr. Herlihy could roughly peck out our names in the rock with his small hammer and chisel.

Mr. Steitler sat for a long time, making a sketch in his little book of the view from the top. We took a bucket of tar from our wagon so that we could fill in the letters, below the date and the notation of 'Kettering Company'. It was a rare day. We could sit on a ledge which ran across the dome close to the top, our legs swinging and look down at our camp below, with the wagons appearing as small as toys.

Choctaw Joe pointed out the place where he had carved his own name, many years previous, and when we all climbed and slithered down again, Jon and I had a nice supper. When we went to bed, we could hear Mr. Steitler, Henry and the German boys singing. As I drifted off to sleep, I was content, thinking how very much closer we were to the end of the trail, grateful that we had not really encountered any of the dangers and hardship that Aunt Rachel and all at home back in Ohio had feared for us on the morning that we departed.

We passed into rocky and broken-up country, about a week after passing through the place which Choctaw Joe said was the backbone of the continent. He told us that there were two little pale mountains which marked that very spot. After passing that place, every stream and river which we would see would run to the west, or south and west. I remember this particularly, because it was at about this time that Daisy ran dry of milk; Pa sighed and said that the pasturage did not agree with her, and neither did the long days of travel. So there was no more milk every morning for Jon and I, and no more butter, churned every day from a covered can of milk hung from the back of our wagon next to the tar bucket.

The tragedy which the home-folk back in Ohio had feared struck us, all of a piece and all at once. On that morning, it seemed a usual journey as we had become accustomed to it all; rise before dawn, Mr. Glennie, Oscar and Henry mounted their horses, seeing to rounding up any of the cattle which had strayed from the grazing ground during the night. Harness the oxen, hitch the chains to their traces, harness the Glennie mules to Mrs. Glennie's buggy. Strike the tents in which most everyone but children had spent the night, rolling up thick bed-pallets and stashing them in the wagons. A hurried breakfast under a dark sky lightening in the east, pale and rose, the odor of salt-bacon crisping in the three-legged spider, and fresh-ground coffee perfuming the still morning air. It was a routine so regular that I think we all could perform it halfway asleep. Indeed, I do believe most of us were half asleep on such mornings, undertaking those tasks as if we were still dreaming. We had come across a long desert stretch – no water but what we carried in casks and barrels, no green fodder but what we cut and carried with us. It took us a day and a half to reach the Green River. We had expected the haul over that dry patch to be long and hard. What a relief it was to reach the edge of that desert, look down from the edge of the low bluffs and see the flowing river below.

The oxen scented water, of course and they were powerfully thirsty.

"It's not a steep drop," Mr. Glennie told Pa. He and Henry had ridden out ahead, as was usual. "No need to chain the wheels. Just take it nice and slow. I took a gander at the river, though. The water looks pretty deep and running fast. We might have a time, finding a good fording place."

"Good," Pa nodded. We needed sometimes to chain the wagon wheels or run a long length of tree branch through them, to prevent the heavy-laden wagons from rolling down a hill faster than the oxen moved.

So the oxen stepped out eagerly enough; and honestly, we were all relieved to see the water, chuckling over rocks and streaked with green weeds at the river edge. A few scattered stands of cottonwood trees stood with their roots twining deep into the soil along the banks. We had already learned that cottonwoods were thirsty trees; wherever they grew to a good size, or any size at all, there would be a promise of water. Henry and Oscar had already brought the herd of loose cattle down to the river – they were milling about, drinking their fill. Not being hitched up, they had moved faster, advancing at a quicker pace since they were not in harness.

We threaded our way down the side of the bluff, a bluff deeply scarred with old wagon tracks and the gullies that rain or snow-melt or just the blowing wind had scored into the hard soil. We were going by several paths, as we had spread out on the trail. Mrs. Glennie was the first, in her light mule-drawn buggy. Then I think it was the German boys light wagon, with the ragged canvas top, and Deacon Zollicoffer's mule wagon, with Choctaw Joe at the reins. Then the Herlihy wagons, heavier-laden and slower moving, followed by Mr. Steitler's wagon. The rest of our company made our scattered and slower way down the bluff towards the water, or if already there, with team animals unharnessed so that they could drink their fill without impediment.

I did not see exactly what happened then, since we were watching our footing as Ma and I picked our way down the bluff a little apart from the wagons, while Jon had already run ahead, down to the waterside. We were almost to the riverbank. Ma was wondering out loud if we would have difficulties fording the river, and was Jon going to fall in and get all his clothes soaked? I was about to reply that I didn't think so, although the water level looked middling deep, almost to the level of our wheel hubs. I had gotten very trail-wise and observant, in those months since departing from Marion County.

"I believe we will camp here a day, as tomorrow is Sunday ..." Ma was saying, when the sound of an ox bellowing snapped our attention around to a horrible spectacle a little way behind us, still on the down-slope of the bluff. The Steitler wagon overturned in a massive cloud of dust, and the crack and crunch of splintering wood as the wagon contents spilled out. We heard the agonized bellowing of Mr. Steitler's oxen as they were overturned or forced to their clumsy knees. Men shouted, and another woman screamed – Shivaun, I think. Ma gathered her skirts in her hands and ran towards the wreckage. I was on her heels, and out of the corner of my eye, I saw Choctaw Joe halt the mules of Deacon Zollicoffer's team, on the gravel at the water's edge and leap down from the wagon. He ran towards the wreck – as spry as a much younger man, almost as fast as my brother Jon.

The most horrible sight met our eyes; Mr. Steitler's team of two yoke lay all jumbled together, some still and some thrashing feebly but moaning in the way that oxen had, their eyes showing white all around. They were still hitched to the wagon tongue. The wagon itself was off the wheels and lying on one side, having rolled all the way over and then half again. Worst of all, Mr. Steitler himself lay beside the wreckage with his face up to the sky, broken bits of wood and the contents of the wagon all scattered on the slope below the overturned wagon. His ox whip had fallen from his fingers. He looked vaguely surprised. I saw that his chest was curiously flattened, dented inwards, in an unnatural manner and that there was dark blood spreading into the scuffled dirt around him, and another trickle of it coming from his mouth. He wasn't moving. Ma took my shoulder and spun me to face towards her.

"Stay with your brother by the water," she commanded clearly. "He need not see this! He will wake up screaming with bad dreams and we do not need that!"

"Yes, Ma!" I stammered. Jon had not reached us at that moment. I did not want to see any more, so I grabbed Jon by the hand and hustled him away from the Steitler wagon, back down to the riverside. I did not want to see any more, either. My throat hurt from trying so hard not to cry. Mr. Steitler was our friend. Ma and Pa liked Mr. Steitler enormously, and … and… Henry was our friend, too.

I bit back a sob as I dragged Jon by one hand. There were people from the company all around us; Deacon Zollicoffer, Mrs. Glennie, Shivaun and Mrs. Herlihy and the boys. Shivaun and I kept the children apart, while Mrs. Glennie sat on the bank, fanning herself while the other women whispered together.

"What's the matter with Mr. Steitler?" Jon's lip quavered. "Is he hurt real bad, Sally?"

There wasn't anything comforting, any lie that I could tell him. "I think he's dead, Jon. He looked too bad hurt to live." I answered, and Jon's face crumpled.

"What will happen to Henry?" He asked then, between sobs. "He hasn't got a papa, now."

That was something painful to consider. Henry's mother was dead back in St. Louis, and now he was orphaned and alone. If there were any kinfolk, they were way back in Germany, on the other side of the world. We were all in the wilderness, months of travel from California, still.

It looked to me that the Steitler wagon was wrecked; I thought that one wheel was completely smashed into kindling wood. None among our company was a wheelwright, although Pa and some of the other men were pretty good at rough carpentry, and Mr. Herlihy could work his forge to fix the metal fittings.

Later, Mrs. Glennie told us that she thought one of the front wheels on Mr. Steitler's wagon broke on the way down the hill, and that was what had pitched the wagon over. She had been watching as she waited for everyone at the bottom of the bluff. She said that it happened so fast, there was nothing anyone could have done.

"I don't know, Jon," I took a corner of my pinafore and wiped Jon's face with it. "But Pa will think of something. He's the captain – and I believe that he will take charge of Henry."

Of course, Henry was fourteen; nearly old enough to take charge of himself. If our family stories were true, Grandfather Reverend's Grandfather Tobias hadn't been much older than fourteen when he took an indenture and came to America, all alone, leaving kin and friends behind. At least, Henry had us – the German boys, the Herlihys, Deacon Zollicoffer and Choctaw Joe.

It seemed that every man in the company converged on the wrecked wagon and the feebly-thrashing oxen still hitched to it. I saw Henry, his bright fair hair under that foreign-looking cap of his. He was standing on the far side of the wagon looking down at the body of his father, now decently covered with a dusty quilt that someone had retrieved from the goods strewn around. He looked almost as if he had been pole-axed, stunned into silence; Pa and Deacon Zollicoffer stood either side of him, Pa with his arm around Henry's shoulders.

"Pa will take care of Henry," I assured my brother.

It was a sad camp, on the banks of the Green, that evening, and for the several days following. We had to bury Mr. Steitler, of course, and work to gather what could be salvaged from his wagon. Two of his team oxen had broken legs or their ribs stove in. They had to be dispatched and butchered on the spot, for the meat left on them. That left only a single yoke – bruised and very unhappy with their lot in life, but otherwise whole and fit to work.

Mr. Herlihy came and talked to Pa, as Mr. Martindale and the other men took a hand with taking heavier things from the wreck. Henry, white-faced and silent, was helping too, in a half-hearted way. He still looked stunned, disbelieving, as if he had been walloped over the head himself. He didn't talk much, but as I didn't know what I might say to him that would be comforting, that didn't bother me none.

"I can't repair the wheels," Mr. Herlihy said, regretfully. "One is smashed to kindling, and the other is not much better. What I have in mind is to cut the wagon down to a cart – what can't be carried in it ... well, we can all pitch in, put some small things of yours in our wagons. What do you say to that, young Henry?"

Henry nodded wordlessly, his eyes fixed on the ground, and Mr. Herlihy continued, sounding as if he were forcing himself cheerful. "It wouldn't take more than a day or so – a good sound little cart! Two shakes of a lambs' tail, I promise ye!"

Henry just nodded again, and Pa said. "We'll look after you, lad, ust as your father would have wanted. We'll get to California, all in a company, I promise you that."

Henry just nodded again. I felt so sorry for him again that my own throat hurt. Jon and I, with the Herlihy boys and Shivaun were combing the hillside below where the wagon had smashed, picking up small things that might have fallen from the wagon, or been thrown out. A barrel of flour had burst, and scattered the contents over the dirt; that was thuroughly ruined. I was collecting coffee beans one by one from a sack which had burst. Ma thought the coffee might be salvaged. Mrs. Herlihy and Shivaun were shaking dirt out of bedding, a bundle of which had rolled down the hill nearly to the water's edge. Ma found Mr. Steitler's flute, still fortunately in the padded case, under a sage bush. Jon had already found Mr. Steitler's sketchbook, the cover bent and some of the blank pages creased and dirtied.

Deacon Zollicoffer was going to preach the funeral sermon to bury poor Mr. Steitler. Pa and Choctaw Joe found a level place, well above flood level of the river. Choctaw Joe took a sighting on a gnarled and weathered half-dead cottonwood tree, and allowed as how that would mark the place as best as could be.

We would not be able to mark his grave. Choctaw Joe confessed with deep regret,

"Them Injuns is powerful curious – they spot a place that looks like we cached something in the ground, they're liable to dig it up, just to see if it was something valuable. Best just settle that poor man in his grave, and then pasture the critters on that spot, so they trample up the ground real good. Now boy," he added to Henry. "I'll make note of the bearings, and mark on a map of this place, ezactly where we planted your daddy. Someday, mebbe you can come back here, and mark it proper."

I thought that it would be a funeral like for Granny Elizabeth, or for little Cousin Matty, but observances to bury Mr. Steitler wasn't anything like that. It was all outside, on the hillside in the bright morning under a wide blue sky freckled with white clouds, birds singing, and the cottonwood leaves whispering secrets to each other in the breeze. The river was at our feet, white where the water rushed around the rocks, and there wasn't anyone wearing black. Just our ordinary clothes. Mr. McNabb played the hymn *Abide with Me* on his hurdy-gurdy and we all sang. Deacon Zollicoffer stood up in front of us, his arms clasping his heavy old Bible, and he didn't say any of the usual funeral words or preach a long service. Instead, he said that he was going to share some comfort from a saint back during medieval times, whom he said was called 'The Venerable Bead" which brought such a funny picture to my mind that I nearly laughed out loud in spite of it being a funeral.

Deacon Zollicoffer stood there, by the open grave and Mr. Steitler's coffin already lowered down in it. The breeze blew his white hair and the tails of his clawhammer coat this way and that. He spoke as if he was talking ordinary to us, not preaching from a great height like Grandfather Reverend.

"My dear brothers and sisters! We seem to give them back to you, O God, who gave them first to us – our dearest ones! Yet as you did not lose them in giving so we do not lose them by their return to the shelter of your arms. Not as the world gives do you give! What you give to us, you do not take away. For what is yours is also ours. We are yours and life is eternal. Love is immortal and lasts forever! Death is only a horizon, and that is a horizon which is only limited by our own sight!" Deacon Zollicoffer paused for a long moment, and I was a bit relieved. I couldn't see where a long oration would have helped Mr. Steitler, and in any case, everyone had other things to do than sit around listening to a long sermon. Deacon Zollicoffer was done, it seemed. He added, "In the name of the Father, the Son and the Holy Spirit, we commend the body of our brother, Manfred Heinrich Steitler to the ground, but his soul returns to your tender and loving care. Amen!"

The Herlihys and Shivaun all made a sign of the cross at those words, and the German boys sang a gloomy hymn in their language, while Mr. McNabb made a stab at accompanying them. It sounded like they couldn't recall most of the words of the last verses. Deacon Zollicoffer nodded –

that was the signal for Pa and Choctaw Joe to begin shoveling earth back into the grave. Henry stood by the side as they worked, still looking pole axed. Mr. Herlihy had managed to cobble together a coffin from the broken scraps of the Steitler wagon box, so at least there was a little decency involved in that funeral. I was sorry for there being no proper grave marker. *How would anyone ever know where to leave flowers?*

At twilight that evening, I saw Henry sitting there, under the half-dead cottonwood – just sitting and looking out to the west, where the sun was setting in a blaze of orange, gold and purple. I also saw Jon walking up to him, with Mr. Steitler's sketchbook that we had found in his little hand.

I was some distance from them, so I couldn't hear what, if anything that my brother said to Henry Steitler. But I could see that Henry took the notebook, reverently smoothing the pages, and smiling at Jon. They sat together, quietly and side by side for a long time, a pair of indistinct shadows, a bigger one and a smaller, outlined against the darkening sky, until Ma called them for supper.

From that time on, Henry ate meals with us, and shared the chores of gathering wood with Jon and I. He set up his small tent at night on the other side of our wagon, next to his cart. If Henry was on his pony, scouting the trail or helping to chivy the loose herd, Fritz, one of the other German boys drove the cart cut down from the wagon for him.

It took Mr. Herlihy and his brothers nearly a week to salvage the Steitler wagon; to take apart the broken wagon box and nail the sound pieces of it all back together to make a cart. They mounted two undamaged wheels on the soundest axle and fixed it to the trimmed-down wagon box. It wasn't large, but it would have to do. Not that Henry had all that much left in the way of things now. Mr. Herlihy set up his forge, as several of our wagons needed their wheels fixed. The dry air made the green timber they were made off to shrink and rattle in a way that caused some to fear that they would break, as the Steitler wagon wheels had. Meanwhile we camped on the Green River, rested our oxen from the desert crossing, and made ready to ferry our wagons over the river, which was running too high and fast to ford. Choctaw Joe and his mountain man friends warned us that the journey would now get more difficult; desert and mountain, and by the end of all, the passage of the terrible Sierra Nevada, the last wall before California. We had best take the rest and refreshment from sweet water and good grass that we could, whilst they were available.

When the work on Steitler's cart was done, Ma and Mrs. Herlihy and Shivaun and I repacked the salvaged supplies and the few home things in it. We sure did miss Mr. Steitler playing his flute of an evening, though. And it was a long time before we heard Henry laughing.

Chapter 11 – The Cutoff

In this telling of my family's journey to California in 1846, I rushed over the episode of that letter which Mr. Hastings, the famed explorer and writer of the *Emigrant's Guide,* had left for us and for other parties at Independence Rock. It was a letter in big letters nailed to a board, saying that he would wait at Bridgers' Fort to guide any parties who wished to take his short-cut. Bridger was another old mountain man; Mr. Clyman knew him well, and so did Choctaw Joe.

"A good man and tells the most original lies you have ever heard – but that is purely for entertainment value among other gentleman of the fur-trapping persuasion. See this, though," and Choctaw Joe scratched his chin. "Jim Bridger has got hisself a nice little trading post downriver on the Green. Settled in real good with his Shoshone lady-wives and his pal Vasquez. He's set to make a bundle from wagon trade if folk take Hastings' route. He wouldn't knowingly steer you on a bum trail," Choctaw Joe looked thoughtful when he added this, "But he will stand to make a good profit out of folk coming past his trading post. Not that I wrong him on that," Choctaw Joe added, apologetically. "Folk gotta make a living, one way or another."

Pa and Choctaw Joe were sitting at our fire when they said this, the evening of the day that we had buried Mr. Steitler. Mr. Herlihy said it would take another four or five days to finish cutting down the ruin of the Steitler wagon to make a usable cart. On account of this sorrowful accident, and the need to prepare our wagons to cross over the river, we had a few days of holiday from traveling, unfortunate as the happening which led to it.

But it was also the point where Pa and the rest of the wagon-owners would have to decide about Mr. Hasting's shortcut towards California. The choice was to either turn more or less south after we crossed the Green River, to where Mr. Hasting's trail led mostly straight west, across an untried cut-off through what Mr. Clyman testified was too rough for wagons, not without a lot of work. Or should our company continue on the well-traveled path leading more or less northerly, towards Fort Hall, instead? This path described a kind of arc; a long way about, which many had already followed, either towards Oregon Territory, or south again from there, to that last pass over the treacherous and rocky Sierra Nevada.

We had come to that place where Pa and the other men must decide, a choice which they had put off until this moment. The choice was stark: Once decided, it could not be undone, not without wasting many days of travel. On one of the evenings that we camped on the shores of the Green, Pa called a meeting of all in the company. They met at our campfire, since Pa was captain and all, and since the Steitler wagon/cart – which was now Henry's was drawn up close to ours, and the Herlihy's two wagons were next to ours – it just seemed natural and logical.

Ma hustled Jon and I into washing up and going to our sleeping place in the wagon, more or less to keep us out from underfoot, and to make space for everyone else. I was a bit annoyed at that, since I was twelve and almost thirteen. Henry Steitler, who wasn't all that much older, would be at the meeting since he counted as the owner of a wagon, now. Or at least part of a wagon, with one yoke of trained oxen and a tamed Indian paint-pony. *Sometimes, it just wasn't fair, being a girl.* I said as much to Jon, as we settled into the bed that we shared. At least from there we could listen to the meeting, hear what the men would decide. On the other hand ... poor Henry. I thought about how awful and grieved I would feel if something dreadful happened to Pa and Ma. I reckoned that Henry would have felt the same. I recollected how pale and shocked Henry was, when he first saw poor Mr. Steitler looking up at the sky with empty, lifeless eyes.

Jon remarked, thoughtfully. "I like Henry very much, Sally. Do you think we could ask him to be our big brother?"

"That would depend on what Pa and Ma think," I answered. This was a new thought to me, and to be honest, I rather liked it; Pa would need so much help on the new farm in California, and Jon was still way too little. "He would be a nice brother – better than those rough, rude Herlihy brothers, Seamus and Darragh – and a good help to Pa with the farming and all – but I think it would be too early to talk about it to him now. Maybe when we get to California, we can ask if he would like to stay with us and be a Kettering."

I wanted to get to California as soon as we possibly could. If Mr. Hastings had found a better and faster way, then I certainly hoped that Pa and the rest of the company would vote to take it. I was already tired of sleeping nights in a wagon, under canvas, wondering if wild critters like bears or wild cats would break in at night, walking every day for hours and hours, while the oxen complained, and the wheels of our wagons raised clouds of dust. If winters in the high mountains were every bit as cold and miserable as winters in Ohio, then I wanted to be done with this journey as soon as was possible. I knew also that Ma was tired of cooking over an open fire, every single blessed day, and having to do washing any which way that she could. Ma had always been proud of keeping a pretty house; now, she had no house at all.

But still ... there were all those disparaging things that Mr. Clyman had said about Mr. Hasting's short-cut. I was certain Choctaw Joe would argue against it and Pa would agree. But what would all the other men say? Mr. Glennie was in a great hurry and thought much of the *Emigrant Guide*. Mr. Herlihy was in a great hurry as well ... and all these families and their wagons had chosen Pa as captain, after we broke from the Major, mostly because Pa wouldn't countenance shooting the dogs or traveling on Sunday.

I will never forget that scene; my brother and I peeking out from behind the wagon cover; the firelight and the golden sparks rising up from it into a dark sky, pin-pricked with silver stars; the faces of Pa and the other men, as well as those of Ma, Mrs. Herlihy, Mrs. Glennie and the other women, lingering at the edge of the firelit circle. This was a choice which would affect all. Of course, the wives and mothers had an interest in the decision that the men would make. The men gathered, bringing something to sit on; an empty keg or a box, a chair from their wagon. Mr. Glennie had a fancy folding camp chair for himself. Henry Steitler, with his pale hair looking as white as Deacon Zollicoffers' in the twilight, sat on the ground with his legs crossed like an Indian's. Pa stood where the light from the kerosene lantern hung from the first wagon bow cast a light on his face, leaning against the wheel of our wagon. I could just see his profile, outlined against the dark, star-speckled sky. The men talked for a while, in the way that they usually did, joking, joshing with each other and talking about practically anything else, before getting down to the brass tacks. Pa had his pipe; I could smell the scent of his tobacco, as he leaned against the wheel of our wagon, calm and casual, speaking when he was asked a question. It was as if he had no more than the usual number of cares in this world. Pa was taking his time.

"So, folks," he said finally, without much fuss. "This is where we must make up our minds about Mr. Hasting's shortcut. Do we go straight from one side to the other, instead of going the long way around. Fish or cut bait, like they say. We've come a long way and have a mite farther to go before we're done. Once we cross over the river, we all need to have our minds made up and move on with a whole heart ... I know," and Pa held up his hand against the murmur around the council campfire, "We done a lot of talking about it, what our chances are, one way or t'other. I don't like to think of myself as a gambler, although bein' a farmer made me pretty much of one, but of the respectable sort."

That brought a rustle of laughter around the campfire, Mr. Herlihy was a blacksmith by trade, and I had no notion of what Mr. Glennie did for a living, but all the rest were farmers, in good times and bad. Mostly good farmers, since they could afford to fit out a wagon, teams, and supplies for a year, for the overland journey. Pa continued, "For one, I done made up my own mind, after talking with Mr. Clyman and Ol' Man Greenwood, and others present here tonight ..." I think Pa flashed a smile towards Choctaw Joe, before he continued. "See here, gentlemen; I don't much like what I've been told about Mr. Hastings's shortcut. Especially since the folk telling me about their doubts are men who have no reason to lie, and considerable experience regarding trail matters. Mr. Clyman told me that the Hastings trail is not fit for wagons, or anything but horseback with a packtrain and hard going at that. They done traveled that route, just this spring. I'm inclined to take his word for the difficulty of it. Likely, Mr. Hastings has his reasons for urging folk to take his way – but they ain't mine, or ones that I think fitten'." Pa straightened his shoulders, and I could see from where Jon and I watched, that he was looking at the other men, one by one, before he continued. "So, once we cross the river, I reckon that I'm gonna continue with me and mine and any of this party who want to come with me in following the regular trail to Fort Hall, and then around to the Humbolt Sink. You all done elected me to captain this company; going against my own good judgement in order to keep that office ... well, that's not a thing that I will countenance. Should y'all wish to elect another captain and roll out in the morning for Bridger's place ... well, folks – that's your right, and I won't stand in your way if you chose that. That being said – how many of you are heading to Fort Hall with me, once that we are moving again?"

I saw that Henry Steitler only nodded, shy and silent, but Mr. Herlihy spoke up loudest, amid a chorus of 'ayes' and 'yeses'.

"Of course I'll follow after ye!" he roared, "To Fort Hall and beyond! For Hastings is a cracked wee man, who looks in his mirror of a morning whilst shaving and thinks that he sees a giant! Ye talk sense, and so did that Mr. Clyman! Wee Joe of the heathen Choctaw, he talks sense, too. Better the evil that ye know, indade!"

Mr. Herlihy's brothers were with him of course. Mr. Martindale took his own pipe out of his mouth, and said,

"Aye, my father always warned me 'bout something that seemed too good to be true – telling me that promising shortcuts make the longest journey in the end. Haste do make waste, my father also used to say, and I'd sooner be careful

187

than hasty! I'll be with you, Cap'n, on the regular trail tomorrow. I might have been born at night, but it wasn't last night."

The German boys all spoke in a chorus; Yes, they would follow Pa where he led the company over the old trail. They were all just boys and new to the country at that. They had looked towards Mr. Steitler to lead them, I think. With him gone, perhaps they looked towards Henry, for a hint as to what was to be done.

Deacon Zollicoffer, with his precious Bible held to his chest, spoke after the German boys.

"I will abide with the company, Captain Kettering. In any case, I am bound for Fort Hall, so such a deviation in the trail is of no relevance to my call. Upon reaching that place, I will pray for further guidance from Our Lord. It may be that I am meant to minister to the tribes in the Oregon Territory."

Mr. Glennie was the last to speak, looking meditatively into the fire.

"I'm as eager for California as the rest of you," he said, at last. "And I considered Hastings and his *Guide* to be trusty... the man has been down the trail before! He's a notable frontiersman, so all but Mr. Clyman and his friends do say. Mrs. Glennie and I ... well, we hoped to be in California, by the time our child arrives. I do not care for knowing that we will all still be in this wilderness, wandering like the Jews out of Egypt! There's many a man who can say that Jeptha Glennie knows his own mind once that I have made it up! It's a galling thing to me or any a man, to admit that they might be wrong in their thinking. But I was wrong once before, in the matter of the distance to Chimney Rock, and may be wrong again. I don't know. I like not the dangers of a longer trail … but even less than the risks of an ill-advised detour." Mr. Glennie lifted his head and looked straight at Pa. "We'll stay with the company on the main trail. But if misfortune come to me and mine on it, a misfortune that might have been avoided by taking Hasting's guidance … I will have satisfaction, Kettering. Depend on that."

Pa looked straight back at him, and replied,

"I do not think we will regret the decision made tonight, Jeptha. Agreed then; we follow the trail to Fort Hall, once we have gotten across the river."

And that ended all discussions concerning the possibility of our wagon company following Mr. Hasting's new trail. That decision turned out to be very fortunate for us, but we did not see how fortunate until many months later, after weeks of toil and hardship.

Chapter 12 – At the Green River Crossing

While we camped at the Green, waiting on Mr. Herlihy to finish repairing the Steitler wagon, and for the oxen to recover from the hard crossing of the desert, Mr. Glennie, Oscar, Henry and Choctaw Joe had leisure to search out the best place to ford the river. They cast upstream and down and returned with depressing news; no good place that that they could find. We must cross over, though – and make the wagons ready for a hazardous venture.

"The Green is one o' them chancy rivers," Choctaw Joe explained to Pa and the others. "Sometimes, she runs high and fast with the snow-melt, and it's a treacherous crossing. Other time – 'specially late in the season, it's no more trouble than fording a shallow creek."

"It looks like we have reached the Green in the first condition." Pa asked, with a grin behind his beard. "So, what do you advise that won't waste many days travel?"

"Waal, hoss," Choctaw Joe scratched his head thoughtfully. "We're at mid-summer, but I reckon that the snow last winter piled up something fierce in the mountains. The current is running fast, and higher than I like to see. I'd say swim the stock and float the wagon boxes over, just to be on the safe side. Or you can caulk the boxes tight, raise them off the running gear, and ask the Deacon's guiding angel for a spot of mercy on our poor sinner's account!" Choctaw Joe added, carefully, "Just my considered opinion, Captain. Not that I have been hired in any capacity as a guide, so don't take it personal, if I am mistaken."

"Taken into consideration, Joe," Pa replied. The men talked some more, considering how best to make a crossing, with the water too deep and current too strong to risk double-teaming the wagons and fording, as we had crossed the Platte. There was no ferry – and few trees large enough to fell and build a raft big enough to carry even just a single one of our wagons in the time that we could spare. It was finally Mr. Herlihy the blacksmith, who proposed the most workable solution to move our wagons across. He took his time in explaining, which was his way, for Mr. Herlihy loved to tell a story by way of getting to his point. He was a good man, so I think that Pa and the other men indulged him in this.

"Where there's a will, there is a way, indade!" It turned out that Mr. Herlihy had supplied his own wagons with a store of long, sturdy chains and a lot of lengths of stout rope, having heard through various means that such items might prove useful on the trail. "A capital fellow from Derry that I met on the waterfront in Independence advised me such," Mr. Herlihy explained. "He was by way of being a cousin of mine, since it turned out that our mothers – mine and his were both McGowans from Clogher. Ye canno' throw a stone in the County without you strike a McGowan who is a cousin o' mine! Y'see, he was a teamster for several seasons on the Santa Fe trade, and before that a sailor ... chains and ropes, and plenty of both are a capital item to have! I propose a way to tow our wagons over, one by one, by setting up a means of towing them across ..." Mr. Herlihy went on at some length, demonstrating with sticks and drawing in the dirt at his feet- pulleys and ropes, and a pair of long chains laid across the river, attached to the wagon box, and with another length of rope to pull the chains back, to attach to another wagon.

Ma sighed, at seeing this. "Elkanah, we shall have to unpack everything and make certain that the wagon-box is water-tight! Otherwise, everything shall be wetted, and certain to spoil."

Pa agreed, saying, "Sue, I know that ours is tight and trim, and of well-seasoned wood – but the long miles and the dry air in the west have shrunk almost everyone elses' wagon box and wheels ... better safe than sorry, then."

All the time that we were waiting to bury Mr. Steitler, and for Mr. Herlihy to finish cutting down the Steitler wagon to make a cart, Ma and I and the other women were working at unpacking the wagons, so that Pa and the other men could make certain that the wagon boxes were as watertight as they could be made. We had already used nearly half the food supplies that we carried, so this chore was not nearly as onerous as it would have been earlier in our journey. Still, we could not risk damaging and spoiling any of that which remained; the flour and cornmeal, the salt meat and all – especially not the German boys, who had barely sufficient to begin with, or Henry Steitler, with much of his own supplies lost or ruined in the accident which killed his father.

There was some good from that, though. Steitler's two oxen which had to be slaughtered through being injured; we had the fresh beef from them dried what we couldn't eat right away, although even the fresh beef was almighty tough. Mr. Herlihy and the other men made use of the fresh hides to patch over places in wagon boxes which gaped and cracked. Quantities of unraveled rope and soaked in tar, or shreds of rags were used, too. Some of our party used the opportunity to lighten their wagons of things they had brought along, thinking that they would be useful, but which had turned out to be useless weight.

"I wish I may know why Martindale thought it necessary to bring a couple of hundredweight of Pennsylvania brick in his wagon," Pa lamented one night, to Ma, who laughed softly and replied,

"Because Mrs. Martindale wanted their new house in California to have a good bread oven made of finest quality bricks!"

"Well, whatever Indian tribe frequents this part of the country can have their joy of the bricks," Pa replied. "I s'pose they can build a stout chimney for their tee-pee with them."

When we had repacked the wagons and finished such repairs as were necessary, the river had not gone down much at all, a thing that we had hoped for while we waited. At midmorning, Mr. Glennie and Henry Steitler crossed over, laying out a pair of long ropes all the way across. They carried more lengths of rope with them as well as a pair of pulleys. The ends of the longest ropes were anchored to the biggest cottonwood on the near bank, while Henry and Mr. Glennie meant to carry the other ends across the river. Their horses had to swim for it, with Mr. Glennie and Henry holding tight to their saddle-horns. We watched them struggling in the deepest part of the river, as the current pushed them down-stream and nearly out of sight around the next bend.

"It's all right, Sugar-plum," Pa said, upon seeing my worried face. "Their horses can swim. They'll be all right, as long as they keep tight hold of their horses."

Henry and Mr. Glennie soon came in sight again on the far bank, leading their horses along the water's edge. Henry saw us watching and waved. He looked cheery enough despite being dripping wet. I thought he was ever so brave, going into that river, the river being in flood and all. Nearly as brave as Pa.

They had carried with them lashed to their saddles more lengths of rope and a pair of very large and sturdy single pulleys; great iron and wood things, nearly as big as Jon's head. Well, at least they were lighter than Mr. Martindale's hundredweight of bricks, although given how long the chains and ropes were – a sight more useful, especially in the circumstances. There was a stand of big cottonwood trees on the far bank, Mr. Glennie and Henry attached the pulleys to the biggest pair of trees. They waved to us, all watching with hearts in our throats, and threaded the long lengths of rope which they had carried across the flooding river – and then carried the ends of that rope back across. They emerged from the river, soaking wet as to their clothing, and the water dripping off making runnels through the coats of their horses.

"Right and tight and Bristol-fashion secure, Cap'n!" Mr. Glennie assured Pa. He sounded exuberant, as if he had just had the most exciting time imaginable. "I think that we can commence crossing the wagons ... I suppose the smallest and lightest first? Mrs. Glennie's buggy, then ... but I will not countenance her riding in it for this crossing – not untried, as Herlihy's system might be. Then young Henry's cart following." Mr. Glennie looked to Henry for approval, and on receiving it with a nod. "All right then – haul away, boys, haul away!"

"If you like, Mrs. Glennie can ride in my wagon, with my own family," Pa replied, and Mr. Glennie agreed with another brief nod.

It was a complicated business, that crossing. It took us all that day to cross the wagons, the mules and the ox herd over. Pa and the other men had the wagons brought down to the water edge, almost axle-deep in the river, before unharnessing the oxen and sending them swimming across, with many a shouted word and a cracking of whips. Then – they attached chains and ropes – chains to the tongue, where the oxen would normally be hitched and ropes to the back, to steady the wagons against the current. And then – they pulled from the bank, and ferried the wagons across, floating and bobbing like corks in a flood, even as heavy-laden as all were, after Glennie's buggy and Henry's light cart.

Jon and I sat on our bed, with Boomer curled up between us, for the crossing, while Ma and Mrs. Glennie huddled close together on the wooden seat. Boomer whined softly in his throat, as the wagon lurched out into the stream. The feel of the heavy wheels bumping and bouncing over the rocks suddenly went away – and we were floating free and rocking gently on the current with a sudden sway and swing ... free save for the chains hitched to the wagon tongue.

"Oh, my!" exclaimed Mrs. Glennie, and I saw that Ma was clasping Mrs. Glennie's hand.

"There's nothing to worry about, Abigail ... it's just a short way across, and the men have a good hold on the ropes. They won't let us come to any harm, not if they can do anything to prevent it."

Boomer whined again. He did not like the sensation of floating on the water as we did. He had not been happy when we traveled from Independence to the start of this trail, all these months ago. I ruffled Boomer's ears and looked down at Jon's face; tense, but confident. I should not be worried, because of course Ma was right ... but in those days, it was not often that people learned to swim. Folk drowned often on the trail, which was odd to think, when we were in the middle of land! That was why we took such care in crossing rivers, I think.

It was only a short way across this river, but the powerful current swung our wagon in almost a half-circle, before the iron-shod wheels underneath us struck and bit with a crunching sound on the rocky shore opposite. Mr. Martindale and Darragh Herlihy came up leading our oxen as river water sheeted off the running gear and box. I do not think that anything of ours was seriously wetted. Darragh Herlihy helped Ma and Mrs. Glennie down, and Ma slapped our lead ox, Star, on the shoulder, told him that he and his yoke-mate, Brandy, were good obedient critters and the best oxen in the world, and had them pull the wagon up and away from the shore towards a patch of level meadow where we were to rest and camp for the night before moving on. The riverbank was as busy as the floor of a mill, when all the farmers brought their grain to be milled into flour, what with the wagons coming across, and being hitched to their teams for a short way up to a higher place on the bank. But the last wagon was about to come over.

"Well, that's done," Ma dusted her hands on her apron. "I think I have time enough to set some bread to rise. As soon as your father crosses with the last wagon, we'll set up the tent. And if any of the bedding got wet, Sally – help me hang it all out to dry."

We had spent most of the morning watching nervously, while the men and older boys pulling at the ropes that ferried our wagons over the Green or swimming the cattle across. Now that crossing was nearly finished, with just the Herlihy wagons on the far side. Pa had planned that he and Mr. Herlihy and those men who had pulled the ropes to draw the wagons over the river would all get into the Herlihy's last wagon – which held supplies and all of Mr. Herlihy's forge tools. It was all Mr. Herlihy's plan, you see – to pull themselves last over the river, with Mr. Glennie and Henry Steitler following on their horses. We would camp there for another night and get an early start in the morning.

The Herlihy's family wagon came over, with Shivaun, Mrs. Herlihy and the boys all crammed together, watching the ropes and the water so nervously as the wagon swung wide in the current and finally came safe to the shore. Ma and I were busy, taking our bedding out, shaking out the quilts and blankets, while I went scrambling up and over the tailgate into the back of our wagon, making certain that nothing in it had been soaked by water seeping in. Jon was hopping from one foot to the other in his excitement over seeing his friends, Wee Donal Herlihy and his brothers Rory and Liam. joining us at last.

"Don't go into the water now!" Ma called after him, as he ran to join his friends. "Not any deeper than your ankles," she added, in a mildly despairing tone. "You'll catch your death of cold!"

Jon only looked over his shoulder and waved. He and Wee Donal were mad for fishing minnows, catching tiny frogs, and making little boats from twigs, wood scraps and leaves for sails, which pleasant diversion had entertained all the small boys during the days that we had been camped on the Green.

Now the last wagon was safely over, and Mr. Herlihy and his brothers, and the other men were stretching their arms, and slapping each other on the shoulders, congratulating each other over having managed a successful crossing without having lost a single ox or toppled a wagon over in the water. Henry and Mr. Glennie wearily slid down from the soaking-wet saddles on their dripping ponies. They both looked exhausted and shivering. They had both spent most of the day in the water, and I just knew that the afternoon breeze was cutting directly through their soaked clothing. Deacon Zollicoffer beamed pacifically over the scene at the riverbank, and Choctaw Joe seemed the most pleased at all.

"Not bad for a bunch of clod-hopping farmers," he was saying, and Ma told me to go fetch a pail of clean water, from upstream, where the horses and oxen hadn't been piddling into it and raising the bottom mud.

"Poor Henry," she said to me. "Now, if he hasn't a care for health, I just know that he's the one who will catch his death! If he has a change of dry clothes to put on, I will make him take off those wet thi..."

A dreadful scream interrupted Ma's very words; Mrs. Herlihy, crying and carrying on something awful. I dropped the pail, and Ma looped up her skirts and we ran to where she stood, pointing at the river, where the current dashed up white foam along the edges, but the current ran cold and smooth and deadly.

"Liam! He fell into the water! And it's too deep and the current took him!" Shivaun shrieked. She was running towards the river, where the boys were crying as well.

I felt sick. I could see little Liam's copper-red hair, and the pale cream homespun of his shirt, but he was already well out in the water, struggling, frantic and gasping, until the swift current carried him out of sight beyond the next bend. Mr. Herlihy and some of the other men were already running along the bank. Mr. Herlihy had a coil of rope in his hands; I think he hoped to throw it to his boy.

How could this be happening? We had all gotten safely over the river, and now ... our party was faced with another awful tragedy, and a certain prospect of Deacon Zollicoffer saying the mournful words over another open grave? How could Mrs. Herlihy bear such grief, leaving her little son in an unmarked grave, on the shore of a wilderness river?

Jon flung himself into my arms, in tears.

"Sally, I didn't go into the water! Ma said that I shouldn't and I did like Ma said! Only to my knees, but then Rory said ... and then Liam ..." the last words were lost on a sob. I hugged my sorrowful little brother to me. I was certain that poor little Liam was gone, and maybe his body was never to be found.

Then Henry Steitler went running past us, running all-out, as if he had a race to win; he had shucked off his shoes and jacket. He ran into the river, and then plunged full-length into it. I saw that his arms broke the water in a regular rhythm; and then the current bore him away, the pale head and the smaller copper-haired one.

Henry could swim! I don't think anyone knew that he could, although thinking on it later, we should have guessed, since he showed no fear about going into the deep water on that Indian pony of his. Anyway, there we were, Ma and Shivaun keeping Mrs. Herlihy from throwing herself into the river, while Wee Donal and Rory clung to her skirts and Jon hung on to me, while Mr. Herlihy, Pa and Mr. Martindale ran along the riverbank. Mr. Glennie was on his horse again but making his way no faster because of the stones and timber wrack left by higher water along the shore. Ma and Shivaun were begging Mrs. Herlihy to calm herself, for the sake of the other boys, pleading for her not to give up hope. It was all no good. She continued rocking back and forth, screaming Liam's name, incoherently calling out curses and pleading with the saints ... I could not make out if she were damning them for letting her son fall into such peril or begging them to save her child. It was all very upsetting to me. Even Aunt Rachel had not carried on so when our little cousin Matty died.

It hardly seemed any time until Pa and Mr. Herlihy reappeared around the downstream bend, on either side of Henry Steitler, who was limping on his stocking-feet. Mr. Herlihy carried the body of Liam in his arms. Mrs. Herlihy screamed, seeing that. She ran to them, and took Liam from them, sinking to her knees in the cold shallow water. She rocked back and forth, keening her grief as she held Liam's body in her arms – soaking wet, limp as if entirely boneless and ashen-white, like nothing so much as one of our barn-cat Cally's poor stillborn kittens, back in Ohio. His eyes were half-open, but sightless. I turned Jon's head into the front of my dress so that he could not look at that awful sight. But I could not make myself look away, so I was looking on when Ma touched Liam's chest, then put her ear to him and said something to Mrs. Herlihy. Shivaun exclaimed,

"*Mo chroi* ... let her see to the lad! You're making a scene in front of the English, and Mrs. Kettering has the healing talent!"

In front of my eyes, Ma took Liam into her arms. She said to me, crisply,

"Look to your brother, Sally – there's a good girl, now!"

Ma parted the wet shirt and pressed her ear to poor Liam's bare and skinny little chest – so white and still. In a moment, she sat up straight and did something extraordinary. She laid Liam across her knees and pressed on his chest. A bit of water came out of his mouth, and Ma looked up at Pa and Mr. Herlihy and the others, all standing over us.

"He has a heartbeat – only faint, but it is there!" She pressed again on Liam's chest, and some water seeped from between his lips ... and then the miracle happened. His pale face twitched, and he coughed and began to gasp and cry, and vomit more water.

'Holy Mother and all the saints!" cried Mrs. Herlihy, and began to weep again, but with relief. Shivaun was crying, too, as she hugged Wee Donal and Rory to her. Mrs. Glennie most sensibly took off her shawl and helped Ma wrap it around Liam, and from somewhere, Deacon Zollicoffer produced a blanket to go on top of that.

"He must be kept warm, now," Ma said. She sounded as if her own voice would shake, if she let it. "Hot stones at his feet, wrapped in flannel. Let him have warm broth, or tea ... stimulants, if you have brandy or suchlike, but in tiny amounts, a little..."

"Our Savior has blessed us with a miracle," Deacon Zollicoffer exclaimed. The Herlihys all agreed, invoking all manner of saints and the Holy Mother, and Ma shook her head.

"When my mother was a little girl in Downingtown, the miller's little son ... they couldn't find him, one day. He was at the bottom of the millpond, and it was nearly winter, so the water was ice-cold. The boy was cold, too, when they fished him out, and they thought he was drowned and beyond all aid ... but he wasn't. Her father was the doctor they called. He rubbed the boy's chest and listened for a heartbeat ... and it turned out the miller's boy was alive..."

"It is still a miracle," Deacon Zollicoffer insisted, "Since you remembered the previous example and did not despair of his life!" The Deacon looked up at the sky and added, "He works in mysterious ways, his wonders to perform. We have been blessed, all of us," Deacon added, and Mr. Herlihy rumbled,

"And so we have, indade! Mayve, stop geeting! Take the lad to our wagon, put him to bed with plenty of hot stones to take the chill from him," That was Mr. Herlihy, looming over us all like the big, red-headed colossus that he was. Pa helped Ma to her feet. Darragh Herlihy took up the bundle of blankets and shawl around Liam, who was still coughing and shivering. Henry Steitler looked cold, wet and as miserable as Liam, and Ma turned her attention to him,

"Oh, you will certainly be catching your death of cold! Let me find you some dry clothes now..."

"You were very brave, lad," Pa said. "But for you thinking so quick and going after the boy..."

Henry looked embarrassed, blushing red. He mumbled something and looked at the ground. He looked about the age of Jon, and even more miserable at that moment.

"Indade," Mr. Herlihy rumbled. "We owe you a great debt, young Steitler – one that I think we will never be able to repay entire! Know you this – and your missus, too, Kettering; if ever you need friend or aid, all you need do is ask, and a Herlihy will come to you, even if it is to the brink of hell."

Ma nodded. "Thank you, Mr. Herlihy – but I only looked after your son as any sensible woman and mother would – never despairing of life as long as there is breath and a heartbeat!"

"We are in your debt regardless," Mr. Herlihy insisted stoutly. At that, Ma took me by the hand.

Pa put his arm around Henry's shoulders, and replied, "Be at ease, Donal – tomorrow, we may be in your debt to the same degree, for we are all pilgrims on this road together, and bound to look after each other as best we can."

Deacon Zollicoffer, who was walking with us agreed most passionately, but I didn't hear much of what he and the men were talking about, for Ma was hurrying us on, pleading concern for Henry Steitler's health, clad as he was in his soaking wet clothing, and that she must get started on supper. The Herlihy family had already gone with Liam to their wagons to set up their camp for the night. It seemed as if there would be no more exciting incidents happening that day. I was grateful for that. Crossing over the river had been quite enough for one day, little Liam all but drowning in it and then being rescued by Henry Steitler ... it was all more than enough.

Later, as the sun slid down the western sky in a blaze of orange, gold and purple, and my brother Jon yawned, leaning against me, half asleep, Ma tousled his hair and mused,

"I declare, why do boys court danger, the way they do? I told Jon not to go into the river any deeper than his ankles and Mayve Herlihy told her boys the same ... and still, Jon and Dougal Herlihy and his brothers were flat-out disobedient, and Liam Herlihy carried away and nearly drowned!"

"A fair question, Mrs. Kettering," Choctaw Joe knocked out shreds of burnt tobacco out of his pipe into fire. "And the plain answer as I see it... it is the nature of boys and men, too – to court danger. They cannot help it, like salmon rushing up-stream." He looked across the fire and exchanged a grin with Pa. "Young Injun boys in the tribes ... they vie to outdo each other with feats of strength and daring. I daresay it's the same with your young 'uns. Young Henry here, now..." Choctaw Joe nodded at Henry Steitler, now dressed in one of Pa's warm homespun shirts, with one of Ma's plain scrap quilts around his shoulders. "He went arter the Herlihy sprout like a young Hero..." Choctaw Joe added with a rich chuckle, "It's not only the young boys daring each other ... sometimes it's to attract the notice of a pretty young girl."

Henry blushed deep red. It showed even in the firelight, and protested, "No ... no, it was not that, Herr Bayless ... it was because... it was necessary! The *kleiner junge* ... the boy, it ... I did not think anything..." embarrassed, he seemed to have forgotten all English.

Pa said, "No, of course it wasn't like that, Henry. But you did very well and didn't even stop to think about anything else – much less impressing the McCarty miss. Of course, we are all grateful. Although," Pa added with a smile under his scruffy beard, "A proper man never hesitates at all, when it comes to looking after ladies and young 'uns in danger. It's set in us, just like it is for those salmon-fish. And speaking of young 'uns, it's well past time for these young 'uns to be in bed!"

Very well true, for Jon was all but asleep at my side. As we settled to sleep, buried deep under the quilts in the wagon, I thought somewhat resentfully that Pa assumed that Henry was impressing Shivaun McCarty. *Why didn't Pa think of me, that Henry might think of impressing me, as well.*

Chapter 13 – Across the Top of the World

We were traveling through a very curious country now – the trail being mostly level, but with many crags of rocks on either side and the sight of mountains always in the distance. Even though it was now late summer, the highest and most distant mountain crags still bore rags of snow at their peaks. We were never very far from water. Mostly we traveled close to shallow rivers or creeks, so the oxen did not suffer from lack of water or good grazing, as they had in that stretch of desert before reaching the crossing of the Green.

"You'll have easy traveling for now," Choctaw Joe told Pa one evening, as he drew on his pipe beside our campfire. "Leastways, until the long haul across the desert stretch between the Humbolt Sink and the Truckee River. That's close on to forty miles of hard going, and there's one hot mineral spring halfway along and not a blade of grass to be seen. The party that Old Greenwood led up that way, two-three year gone, it was … they loaded up on grass and water at the Sink and traveled as soon as the sun set. Heat's not so much of a killer, then. Speaking of water and springs … some will tell you that Beer Spring water does taste like beer. It don't. What it mostly tastes of is sulphur, and powerful enough to gag a hungry buzzard."

"Is that true?" Pa began to laugh. "Indeed, Oscar and the other boys will be disappointed! They were all looking forward to a natural spring that gushed beer! I hear tell that some of the other springs bubble out of the ground, fizzing and sparkling."

"They do, in some places," Choctaw Joe sat back, as if to relish the telling of a good yarn. "And it is sight to see, indeed – regular geysers spouting out of the ground, great pots of boiling mud, pools of water all the colors of the rainbow and so hot and caustic that it would render the flesh off your bones in about five minutes. There are wonders out west, that we poor fellows can hardly dream of ... only that it is a painful long way to get to see them. Water from the other bubbling springs taste pretty fair, like soda water without any sweetening ... but don't let your critters drink too much of it."

"We won't camp there long," Pa decided. We had been overtaken by two small parties, in the days since fording over the Green – one of a dozen young men with mule packs, and another of four men with just two light wagons. I could tell that circumstance unsettled Pa. The next day when I walked next to Pa and Star and Brandy, I asked him why. Ma and Jon were walking with the Shivaun and the Herlihy boys, so I knew they couldn't overhear.

"Mr. Bayless said that when we reached Fort Hall, we'd be two thirds of the way to California," I said. "I thought that you and Mr. Herlihy and Mr. Glennie would be right pleased ... but instead, I heard you tell Deacon Zollicoffer that we might consider traveling on Sunday now, and Deacon weren't happy about that at all."

"Ah, Sugar-plum – another round of your questions!
But I think you're right, and we should be right pleased to be
so far-along, and it only being the end of August," Pa replied.
He tapped Brandy with the stock of his whip. Brandy was
lagging, turning his head in the direction of a particularly lush
clump of grass. Brandy, so tame and biddable that he would
even obey Jon, who barely came up to his nose. Pa had raised
Brady and Star from calves, so young when he began to train
them that they were hardly larger than Boomer. Brandy
switched his tail, and I think even looked a bit guilty for
having let his attention wander. Pa continued, "It's worrisome,
though, Sugar-plum. Choctaw Joe reckoned that when we
reached Fort Hall, we would be better than two-thirds of the
way to California. He told me straight out, what others told me
before – that last third would be the hardest haul, and one
when we would be worn-down from the long, long journey. A
stretch of desert, longer and dryer than that we came over
before. Then a long hard pull going up a steep canyon river,
and finally a big ol' rocky pass at the end of it. Likely your Ma
will not like that I shared this with you, Sugar-plum, but
you're nearly a grown girl now and been such a help to your
Ma and I and everyone, I figure you're old enough to share
concerns. That's the whole of it. We'll be at the hardest part of
this trail just when we are wearied and worn-out with
traveling all summer. That's what frets at me, Sugar-plum.
When you are wearied and worn-out, that's when folk will be
hasty and careless, and liable to get themselves hurt."

"I see, Pa," I replied, upon thinking seriously about it. When I was tired and impatient at mending or piecing quilt squares – that's when I was most like to run the needle into my finger.

I had begun to understand how much Ma and Pa and the other grownups worried about this, as the weeks of summer turned into autumn. I could see that snow on the highest mountains around us even now. What if winter came early, just as we reached that last mountain barrier? I knew that possibility haunted Pa. I heard him say so to Ma, late in the evening, when they thought that Jon and I were fast asleep. That was the reason that Pa and the other men pushed the oxen so hard on the days that we traveled, made them keep as close behind Deacon Zollicoffer's and Mrs. Glennie's faster-moving mule teams.

I was reassured and not a little proud of being talked to like this by Pa. I must be near to growing up. Maybe Ma would make my next dress with a skirt down to my ankles, like Shivaun McCarty's dress, instead of a little-girl dress with a hem somewhere about my knees. I had already outgrown my last pair of shoes – they rubbed my toes and heels so awfully that Ma now permitted me to wear my Sioux moccasins.

We reached Fort Hall on the Snake River after a journey of some ten days, or so. To my eyes, Fort Hall didn't look nearly as much a proper fort as Fort Laramie. It was just a quadrangle of white-washed mud-brick walls with a taller peak-roofed tower at one corner. The inside of those walls were lined with huts made of unpeeled logs, and irregular shake roofs that sagged alarmingly in places. There wasn't much in the way of food stocks; such were alarmingly expensive, even more so than at Fort Laramie. The fort itself was so distant from anything like settled country. It had changed hands once again – from the British Hudson's Bay Company to American, what with the cession of the southern portion of Oregon Territory to American governance.

The only supplies to be had in quantity and at no charge were scraps of wagons scattered in the vicinity of the fort; lengths of lumber from the boxes, wheels and parts of wheels, axles and wagon-tongues. So many, that Shivaun said one could build a whole wagon several times over, if one was so inclined as to piece all those bits together.

"See, many of them headed to the Willamette valley settlements, they've had to cut down their wagons to carts," a man from the fort explained to Pa when Pa made mention of it when trying to find someone who would take letters back home for a small consideration or even just good fellowship. "Oxen worn out, not so much left of their trash and traps ... so, makes sense to make a cart and lighten their load somewhat."

Still – we could post letters at Fort Hall, in the hope that any travelers going east could carry them back to the States. Ma wrote again to the folks back in Ohio. I wrote another letter to Ginny Reed, in the hope that Mr. Clyman had been able to persuade her father to follow our party on the established trail, in several weeks, and not chance taking Mr. Hasting's shortcut. I addressed my letter to Ginny, care of the Reed company, traveling in the palace wagon, and described the wagon to the storekeeper at Fort Hall, who smiled down at me and patted my cheek as if I were a little girl, hardly the age of Jon. I did not bristle at him indignantly, for he was doing me a favor. Still, I wanted to tell him that I was nearly grown, and ought to be treated respectfully as a young lady.

(I do not believe my letter was ever delivered to Ginny. I have no notion of what became of it. Likely used to light a fire, or something.)

There was good water and pasturage, so we took two days to rest and prepare for the hardest last-third of the journey. But we did have good news. Deacon Zollicoffer and Choctaw Joe would continue with our party. We were camped by the white-washed walls of Fort Hall on the second day, when Choctaw Joe told us. We had all assumed that Deacon and Choctaw Joe would carry on to Oregon, as Fort Hall was where the trail forked. Choctaw Joe appeared that evening, as was his custom, while Deacon Zollicoffer communed in prayer for hours on end, which Choctaw Joe complained gave him the yips. Also, Choctaw Joe much favored Ma's bread-baking, nearly as much as he favored Pa's conversation, and Pa relished Joe's advice.

"It seems that Deacon Zollicoffer has received new orders from his spirit-guide," Choctaw Joe replied, scratching his jaw, reflectively. "Of late, the Deacon's been considering

California, after all. Seems that Colonel Fremont made friends with them mountain Paiutes and their old Chief Truckee, who's well-disposed to whites in general. The Deacon thinks that the Lord hisself has issued a new set of orders, directing him to a fertile ground for his preachifying." He lit his pipe with the end of a smoldering twig and puffed heartily to get it going.

"We'll be glad to have you both with us a little longer, then," Pa sounded relieved. "It's a flat-out relief to have your experience to draw on, rather than Mr. Hastings' guidebook. What can you tell us about the Indians we might encounter – are they friendly, or … not so friendly. Any chance of trading, as we did with the Lakotah Sioux? What about game?"

"Round these parts, the Snake and the Crow are friendly enough, most times," Choctaw Joe replied, with a chuckle. "Hunters and trappers mostly. They looked to the white men as allies in the war against their enemies – the Lakota Sioux, mostly. They hunt for deer, elk and suchlike. No buffler, though. Now, them Bannock Indians just never took to the horse. No need. They're a bit hostile-like if provoked. I'd advise not giving them a reason to have a mad fit with you. Then we got them Shoshone – folk call them Diggers; they're a sorry lot. After that, there's them desert Paiutes…" Choctaw Joe considered his words for some little time. Pa waited patiently. We had got accustomed to the curious manner of Choctaw Joe putting his thoughts into words that we could readily understand. "It's a harsh country," he said at last.

"Hot, dry, mostly. Sand and sagebrush, spikey trees and cactus. Little in the way of water, and far between those places. Full of life, though – but small life. Little foxes and rabbits, mice, snakes, lizards and such. Beautiful in the spring, when it rains and for a few days, meadows of wildflowers. Like the Deacon's Almighty went mad with a cosmic paintbox. But the flowers don't last..."

"Nothing beautiful ever does," Ma remarked, unexpectedly, and Choctaw Joe nodded.

"No, it don't, Miz Kettering, and maybe that's so's we'll appreciate it all the more. Anyway ... them Paiutes live a hard, harsh life out there, but they're mostly friendly, but them Digger Indians along the lower Raft live even harder. Ain't an easy one, by any means. They don't have the room to be lordly and generous to outsiders ... especially if those outsiders might do something ... unconsidering-like, which makes their lives a mite harder. And it might be real easy for one of us pilgrims to do that, without bad intent or even not just knowing."

"We'll be as careful as we can, to not provoke them," Pa replied, and Choctaw Joe grinned.

"With luck, you mayn't even see them," he replied. "Although I don't know if that'll be good or bad."

"Sufficient to the day," Pa said.

We departed from Fort Hall at the end of August. Pa's expectation was to be over the tall mountains into California by the end of September, well before what was said to be the worst storms and heaviest snowfall. In expectation of a hard journey, the German boys repaired and reinforced their rattletrap farm wagon from the bits and ends left by previous parties. Mr. Herlihy again set up his forge fire, bellows and anvil and set about reshoeing Mr. Glennie's horse and setting to rights all the rattling wheels of wagons which had shrunken and become loose in the thin and dry air.

We all took heart, I think, knowing that we were so close to the end of that journey – but we were also so very tired of the vagabond life, following the long, dusty trail. The sense of being on a great adventure, with amazing things to be seen around every bend had long worn thin. I think we all just wanted it to be done.

I know that Ma was tired and frazzled about the dust that got into everything, about never having anything that stayed clean, tired of cooking over an open fire, living all day, every day in the out of doors, as splendid as the out-of-doors could be, sometimes. I was tired of the sameness of the country, although when we came to the branch of Kassia Creek, where the road to California made a definite turn, there was a splendid assembly of rock bluffs and standing spires of rock.

Jon and his bosom friends, the Herlihy boys, though – they seemed just as excited now, about the daily travel and everything that they saw, as they had been at the beginning of the trek.

Little boys can be so very exhausting. I said so, about this time to Miss Pierson, who was now Mrs. McNabb, although I still couldn't bring myself to call her by her given name. I had that much respect for her, as an older person. I just couldn't bring myself to do it, although she urged me to do so, many times. We were trudging along the trail, trying to remain upwind of the dust that the feet of the oxen and the slow grinding iron wheels of the wagons kicked up

"It's the nature of boys," she replied. "Especially the small ones. They are inexhaustible little engines of energy. Possibly they have discovered a means of perpetual motion."

"I wish that I could find that," I replied, "Or a way to still it. Like keeping a clock pendulum from swinging."

Later, I wished that I had not said that.

It happened on the third – or maybe the fourth day – as we followed the meandering, swampy and slow-flowing Humbolt River, farther and farther into the desert. It was desert, clear and dry, where no wood that we could burn for cookfires but sagebrush; sagebrush that the men and boys cut for us and piled into a shallow pit dug in the ground. It burned brightly and long, better than the buffalo chips of earlier along the trail – and it certainly smelled a lot better. Remembering it all now, I think that was the only advantage to burning sage; that it was aromatic and burned down to hot coals that lasted a long, long time.   The dust was a particular plague to us at that part of the trail; fine gritty clouds of it blowing on the lightest breeze, and getting into everything – hair, clothing, bedding, even our food. It made a sticky paste when we sweated. It made me feel like I had rolled in thin, slippery mud. It even gritted in our teeth. I believe Ma despaired of ever being wholly clean again.

For some reason – I think perhaps because the trail was mostly sandy and not all that rough, so our wagon rolled smoothly, Jon and I were riding for a while, until the moment when I decided to climb down from the wagon. I saw Shivaun McCarty a little way ahead, walking next to Henry Steitler, leading his Indian paint-pony by the reins.

"Let's go walk for a while," I said to Jon. I climbed over the side of the wagon, and across the slow-turning wheel, as I had done hundreds of times before. I reached the ground, and looked ahead, knowing that Jon was following me. I'm not at all certain what happened then, as I wasn't looking in his direction, but ahead – when Jon fell.

Jon fell awkwardly, clumsy. Before I saw anything at all, the heavy iron wagon wheel rolled straight over his left ankle, and he screamed.

It was a horrible sound – that scream and the awful sort of crushing, grinding crunch. I think that I must have screamed, also. As quick as anything – even before Pa shouted *whoa!* At the oxen to halt them, I pulled Jon by the shoulders of his shirt, pulled him out from under the wagon before the other wheels could roll over him. As pale as a linen sheet, Ma was at my elbow.

"What happened?" she cried, and I said,

"He fell! And the wheel went over his leg!"

Jon was sobbing now, and my heart was wretched cold in my chest, because he was hurt, my baby brother was hurt, Boomer was nosing at my elbow while Pa stood with his ox whip in his hand, and now there was Henry Steitler and Shivaun hovering at his shoulders. Pa knelt and Ma knelt on either side of Jon, who had grabbed ahold of my arm, my hand – so hard that I found bruises there later.

Pa said some words under his breath that I had only heard from men when they thought that no women or children were around. Aloud, Pa pleaded, "Easy, Jonny-cakes! Let your mother look at your leg, now!"

But Jon only squinched his eyes tighter together, and rolled away from Ma, who was trying to roll up his trouser-leg – and there was blood seeping into the rough jeans fabric and the knitted sock cuff underneath, spilling into the dusty ground over him. He screamed when Ma touched his ankle, a scream that went straight to my heart, as if someone had plunged a dagger of ice into it. Boomer nosed between us. He was frantic to be beside Jon, and Ma cried,

"Get away, Boomer!" but Boomer lowered his head, and whined deep in his throat, the very picture of puzzlement and distress.

"Is he going to die, then?" That was Young Donal's interested voice, piping up over my shoulder, followed at once by a chorus of Shivaun and Mayve telling him to hush. About half the company had gathered around, because everyone had heard our voices and run to see what was the matter. After Mr. Steitler dying in the accident with his wagon, and poor little Liam Herlihy nearly drowning – everyone dreaded the worst. And that it was a child, hurt to the bloody bone ... I believe this incident cut to the heart of every mother and father in the company. It certainly cut to mine. I was grateful for the calming presence of Mrs. McNabb, who had halted the McNabb wagon. That wagon was the nearest to us. She ordered the team to 'whoa' and stand fast and come running to our wagon.

After some fraught moments, Jon's sobbing abated, somewhat, although he still clutched frantically at my arm. Ma peeled back the bloody trouser-leg and the sock cuff under it ... and such an awful sight it was, although it was even worse when the bruises colored up over the next few days. I was surprised that Ma's hands were steady, and that she was as calm as when she found Liam's heartbeat when everyone thought him drowned and dead. She felt along Jon's ankle, and he cried out again, and would have pulled away, but for Mrs. McNabb and I having a firm hold on him. Pa's breath hissed through his teeth. It was as if Pa felt the pain, too.

Ma sat up straight. "Elkanah, can you find my medicine box in the wagon? I do not think the bones are broken. Only that the flesh was crushed under the wheel, but it was going over sand, which was the saving of that limb. Jonny-cakes, I am sorry – that your leg will hurt for some time, until it heals, but you will not be crippled for life because of it."

"Thank God for that mercy," Pa said. He looked as if he would be sick with relief. At that moment I had a curious realization; Ma was the stronger one, when faced with pain and illness. Pa could not long endure the sight of suffering and injury, especially when such involved Jon or I, although as a man and a farmer, he would certainly have encountered such often enough. It was just that Ma was more resolute and calmer when dealing with it.

We halted our wagon for an hour or so, long enough to build a small fire of dry sagebrush, and heat water, so that Ma could brew up a kettle of sage-leaf tea to wash the cuts and abrasions on Jon's ankle clean. Ma was a great believer in the healing properties of sage-leaf tea for inside and out. She made Jon drink some of it, then gave him a little bit of syrup of laudanum to take the edge off the pain and put him to bed in the wagon. Boomer insisted on curling up next to him and wouldn't be ordered away. Then we went on, catching up to the rest of the company. Jon slept fitfully, then and later. His ankle pained quite dreadfully, and he could not walk for days. The constant jolting of the wagon on the following day's journey made him fretful and sobbing.

Mrs. Glennie, whose stomach bulged out most noticeably now, came to confer with Ma that afternoon, when we stopped for the midday rest.

"The baby is wriggling dreadfully," she complained. "Is there any tonic that you can give me that will make the Little Stranger calm down?"

Ma laughed. "I'm afraid that there isn't – and it is rather a good sign! That means that Baby is almost ready to come out and meet the world."

"And when will I get any rest?" Mrs. Glennie pleaded, and Ma laughed again.

"About the first day that you send him or her off to dame school," she replied, laughing again at the woeful expression on Mrs. Glennie's face. She did ask after Jon, though.

"Would he be more comfortable, riding with me, in my buggy?" she ventured. "It rides very easily, over the rockiest trail. As it has been restful for me in this journey. I believe that it would be easier your sons' poor little leg."

Ma looked as if she would cry for gratitude. "Not if you mind Boomer, following after you – we can't keep that dog away from the boy!"

"I'll make certain that Portus behaves," Mrs. Glennie promised. Portus was her little brown and white spaniel. You wouldn't have thought Portus was much of a dog, being a coddled little lapdog, but he had turned out to be quite bold, given to tussle fearlessly with other dogs and chase after critters much bigger than himself – even the Herlihy's two big coachdogs, and Mr. McNabb's big black hunter.

Pa carried Jon to Mrs. Glennie's buggy – a light little vehicle on sturdy springs, so it rode quite easily over the roughest trail. For the remainder of that day, Jon rode with Mrs. Glennie. Ma was grateful for her offer to have Jon travel in the buggy with her. We were at our wits' end, trying to keep him comfortable in the jolting wagon. His ankle was dreadfully swollen; bruises that came out almost to his knee, all dark blue, purple, and almost black. Not all of Ma's potions and poultices could give Jon ease from the pain of where that iron-shod wagon wheel had rolled over his ankle, crushing that limb down into the pebbly sand. I could not tell if Jon was cross from the pain, or from forced inactivity. He could not romp and play with his friends, Wee Donal, Liam and Rory, or adventure with Henry Steitler on his fleet-footed Indian pony. We would not know for weeks if he would suffer lasting damage from this awful accident.

Oh, this was a tedious stretch of the trail, following along the slow-flowing river, as it wandered farther and farther into the arid desert – a river which degenerated more and more into a stagnant swamp as we traveled. We never saw any Indians, not hide nor hair of them, although once or twice, the men found our cattle of a morning, with fresh arrow-wounds, or their limbs cut by sharp blades. Those we were forced to slaughter, and Choctaw Joe showed us how to cut the meat into thin strips and dry in the hot sun to make jerky.

Our milk cow, Daisy, wandered off one night. Either that, or Daisy was stolen and slaughtered by the Indians. I missed that cow, and the milk and butter, but not milking her on a dark early morning since she had gone dry weeks before, so my feelings were mixed on that loss. Mr. Glennie, the Taylors and Mr. Martindale also lost seven of their critters between them, as we followed along the Humboldt. That, or the poor things went off looking for better grazing. In any case, we never saw them again. This reduced our herd of loose oxen to a handful, which would have affected us more, but since we had lightened our wagons at Fort Hall ... well, other companies were affected worse than we were, so I shouldn't make so much of it.

Still, I could tell that it did worry Pa and the other men.

Chapter 14 – Desert Crossing

We finally reached the Sink, where the slow-flowing Humboldt River finally spread out into a stagnant swamp and sank into the desert. I thought then that this was a very odd thing for a river to do … to just sink into the sand like that. In Ma's books of nature and geography, proper rivers ended by pouring into the ocean. In any case, the Humboldt Sink was the last bit of green we would see for what seemed to be hundreds of miles. For many days of travel, we had been able to see a faint jagged blue line of mountains on the far west horizon – most clearly at morning and in the evening, when they were outlined against the setting sun. The mountains made a line like something cut from dark blue blotting-paper, stretching across the horizon as far as I could see in either direction.

We had reached the place where the trail led from the Sink somewhat later in the afternoon than we had expected to travel that day. We were all so tired – tired, dirty and worn ragged, as we made a late camp. The moon rose, pale and luminous. The swamp of the sink seemed to be as alive as the desert in other directions was dead. Frogs cheeped in chorus among the tall green bullrushes, and waterfowl had settled for the night. It had been such misery, those days following along, while the flowing river shriveled, and the dust invaded everything. The track left by wagon companies ahead of us, and in previous years were gouged deep into the desert sands, heading away from the Sink. All that we needed do, Choctaw Joe told Pa the day that we got that far, was to follow them. It was hard to contemplate yet another three days of worse travel, and travel without any comfortable break.

In fact, the only comfort that I could see in our present condition was that Jon's ankle, although near-black with bruises at first and very painful, was not broken. He could not bear to walk on it without limping, but at least the pain did not keep him from sleeping well.

Around the twilight fire, Pa and Choctaw Joe, Mr. Herlihy and Henry gathered with some of the other men. Mr. Glennie was there, and so was Deacon Zollicoffer. I recollect that because of the stifling heat, Deacon Zollicoffer had even taken off his dignified black clawhammer coat and loosened his collar and neckcloth. I watched from our bed in the wagon, where Jon had mercifully fallen asleep with Boomer curled at his feet.

I was so glad for the presence of that dog, let me tell you. We had left Cally, our sweet barn cat and her kittens far, far behind in Ohio. Daisy, the milk cow, so tame and biddable – she had vanished a few days previously, as we followed the stagnant river. I wondered how likely it was that Brandy and Star would fall to the various perils of the trail, as other oxen had already succumbed. The trail was a hard one, no mistaking that. The odds of any of our oxen living to retirement in a lush pasture in California were vanishingly small. They were critters, you see – bred and trained to pull the wagons, and if something happened and they could not … well, they fed us on their flesh, fresh or dried into jerky. It was lean, and tough, and not really good eating, but as Pa had told us many times, if you are very hungry, anything made a good meal.

But the men were talking; Pa poked a long stick into the fire and lit his pipe from the ember-hot end.

"You see, fellows – we'll be heading out for a long, dry, rough haul when we leave out of here," he said. "We need to spend a while here, taking some precautions. It's a long, hard haul, so say them as has gone there before. Joe – you tell them what you know about it. We had a hard pull getting to the Green, you will recollect – and this is pert near three times longer a dry stretch."

"Cut plenty of fodder for the critters," Choctaw Joe advised. "Carry water in every single blessed thing that don't leak, or leak much, leastways. There's not a scrap of green or a drop of sweet water until you reach the Truckee River. Ol' Caleb told me when we met him last, west of Laramie. It's hard pull, nearly three days of it. Them folks that he guided through in '44, they set out at sunset. Did the worst of it at night when it was cool. Spared the critters considerable hardship, he tol' me. But it's hard going, even then. And one more thing," Choctaw Joe drew deep on his pipe. "Unharness the critters when you get close to the Truckee. Let them run when they first smell water. They'll be frantic with thirst. You don't want to risk them wrecking a wagon, then."

"But will we be able to retrieve them all, after running mad and loose?" Mr. Glennie demanded.

I saw Choctaw Joe shrug. "A couple of lost critters, or a wrecked wagon? Your choice, hoss! Ain't any skin off mine."

Mr. Glennie looked angry. I guess that he wasn't used to being talked to that way by folk that he thought little enough of, but it fell to Pa to smooth it over. Pa drew deep on his pipe, as he looked into the campfire, and replied, "Sufficient unto the day, Joe – Jeptha. Keep it comradely, fellows. We'll cross over that bridge when we get through the desert. For now – tomorrow – I'm suggesting that we set about cutting rushes and grass. Green stuff for the critters. We turn out every empty barrel, every bottle, jug or bucket, make them sound and fill them full."

"Aye," Mr. Herlihy agreed, quite eagerly. "Put them empty into the water to soak, and thereby the wood will swell up and seal the leaks!" He began enlarging on his plans to do just that. I believed then and still do that he was that one man of our wagon company who would back Pa, no matter what Pa suggested. If Pa had had taken it into his mind to tell all the men to strip off their boots and socks and walk barefoot across the desert, Mr. Herlihy would be the first to peel off his boots and throw them into the Sink, and cheerfully walk away barefoot. Likely Henry Steitler would follow, too.

Fortunately, Pa would never have suggested such a silly thing. The men went on talking for some time over their plans for gathering and cutting rush and grass, and what could be done to carry as much water as possible over the long, desolate dry stretch. I was tired, so tired, and the desert turned so cold at night, after the sun went down. *That was another impossible thing – why would the desert be so hot during the daytime, but so cold at night?* That was as much a bafflement to me as the river running into sand and sinking into the ground. I pulled my share of the quilt and the buffalo pelt over me and went to sleep almost at once.

We camped for two days at the Sink, preparing for the desert. It would have been three days, but Mr. Glennie was impatient to continue, and I overheard Pa saying to Choctaw Joe that he thought it best to let Mr. Glennie have his way this time. It was then nearly to the end of September.

"Snow comes early in the high mountains," Choctaw Joe agreed. He looked sober. "Midway through October, so Old Greenwood told us. By the time it finishes falling, they say it'll be twenty feet deep."

"I can't imagine that to be possible," Pa said, "But I don't want to be the one to find out that it is. Also, I can't stand the thought of Jeptha Glennie swearing at me and telling everyone that that he told me so."

The next morning, Mr. Herlihy set up his whetstone and began sharpening tools for cutting rushes and tall grass. Those folk who were intent on farming when they got to California brought out scythes and hand sickles and piled them up by

Mr. Herlihy's treadle-powered whetstone. Meanwhile, Shivaun and I and the other women ransacked our wagons for empty barrels, buckets, washtubs and anything which could hold water. Those empty casks, which at the start of the journey had contained everything from flour to salt-pork, we scrubbed out and carried to a shallow part of the sink and set into the water. We hoped that soaking them well would expand the dried-out wood which they were made from and prevent them from leaking too much.

Ma and I sat down under the shade of the front of our tent, after completing the last of this chore. We were looking at the collection of barrels and buckets soaking in the murky browny-green water.

"I do not see how we can carry all the water that the creatures will need," Ma confessed abruptly. "Look at all those animals now. Consider how much they drink..." She was looking out now, at our herd; the cattle, Mr. Glennie's and Deacon Zollicoffer's mules, the handful of horses and ponies which various members of the company possessed. They were all cropping at the thin grass meadowland, in a kind of half-hearted manner. No, this pasture wasn't anything like what the critters normally favored.

I was heartened by this conversation, in an odd kind of way. Ma was talking to me as if I were a grown woman, already, sharing her heart and her deep concerns. There we were, at the edge of a dry and horrible desert, faced with a horrible two days of travel – two days at least. My brother Jon still couldn't walk on his mangled leg, Pa had the management of the company to distract him, and Ma was looking after Mrs. Glennie, whose' stomach was now bulging hugely. I think her baby was about to be birthed any day and then there was poor orphaned Henry Steitler for Ma to worry about. I thought that my little brother might very well be right, and I said so. I didn't venture to mention that Henry was all but a trusty son to Pa. Which meant that Ma and I would be outnumbered by men in our family. We had best now be close.

"I wish that I could send a letter home," Ma confessed. "Now that we are so alone and far away from home."

"I'd like to write to Ginny again," I said. "I know that the Reed's company will be rejoining the main trail – perhaps I can leave a letter here, for her ... like Mr. Hastings did, at Independence rock. On a stake, addressed to her, out in the open where they can see it in passing."

"You should do that, Sally," Ma replied, warmly. "I'll get out my writing desk and ink tonight after supper. Write your letter before it gets too dark!"

So I did, sitting in the twilight, under the glow of the single lantern hanging from the first wagon bow, listening to the evening sounds of our camp, accompanied by the constant song of frogs, and crickets and other swamp-dwelling small critters. The sky was clear overhead, stained in the west with coral and a shade like the lining of an oyster shell.

Dear Ginny:

I will leave this letter for you at the Sink of the Humboldt River, in hopes that some kind person of your party will spot it and take it to you. Tomorrow, we shall set out across a barren desert. Mr. Bayless says that this is a long, dry stretch, so we are gathering reeds and grass enough to feed the oxen on and filling up every container with water. He also says that we are within some two hundred miles or so of California, which is a bare fraction of the distance that we have traveled this far. So close and still so far!

We have managed very well in our travels thus far, although Liam Herlihy – one of the little boys that you would not know – nearly drowned after our crossing of the Green River. Also that my brother Jon fell while getting down from our wagon. His lower limb was run over by the wheel, which caused him much pain. My mother did not think that it was broken, which is most fortunate. I believe he is getting better. Mrs. Glennie, who is of our party and travels in a light buggy drawn by a pair of fine mules offered to have him ride in her conveyance to spare any further pain.

Otherwise, our family remains well, and in good health. The wagon party which my Pa is captain of remains in excellent spirits. We have every hope of arriving safely in California before the winter snow blocks the highest pass over the mountains. I hope that your company will have the

same safe travel and good fortune, and that we will see each other in California.
Your devoted friend,
Sarah Elizabeth Kettering
Written at the Sink of the Humbolt River
20 September, 1846

Ma made Jon and I lay down and rest in the late afternoon of the day that our company set out into the desert. Pa and the other men filled the barrels buckets with every drop of water that they could hold and horsed them into our wagons. They had already rolled piles of cut green stuff in canvas and tied them like bolsters to the backs and sides of our wagons. Ma laughed with me, saying that it made the wagons look like pictures of court ladies in Elizabethan times, with enormous rolls of stuff tied around their hips to make their skirts stand out.

Pa hitched up the oxen, and they stood in harness, while Ma set out supper for us. The sun was already sliding down the western horizon, outlining the mountain peaks, all jagged and clear; dark indigo silhouettes against a pale saffron sky. The daily heat eased off once the sun went down, so it was not all that unpleasant, walking with Ma a little way from the wagon. Jon, whose ankle still pained him dreadfully, rode in Mrs. Glennie's buggy. Her own ankles were so swollen that Ma and Mr. Glennie absolutely forbade her to walk. Ma and Mrs. Herlihy quietly agreed that Mrs. Glennie was very close to her time, which concerned them both mightily. I thought about how a new little baby would make everyone so happy, and I didn't worry all that much.

"I hope that someone finds my letter to Ginny," I said. I had left it by the side of the Sink, near to where we had camped. Pa cut a long, thick reed stem and plunged one end of it deep into the ground. He had split the top of the reed, and I wedged the letter into it, with the address, inked in big letters; *To Miss Virginia Reed, in the Reed-Donner Company – please deliver!*

"I'm certain that they will," Ma replied. "You left it where anyone passing will see it."

"The one thing that I considered," I reflected, as we walked. "Is that they might be ahead of us... they could be far ahead, couldn't they, Ma?"

Ma considered it for a long moment. The sun had gone down behind the far mountains now, and so she loosened her sunbonnet ties and let it slip off the back of her head. "I don't know, Sugar-plum. I suppose that they might have made good time on Mr. Hastings' shortcut, but I just don't see how they could have gotten ahead of us, recollecting what Mr. Clyman said of the country they would travel through. And," Ma added, after another long moment of reflection. "Mr. Bayless has read what he calls the trail-sign ... the remains of campfires, and the dung that the critters leave, along with the tracks and all... and says that there are only three or perhaps four parties ahead of us on the trail to California this season. One of them with many mules…"

"And they move fast," I agreed. *Oh, I had learned so many things, so far on this journey.* "Especially if they are in a packtrain and don't have to bother with wagons at all."

"Mr. Bayless says the other parties ahead on the trail are traveling with light wagons, or perhaps carts," Ma answered. "I do not think that your friend Ginny's party is ahead. Most likely behind us. I hope not very far behind," Ma added fairly. "Because winter sets in early in those high mountains – so those who know the west well insist. I think your Pa is very wise, for taking the advice of such men. Sometimes men are not wise at all, thinking that accepting such advice from makes themselves look small." In the twilight, Ma looked sideways at me, and she had a tiny smile on her face. "Sugar-plum, when you decide on a man to marry … when you are grown and ready to marry … settle on a man who will be guided by advice of those who know better and accept that advice without anger and resentment. That is a man who will make a good and worthy husband."

"Like Pa?" I asked. I was flattered that Ma should be speaking to me in this way.

Ma nodded. "A man with your Pa's best qualities. Not necessarily a man who looks like your Pa; but one who respects you and will do his very best for you and the children that – with the Almighty's blessing – you and he will raise together."

I thought about this for some moments. The sky had darkened overhead, spangled with a blaze of stars as large as diamond chips, while the faint mist of the Milky Way spanned the sky.

"How will I know that man, then? I don't know of any one as good as Pa ... except for maybe Ginny's Papa."

Ma set her arm around my shoulders and gave me a brief hug. "Oh, likely you will know ... and if you are uncertain, perhaps ask your father and I for our opinion. Although," she added, "I doubt that Elkanah Kettering will think any man on earth is good enough for our little Sugar-plum!"

We walked on for hours; the full moon sailed higher and higher, turning from rich ivory in color to as pale as milk. We could see quite well, as it turned out. The light it shed turned the desert almost as bright as day, as curiously light as those nights in winter back in Ohio, after snow had fallen, and a full moon behind a pale overcast lit up everything clear. It was so quiet at night, but for the regular faint crunching sound that the wagon wheels and the ox teams' feet made as they plodded steadily onward. The trail was just as dusty and hard as it was during the day, but for some odd reason, it seemed to glow faintly.

"'tis the way that the fae made, to mark their roads," Mrs. Herlihy said, when I noticed this and made mention of it. She hastily crossed herself. "The Fair Folk, that is ... and sure you will, young Sally – never to follow a track like that into the side of a hill, for enchanted you will be for a hundred years or more, while thinking that only a night has passed! For when you escape – if you can escape – you will find that all your kin are dead long-since, and your home tumbled to ruin!"

"Like the tale of Rip Van Winkel," Ma remarked, and since Mrs. Herlihy had never heard that story, Ma related it to her. The night and this journey seemed endless, as if we moved on a treadmill, never actually getting anywhere. But it was important that we spare the oxen, who had such a great chore of it, and so we walked for as long as we could put a foot ahead of another. The Herlihy boys, yawning and stumbling with weariness, were finally put to bed in the Herlihy's wagon. Ma asked if I wanted to go to bed in ours, but I knew how important it was to keep on walking, even though I was dazed with exhaustion.

"Up, Sally-Sarah!" That was Henry Steitler, leading his pony by the reins, and I was so tired and half-asleep on my feet that I let him boost me up into the saddle. I think Ma helped me, saying,

"Oh yes – you'll take care, then."

"*Aber naturlich,*" Henry replied, and then he got up onto his pony, and we rode along double on that sturdy Indian pony with me for what seemed be all that night. I dozed, leaning back against his skinny chest while that pony plodded on, and Henry's arms kept me from falling to one side or the other. I felt perfectly safe, for he was the next thing in the world to being a brother to Jon and I.

I recollect half waking up, when Pa said, "You can go back to sleep now, Sugar-plum!" I believe that Pa carried me to our wagon, which for once during that interminable night was not moving.

When I did wake up for real, it was bright daylight, gaspingly hot, and the air smelt funny. I sat up. Yes, I was in our bed in the wagon. The sun was at the highest, in a brazen, burning sky, a sky without a single speck of cloud in it.

The air smelt of wet mud and that kind of alkali stink which I recalled from where we had passed by those odd, bubbling springs back along the trail before reaching Fort Hall. Only this odor was more pungent. I sat up, crawled from the bed and climbed down from the wagon. Ma, Pa, Jon and Henry sat on the sand in the thin band of shade cast by the wagon cover, listlessly picking at cold meat, bread and the beans that Ma had cooked the day before.

Pa made a space for me, and Ma handed me a plate.

"Dinner," Ma said, but I looked at the food, slightly revolted.

"I'm not really that hungry," I confessed, and Ma sighed.

"No one is, really. This awful desert really takes any appetite out of you. Mr. Bayless says that we are almost halfway across."

"Another night," Pa added. He looked as exhausted as I felt, drained and with new lines grooved in his cheeks above his beard. "We'll rest for now, and start out again, once the sun sets."

I ate, without any appetite. When Ma wasn't looking, I sneaked the rest to Boomer. I don't believe Boomer was any hungrier than I was, but dogs are like that; they won't turn up their nose at anything remotely edible, no matter how disgusting.

My legs ached and so did my sit-upon from the unaccustomed hours on horseback. I thought that walking around might ease them. Anyway, I was curious about the spring in the middle of the desert – a series of hot, smelly, steaming seeps in the ground. One of them spurted regularly into the air, at least to the height of twenty feet or so. But all this water bubbling out of the ground came out so hot and muddy that it made domes and walls around itself. The men had to break the solidified crust, and let the water run off so that it could cool. It still stank something awful, from all the alkali or whatever was in it. No wonder that the oxen, the mules and horses didn't really want to drink from it. I wouldn't have wanted to drink from something with so nasty a smell that it made the hairs in my nose curl up.

Those bubbling springs of nasty-smelling mud were a curiosity. Though I could have lived without spending much more time next to them than we did. It was so hot and the air reeked. After a few minutes of walking around, I went back to our wagon, where Pa and Ma, with Boomer at their feet, had lain down to sleep on a blanket spread out underneath. That was all the shade there was. I lay down next to Ma, and I was so tired and sore that I did fall to sleep again, in spite of everything.

We set out again at sunset, just like on the first night. Ma asked, in a very defeated-sounding voice, if anyone was hungry. No one was. I was thirsty, so awfully thirsty, but the draughts of lukewarm water didn't seem to satisfy at all. I think I must have felt every bit as miserable as our poor oxen, trudging through the endless miles of sand. At least, I had the comfort of knowing that there was an end to it.

"By sunrise, we should be close to the river," Choctaw Joe assured us. "We'll not be short of water or fodder for the critters, after this dry stretch. Put a pebble in your mouth, and suck on it – that way, you won't feel thirst so bad."

(I did. It didn't help.)

"We'll hold on to thoughts of that promise," Pa replied. Boomer and I were walking next to Pa. Ma had gone ahead, walking next to Mrs. Glennie's buggy. I think she wanted to be close to Mrs. Glennie, in case the baby came sometime during this night, and near to Jon, whose' broken ankle improved but slowly. Our lead oxen, Brandy and Star often glanced at us reproachfully. Poor oxen. They were miserable and suffering, and everyone knew it. So much depended on them carrying on. At least, we humans had an inkling of how much longer their torment would continue.

The moon sailed up into the heavens, adding a light to guide our footsteps, silvering the desert to the far horizon. The mountains were a distant dark outline against a sky blazing with stars. The pale covers of our wagons bobbed and swayed like sails with the wind behind a ship. This was why our wagons were called prairie schooners when people wrote about them later in history books, newspapers, and in romantic novels of adventure on the plains. At a distance, they did rather look like ship sails, especially as constant sunshine and weathering bleached them as white as old bones.

I walked along with Pa for a long time, with Boomer padding at our heels. I think the long sleep in the afternoon refreshed me considerably. At any rate, I was not so tired as I had been the night before. Sometime during that night, Henry Steitler rode on his pony past us. He and Oscar and Mr. Glennie were herding the bare handful of extra oxen and milk cows left to us, who seemed from the complaint and lowing to be almost as miserable as their fellows under harness.

"All the critters doing well, Henry?" Pa asked, and Henry replied, "All in order, *Herr-Capitan!*" He sketched a salute with the tips of his fingers to the brim of that foreign-looking cap, and rode on.

"A fine young man," Pa remarked, absently, when Henry was gone some distance ahead. "I know you and Jonny-cake like him a lot, too. I'll be sorry to have to part ways with him, when we get to California."

I thought about that, and it made me sad to think of never seeing Henry after this journey was done. Then I remembered how Jon had talked about asking Henry to be our brother. Perhaps this would be a good time to suggest it to Pa.

"We do like Henry, too," I said. "Jon and I talked about that. How we want him to stay with us. Be our big brother. With him being an orphan and all. We could take him in, and he could be part of our family."

Pa chuckled. "You have thought about this, haven't you, Sugar-plum?" Then the tone of Pa's voice turned serious. "I can't say we wouldn't consider it, your Ma and I. The trouble is that Henry Steitler is near enough to grown that he might relish setting out on his own. He might not like the thought of being tied down with family obligations and be real reluctant to say 'no' to us ... since he's a conscientious lad, and grateful for how we've looked after him. I wouldn't want to hamper him in his ambitions."

"Oh," I answered. I hadn't thought of it that way – Henry being keen to set out on his own. It took me back a little, but I persisted. "But you will think of a way to ask him, won't you, Pa? A way that he can say 'no', if it's what he really wants."

I didn't think that Henry would want to be setting off on his own, though.

If he was keen to make his fortune all on his lonesome, I thought that he would be spending more evenings with Oscar and the other German boys, rather than supping with us, and letting Ma darn his socks when his boots wore holes in them. *If he wanted to set out on his own, I thought – he would be mending his own socks!*

That second night crossing the desert passed much like the first, only even more miserable. I think that it must have been close to midnight, when Pa told me to climb into the wagon and try and sleep. He said that I was wavering in my footsteps and he didn't want me to go wandering into the desert and get lost. So I lay down on my bed in the wagon, and dozed fitfully. I'm not certain how long it was.

Our company was moving very slowly. It seemed as if all of us, even the oxen were stumbling along, half asleep.

"It's the sand, now," I heard Mr. Herlihy saying to one of his brothers, "Wicked cruel it is, for the poor beasts!"

The next time that I swam up to the surface of being awake, it was because there was a mind clamor going on; oxen bellowing, the rattle of harness chains being dropped from yokes and wagon tongues, the tense and terse conversations of men. The wagon wasn't moving.

I could hear Ma, solicitously speaking to someone else. "Settle yourself here now. It will be in the shade, once the sun comes up ... Sally – are you awake?"

I heard Boomer wuffling, as he settled down underneath the wagon, and I answered,

"I am, Ma – what's happening?"

"The critters are smelling water," Ma replied. "Your father and the other men are unharnessing them all before they get frantic from thirst. We're settling here to wait for them. Mr. Bayless advised that we camp for a bit in the wagons right here and wait for them all to return when all critters have drunk every bit they can hold."

I scrambled down from our wagon just as Ma lit our kerosene lantern. She looked pale, and tense with worry, just as Mrs. Glennie did. Mrs. Glennie sat on her husband's fancy camp chair with Porteus, that little spotted spaniel of hers in her arms. It was Porteus that Boomer was wuffling at.

Ma had spread out a blanket on the sand, and Jon already lay on it, fast asleep. The desert at night was bone-chilling cold. My brother was already covered with that fine woolly buffalo robe that Ma had traded for at Fort Laramie. Boomer curled up at his feet, although he watched Mrs. Glennie's Porteus with a wary eye.

"When will Pa and the other men be back with the oxen?" I asked. There was nothing at all to be seen beyond our wagons, all the way around us in every direction, just rolling waves of sand, silvered by starlight, and the sky overhead.

"I don't know, Sugar-plum," Ma replied. "Your Pa and Mr. Bayless had no notion of how far we are from water … only that we were close enough for the oxen to sense it. The men were afraid that if the critters might panic and start to stampede, if they couldn't get to the water fast enough."

"My team was getting so fractious," Mrs. Glennie agreed. "I could barely keep them in control. I was so relieved when my husband told me that we should halt here and let them run ahead. I was afraid they might run away with me, and wreck the buggy, and in my condition ..."

She couldn't finish. Honestly, she was so swollen, it looked as if she were holding a watermelon up underneath her dress, corset and petticoat.

Ma patted her hand, "It was the sensible thing to do, Abby. Now, all we need to do is wait. Honestly, I am so happy to be nearly through this dreadful desert. I don't mind waiting. Only," Ma added fretfully, "It's too dim to see to my mending!" That was Ma – never a moment of rest when she didn't have needlework or knitting in her hands.

It was well after sunrise, which sent shadows stretching a long way over the sands, when Pa and the other men returned for us, driving our herd of oxen and mules ahead of them. Almost to California, I knew then. Just this one last obstacle in our way – the wall of mountains which stood before us.

Chapter 15 – Into the Mountains

The Truckee River was, I think, the most beautiful river that I ever laid eyes on, after the crossing of the desert. The water in it was sweet, clean and ice-cold. I drank that water from my cupped hands until my teeth ached from the icy cold of it and my stomach gurgled, so thirsty I was that morning. I can only imagine how the oxen, horses and mules felt, after the purgatory of that crossing. Cold sweet water, splashing over moss-grown rocks, the leaves of cottonwood trees and others that I did not know the names of, shimmering and fluttering in that cool breeze which flowed down from the mountains. We were close to those mountains now, hemmed with hills which rose in gentle waves. When we first got to the river, the hills around were bare and rocky, but as we climbed up into the higher hills, following the river, those hillsides became clothed in all shades of green, and amber. As we climbed higher into the hills, certain of those trees and shrubs had begun to be touched by autumn. I know now that Pa and the other men looked with dread on the leaves turning russet, golden and amber, but I thought only of how near we were to the end of the trail, how close to California and the sweet new land and a fresh start on a new farm which Pa and Ma envisioned when we set out from Ohio.

After the long, dry haul from the Sink, we stayed several days in the meadows along that river; needing some time to recover from the griding torment of those days. One of the days was a Sunday, and Deacon Zollicoffer preached a sermon of especial thankfulness, drawing allusions to the experiences of the Jews wandering in the desert for forty years, before reaching the promised land. Pa and the other men were more concerned, though, with the half-dozen oxen and one of Mr. Glennie's mules which had gone wandering on the morning that they unhitched the draft critters and drove them loose in a body to the water.

"They all went frantic, once they smelled it so strong," Pa explained to Ma. "And went running off in a body even before we got halfway there ... thank the Lord that we had unhitched them all!"

"We were fortunate in that," Ma replied. "It could have been so much worse, if in a panic they wrecked a wagon!"

Mr. Glennie, Henry and Oscar ranged up and down the length of the riverbank on both banks and in either direction, but they never did find those missing oxen, or that one mule. Mr. Glennie made do for Mrs. Glennie's buggy. He had another pair of good mules, intending to sell at a profit in California, but they weren't as well-trained, and one of them got stolen by Indians after Fort Laramie so he swapped the remaining mule to Deacon Zollicoffer for one of his since the Deacon had Choctaw Joe to drive them. Choctaw Joe had a stronger hand on the reins than Mrs. Glennie did.

We set off, following the river farther and farther up into the hills, with the blue line of the mountains ever clearer every day. I think that we had been a week or more at it, when we came to a place where the hills gave way to a gentle, shallow valley. Rolling meadows of late-summer grass reminded me of those first days on the trail. The oxen were happy enough to spend a day of it, grazing at leisure on another Sunday. Jon's leg was so much healed, after the accident with the wagon, back in the desert. It didn't pain him much at all, and he could walk without limping – and romp with his friends, the little Herlihy boys. Ma and I had no more than the usual things to worry over; cooking meals, the way that the dust and dirt got into everything, the chore of making a camp every noon and afternoon, that the Indians might raid our critters again; the usual bothers of life along the trail.

Ma had Henry, Shivaun and I with the Herlihy brothers dipping buckets of water from the river, that Sunday afternoon after Deacon Zollicoffer held church services. She and Mrs. Herlihy wanted do laundry. Mr. Herlihy had built up a good fire for us, with all our kettles and pots heating water for the washtubs. Shivaun had just hoisted up a brim-full bucket, when she cast a glance down the worn and rutted trail east of our camp.

"Oh, look, Sally – strangers! Are they advance scouts for another wagon company! Won't that be a fine thing?"

"It might be!" I exclaimed. Although the two men were still at a good distance, I thought that I recognized one of them; Ginny's father, Mr. Reed, for his elegant gray mare, his fine broadcloth overcoat and flat-brimmed beaver. But all – horse, man and clothing were battered, dusty and sadly worn from the hardships of travel. He even had bandages on his neck and arms; bandages crusted with rusty stains. *Had Mr. Reed suffered an accident?* Still, I was inexpressibly happy at recognizing him. My friend Ginny and her little sister Patty and the rest of their company couldn't possibly be far behind.

I couldn't abandon Ma and Mrs. Herlihy and the pile of laundry to indulge my own curiosity, but I looked over my shoulder often enough, as we carried water, stirred and scrubbed. Mr. Reed – and it was him, no doubt in my mind – spoke first to Hansel, one of the German boys, who was cutting firewood by the wagon circle. I didn't recognize the other man. He was younger, but his shabby clothing was as badly worn as Mr. Reed's. I saw Hansel point to our wagon, and Pa, who was conferring at our campfire with Mr. Herlihy, Mr. Glennie and Choctaw Joe. Henry Steitler was there too, as he most usually was when we had leisure for a day. Then Mr. Reed slid down from his horse, which Hansel led away. The younger man went with Hansel. I thought at first Hansel and the younger man were going to turn the horses unsaddled into the corral made from the wagon circle, all with the long wagon tongues chained to the wheel of the next wagon. Instead, Hansel rubbed the horses' legs, and the places on their backs where the saddle and blanket had been … and then they put the saddle back on the horses!

That was curious, I thought. Did it mean that Mr. Reed and his companion would ride back down the trail to rejoin his own party, even in his sad condition? In some disappointment, I concluded that this must mean they were a far piece behind. Still, I was so very happy, thinking their company would soon catch up to us and that I would see Ginny soon.

Mr. Reed and the younger man spoke to Pa; mostly Mr. Reed. He spoke rather long, and that was when I sensed that something was not right. Pa's expression was somber and worried. I could see the other faces as well. Mr. Herlihy scowled, Mr. Glennie looked shocked ... and Choctaw Joe was shaking his head, almost as if he had been confirmed in his own sad judgement.

I could not walk away from helping Ma and the other women to hear what Mr. Reed was telling Pa and the others. I thought that I might be able to speak with Mr. Reed, but he and his companion were gone again within the hour – their horses rubbed down and saddled again. It looked like they had been given a croker sack of provisions.

I heard Pa tell them both, "Goodspeed and good luck to you, James, Walter! We'll look for your family, and if we can aid them in any way, be assured that we will!" Then Mr. Reed and the other man were gone. To my astonishment, they went riding up the trail towards the mountains!

Shivaun commented, "Holy Mary, they ride as if the very hellhounds are after them! I wonder what has happened now?" I wondered too, but I had to wait until that night to even ask.

But all Pa would say over supper was, "Mr. Reed and his hired man have ridden ahead to implore aid from Mr. Sutter, as his family and his friends are in dire need of supplies. It turned out that Mr. Hasting's route was very much more difficult than had been advertised. Their party has fallen far behind – very far behind."

"Ginny – are she and Patty all right?" I was shocked enough to speak out of turn, interrupting Pa and Choctaw Joe and Ma.

"Don't interrupt the grownups, Sally," Ma chided men. She sounded so serious and stern that I knew better than to ask any more.

"The girls are fine," Pa replied with a sigh. "They are with Mrs. Reed, and the other hired folk, and their good friends. There isn't anything to worry over, Sugar-plum."

Pa still looked somber. Ma frowned in my direction when I opened my mouth to ask another question, but Henry Steitler also shook his head at me. I closed my mouth. Perhaps Henry would tell Jon and I later what it meant, that Mr. Reed went hurrying up the trail, without even stopping for the night.

Not for the first time, I envied Henry for being only a year or so older. And he was an orphan – which I didn't envy – but he was the owner of a wagon. Even it was only a cart cobbled out of the wreck of his father's wagon, when it came to trail business Henry counted as a grown-up, and not a child.

He knew what was going on, for all of that, and I didn't, just because I was a girl and younger, and that simply was not fair!

Instead, I kept pinching myself when we went to bed, so that I could stay awake and listen to Pa tell Ma what Mr. Reed had related to him.

"It was bad, Sue," Pa said, his voice low and serious. "They hardly had an organized company remaining when Reed left them ..." and then Pa's voice went so quiet that I couldn't hear what he was saying at all, just bits and snatches that I couldn't make any sense out of. "Hastings will have a mortal lot to answer for to the Almighty!" Pa said then, and his voice went soft again.

Well, Mr. Clyman and Mr. Greenwood had not said much good about Mr. Hastings' shortcut. But what Pa said next riveted my attention. "... threw him out for committing a murder!"

"Oh, my God!" Ma exclaimed in horror. And her voice went even lower. They spoke in whispers; I couldn't hear anything meaningful after that. No wonder they didn't want to tell me anything. I pulled the covers over my head and shivered in the dark until I fell asleep.

Before I did sleep, I resolved absolutely that I would find out what had happened with the Reed company; Poor Mrs. Reed with her sick headaches, feisty, fearless Ginny, little Patty and their blind Granny Keyes. They must be all alone now, somewhere behind us on the desolate difficult trail to California. In the morning, I would talk to Henry Steitler –

the first minute that I could corner him and speak to him privately. He would know more, I was certain, since I saw him with the other men in the company, when Mr. Reed spoke with them all, while I was helping Ma with the laundry.

Henry would know everything – and I was determined that I would make him tell me.

It took me nearly half the morning to find Henry alone and not doing much save lollygagging on his pony, guarding and escorting what our party had left of the loose critters at the rear of the wagon company. Oscar was off, exploring the trail in advance of the main part of the wagons, and Mr. Glennie was driving the buggy, as Mrs. Glennie was too close to birthing her baby to risk any exertion. *(Or at least that is what Ma had told Mr. Glennie.)*

I had never much liked trailing behind the wagons, what with the dust and all, avoiding the damp splatters of what the critters had dropped of their used food all along the way – but it couldn't be helped, not if I wanted to ask Henry what really had happened to the Reeds and their friends when they followed the Hastings short-cut from Fort Bridger. Pa hadn't said much about that, but I thought it must have been dreadful if it broke the company apart and somehow involved a murder. We had a rough few days, crossing from the Sink to the Truckee River, but that was a torment which lasted only a few days.

I found a place to wait for Henry on his pony, and the half dozen oxen and that single mule to pass by. The mule didn't care for the oxen and I don't think that the oxen cared much either. Henry seemed gladder to see me than the mule did. He swung down from the saddle, smiling all over his pleasant, big-jawed face.

Oh, merciful heaven – his lower face was sprinkled with fair stubble. Henry was so close to being a grown man that he might need to begin shaving every morning if he didn't want to go bearded, and my heart sank. Not only would he not think kindly about Pa and Ma adopting him but he might also treat me as just another silly girl-child.

"Good morning, Sally-Sarah! You are most tardy today! You should be careful; you never might know when there are wild Pawnee about!"

He was teasing me – I just knew it!

"Oh, stuff and nonsense," I answered, much indignant. "We left the Pawnee territory just miles and miles ago. Mr. Bayless told us so! But I did want to talk to you – about what Mr. Reed told all yesterday afternoon."

"And why should I confide in you, Sally-Sarah?" I just knew that Henry was smiling; his eyes were, although his mouth was set in a serious line. "It is the business of men – not so much that ladies need bother themselves."

"Even more stuff and nonsense!" I flared up at him – for certain he was teasing me, and I couldn't endure that for an instant, not when I was so worried about Ginny and Patty. "My friend Ginny! You remember her, and how we all gathered firewood by the riverside, back before we set out from Independence? Something dreadful has happened to their company, and no one will tell me anything! They followed Mr. Hastings new trail and came to grief ... and you tell me that ladies need not bother, when we are put to all kinds of trouble and sorrow on account of the stupid decisions of men! There has been a murder among them, and I am just sick with worry, since no one will tell me anything!"

"Ah ... yesterday." Henry sobered, almost at once. "That was ... *unglaublich* ... unbelievable, Sally-Sarah. You are right to be concerned about your friend. Our friend. Her father – Herr Reed told us of what happened. There was no need to tell everyone, since there is nothing to be done."

"But Ginny is my friend!" I cried. "I want to <u>know</u> – even if there is nothing I can do to help! There is torture in not knowing, Henry! Do you and the other men <u>like</u> torturing us women and girls by keeping us from knowing the worst? Thinking that we are protected? That doesn't work! We can see that something bad has happened, and we are all in knots with worry because of it! I don't want to be protected; I want to <u>know</u>!"

Henry looked down at the trampled ground before us. He looked embarrassed. He took my arm, and courteously guided me around a particularly large and fragrant puddle of fresh ox dung.

"All right, Sally-Sarah. I will tell you. The Reed company; you know they took the straight-way cut-off, following the advice of Herr Hastings?"

"I guess they did," I replied, somewhat chastened. "But I thought that Mr. Reed was too smart not to take good advice when it was offered him."

"I supposed as well," Henry confessed, shyly. "For your papa is a very sensible man. Wise enough to accept the advice of others. But for Herr Reed and his family, they began the trail late, waiting on friends to accompany them on the journey."

"I remember," I agreed. "Because we all left as the grass was just barely grown high enough. Everyone told Pa that it was risky enough ... but he had us set out, and then when we broke apart from the Major's company..."

"That was sensible, also," Henry agreed. "For I think that too large a company will make difficulties of themselves. Herr Reed and his friends fell behind, farther and farther, and so it seemed to them that Herr Hastings way might permit them to make up for that lost time. They thought they had his assurance that he would personally see to guiding them over the correct way and I think they were desperate, seeing that winter would be coming on ..."

"Pa said last night that Mr. Hastings would have to answer to the Almighty," I said. "That much, I heard him say. Mr. Hastings did not wait for them, as promised."

"Ja," Henry nodded. "He had departed from the place where he had promised to wait ... to guide another party of travelers. And they had lost too many days already. They went ahead, trusting in his words. Most unwise, Sally-Sarah. But in desperation, men can be unwise. Especially if they fear for their children, their wives."

My heart sank. This did not bode well for my friend.

"So, what happened then?" I asked. "Who was murdered, and why was Mr. Reed blamed and exiled from his company ... where were all his friends?"

"They went ahead, following on Herr Hasting's trail," Henry answered. "Following after the company he had led. They had already lost too many days to turn around and go back. From what Herr Reed told us, it was not an easy trail. Broken, rough. Much labor to move the wagons ahead. Men quarreled. Oxen crippled and lost. Many more than we lost, coming from the marsh of the Sink. And then they crossed a bigger desert. A desert twice, maybe three times wider than the one that we traversed between the swamp and this river. Perfectly desolate – no water. *Nicht weiden* – no grazing. Many of their cattle ran off, looking for grass, or died in yoke. Some had to abandon their wagons. Their company is broken – there are only families or friends looking to their own. Leaderless, and desperate. Then a quarrel between Herr Reed and another man, a teamster-wagon driver for another family. There was a bad patch at the trail along the Humboldt, a steep sandy place, with only room for one wagon to pass at a time. The other man was intemperate, threatened Frau Reed with his whip. In the quarrel when Herr Reed attempted to defend his lady wife ..." Henry shrugged. "They came to blows. When it was done, the other man was dead. The employer who hired him to drive a wagon and the other man's particular comrades took exception. The dead fellow was a popular man. I think Herr Reed was resented. They wanted to hang him for murder – indeed, from what Herr Reed told us, they had already prepared a noose, to hang him from a pair of wagon-tongues propped up to make a gallows."

"That is so horrible!" I exclaimed. My heart was wrung for poor Ginny, all alone with her sick mother, and her younger sister and brothers. "No trial, no law..."

"There is no law on these trails," Henry agreed. "No magistrate or judge. It is well for us that most taking to the wagon trails are sober folk, inclined to obey the laws that we are accustomed to, in any case. Herr Reed had two or three brave friends, who stood for him. The others agreed that he should leave the party and travel on alone. But without food or weapons." Henry looked sideways at me, and added, "They promised him that his family should be protected."

"Well, that was ever so generous of them!" I exclaimed, in considerable indignation.

Henry continued, "Miss Ginny stole out of camp that evening and brought some food, a pistol and ammunition to him. Most bold – for a girl," Henry added in approval, and I was again certain that he was baiting me. I lifted my chin.

"You have no notion of how bold girls can be, when those whom we love are in danger!"

"I think I might," Henry assured me, with such an annoying grin that I knew for certain that I was being teased and he knew that I was annoyed by it, and I had enough of that. Now I knew everything of what had happened; all those things which Pa didn't want to tell me about.

"I doubt that, very much!" I replied. Tossing my head, I walked faster. Of course Henry couldn't follow after me to tease some more, since he had to mind the loose oxen and the single mule. I had found out what I wanted to know, anyway.

Aggravating boy!

Chapter 16 – To the High Pass

We were grateful for the constant presence of the river that we followed up into the mountains; fresh cool water, and good pastorage for the oxen, mules and horses, but oh, it became such a hard drag for them, always pulling uphill. I lost track of how many times we forded the river, crossing back and forth, wading through ice-cold water. Then the mountains began to close around us, high and blue, steep rock-ribbed slopes clothed in dark green pines, and now and again, groves of aspen trees, dark gold with silvery bark. Only Choctaw Joe was entirely pleased at seeing these.

"Mountains, girl – beautiful mountains! How I longed to set foot on a trail among the pines again!" he exclaimed one evening, when we set up camp. Pa took a bite from the supper which Ma and I had cooked, and replied,

"Glad of that for your sake, Hoss, but I wisht it wasn't so late in the season. When do them yellow trees turn and start to drop their leaves?"

"'Bout now," Choctaw Joe replied, with a wry look at the heights above our camp. "But I wouldn't worry all that much. It's what, now – the first week in October. If there's any snow gonna fall in the next few weeks, it'll be light, and melt before noon. Lessn'n we're really unfortunate," he added.

That put kind of a damper on supper, although I am certain that Choctaw Joe didn't mean it to be taken that way. Ma looked as if she were sick with worry, and Pa's face was grim. Still, even though clouds gathered threateningly, especially in the afternoons, we soldiered on for several more days, climbing higher and higher into the mountains. After another few days, we met up with three men; two young Indians in proper clothes and a white man, with a small train of pack mules coming down the trail. I didn't speak to them, but Pa did, as they were heading east and down the trail in a great hurry. The two Indians were hired muleteers from the California entrepreneur Mr. Sutter, with packs of supplies meant for the Reed party!

"Charlie Stanton," Pa told us over supper, the evening that the little mule train had passed us. The third man was an American. "Nice fellow, Charlie – one of the Reed company. They sent him and another man ahead for more supplies, weeks ago. This Captain Sutter is a charitable man. They say there's nothing he won't do to help out folk in a pickle. So that's some of the good news. The other good news is they told Stanton at Sutters' that the high pass should be open for another month or six weeks."

"That's very good news to hear," Ma said, her face brightening with hope and relief. I hadn't realized how very worried she had been, all these last few weeks. For myself, I was just no end relieved to hear such good news, although I couldn't see how Mr. Reed couldn't have gotten help so rapidly.

"The bad news," Pa continued, "I had to tell him about Reed, and how much worse their condition had gotten. Charlie

Stanton came up from Sutter's by a different trail, so they didn't cross paths. Still – I expect that Sutter will help as much as he can. They're surely going to need all the help they can get."

After another week of hard pulling for our team animals, we came out into a shallow valley, with a lake cradled in the center of it. Mountains rose as steep iron-grey teeth all around. The air was sweet, smelling of pine, clean and cold. So cold at night that Jon and I were grateful for the buffalo robe that Ma had traded for at Fort Laramie. Sometimes I thought that was the only time that I was warm – that and at midday, when thin sunshine sifted between the pines.

"There is a side canyon over yonder," Choctaw Joe allowed, on the evening that we camped by the lake. "It's a higher pass, but the trail up to it is not precipitous. Ol' Greenwood's first party that came this way had to empty out the wagons and hoist them up a sheer cliff."

"I don't think we want to do that," Pa allowed, with a shudder.

Ma and I shuddered too. The mere thought of emptying out all of what remained of our supplies and the rest of the gear and traps in our wagons ... no, that didn't bear thinking about. As for rigging hoists to take a wagon to the top of a cliff? That was purely out of the question. It might take days. The men at Sutters' who said that the pass would be open for at least another month; I think Pa and the others had begun to doubt. The thickening ice in the water bucket of a morning hinted ominously that we purely didn't have many days. We were now at the end of the second week in October. That first morning that we camped in that valley, we woke up to see frost on the ground, and to find a skim of ice in the water buckets, a layer of ice thicker than a sheet of glass.

The various trails were trampled out by parties ahead of us this year, and for several seasons before were all clear in that little valley below the passes. They had cut firewood; either felling small trees entire or cutting handy limbs from larger ones. In an open meadow below the steepest pass which stood like a gray granite wall, there was even a rough cabin, with a roof made of rotting cowhide, half-tumbled in. Nearby, weather-bleached bones of cattle lay barely visible among stands of late-season grass.

We could read the tracks of wagon wheels in the dirt and leaf-mast clear enough, the marks left by tent-pegs and ground-cloths, fire-pits and filled-in privies where they had camped before launching their wagons at that final pass through the mountains. Even I could do that; it didn't take someone like Choctaw Joe, with a nose for the uncharted wilderness to read the signs that others had left before us. Other parties ahead on the trail, this season and others in the years before pointed the way – pointed the direction, in the place where all the various trails, the short-cuts and alternate tracks came together. At least we had gotten there in good time, with the ground still clear.

"You fellows and I will scout the pass in the morning," Pa said, that night at our fire. "And work out the best means of getting up there, without killing ourselves or an ox as soon as we can. None of us want to camp here over the winter." Pa nodded in the direction of the cabin with the rotted skin roof. I overheard that some men had built it, two years previously, and tried to winter over there.

Pa, Mr. Herlihy, Choctaw Joe and Mr. Glennie were with us, planning – as Mr. Herlihy said – our strategy to breach the fortress wall of that final pass. It involved lots of ropes and chains, and double- and triple-teaming the wagons. Pa and the other men stayed up very late, as our campfire spat golden sparks up into the sky. Ma sent Jon and I to our beds in the wagon, after Mr. Glennie came to our camp, twisting his hat in his hands, saying only that his wife had need of Ma.

"It could be that her time has come," Ma replied. "Go to bed, children. Likely I won't be back until very late, or even in the morning, if her labor goes hard. Make certain that Jon washes behind his ears, Sally."

Ma fetched her medical box from the wagon and pulled her warmest shawl about her shoulders. It was cold here in the mountains, especially at night. I could see a faint cloud of folks' breath as they spoke. She walked away from our fire, towards the Glennie wagons with Mr. Glennie. Pa was deep in consultation with them men.

"Do as your Ma said," he told us, absently, and went back to talking with Choctaw Joe and Mr. Herlihy. Truth to tell, I didn't mind being sent to bed – since we would be warm, at least, under the piled up quilts and the buffalo robe.

"What did Ma mean, about 'her time'?" Jon whispered to me, as we clambered up into the wagon, and drew the cover over the front, which kept a little bit of the cold out. We could hear an occasional cry from the direction of Glennie's campfire.

"I think it must mean that Mrs. Glennie is about to have a baby tonight," I answered.

It was dim inside the wagon, but I could see that my brother looked puzzled. "A baby? How is she going to have a baby, Sally?"

I sighed. "A baby comes from inside – like Cally has her kittens. They grow inside her, until they are ready to come out … and then they just come out."

"It's the same as kittens?" Jon asked. "How do they come out?"

I had worked out the correct answer to that through seeing critters birthing, but I didn't rightly like to tell my little brother straight out, so I repeated what I had been told when I was his age and asked about babies. "Through the belly-button … you know. In the middle of your stomach. A woman's stomach, but not a man. But don't you worry if you hear any hollering. Men can't have babies. Nor can tomcats, or bulls, or stallion horses." Jon still looked skeptical, and I added, "Well, that's what Aunt Rachel told me when I asked her after Cousin

Matty was born. Go to sleep, Jon ... you DID wash behind your ears, didn't you?"

I think that Jon had washed up before we climbed up into the wagon, shucked our outer clothes and crawled underneath the pile of quilts and the buffalo robe that made our bed. And if he hadn't – it was too cold to make him go back and wash up for real.

Sometime during the night, I floated up to wakefulness, hearing a quiet and nearly soundless rustle against the wagon-top over our heads. But I went to sleep again, almost at once, as it was still quite dark outside, and no other sound broke the silence, but the soughing of the wind in the branches of the pine trees around our camp.

Jon and I woke to a world covered in white, clean and stark, and bitter, bitter cold. I crawled out from underneath the blankets and the buffalo robe and pulled on my warmest things and my moccasins. I could see my breath in a near-freezing cloud. It was just barely light, and paler in the east. I wish that I could have stayed warm in the relatively comfortable nest of blankets and all – but I had to use the privy, I was hungry, and I could hear Ma's voice, and Pa's as well as Choctaw Joe and Henry Steitler's, amid the rattle of tinware, and the crackle of a good fire going. My brother only whimpered and pulled blankets and the buffalo robe over his head, burrowing deeper into our warm nest.

"Good morning, sleepy-head!" Pa said, as soon as I appeared. There was a good fire going, and bacon sizzling in the tall-legged fry pan over it. During the night, or perhaps in the early morning, Pa or someone had rigged a canvas awning, to shelter us from the weather. Ma huddled in her shawl and a heavy blanket around her shoulders, one of the tin mugs in her hands. She was warming her fingers around it. The snow wasn't all that deep; perhaps six inches or a little more where the wind had piled higher drifts against the trees, but there was a slippery layer of ice underneath of it.

"It's snowing!" I exclaimed, somewhat unnecessarily.

"We know, Sugar-plum," Pa replied, and Henry grinned at me. "Good thing we are at the bottom of the pass – by nightfall tonight, we should be at the top and a little beyond."

"First serious snowfall of the season, I reckon," Choctaw Joe also cradled one of the tin mugs in his hands, as if he also treasured the warmth of the coffee in it. He cast a calculating eye at the dreary grey sky over us, a sky of clouds which pressed close over the mountains hemming us in, just as the buffalo robe lay on our bed. "I also reckon that it will go on snowing for a piece ... but let up by tomorrow, or the day after. If we are lucky," he added.

"But it rained last night, before it b'gan to snow," Henry Steitler put in. "There's ice underneath the snow. I went halfway up the pass this morning, and I think we slid halfway down." He looked somewhat embarrassed at speaking up – but then, he was one of our outriders, and the owner of a wagon; even if it was just a cart. But Henry was almost a grownup, which is why he was bold enough to speak.

"That's why we're tackling the pass today," Pa said. "Rather than wait for the snow to let up. Jeptha Glennie is most insistent on that."

Ma snorted. "He might consider his poor wife's exhausted condition ..."

"Is the baby born, then?" I forgot myself, I was so interested in this matter. Ma shot me a quelling look.

"Don't interrupt your elders, Sally, when we are talking ... but yes. A sweet little baby girl. It all went well, then," Ma added. "If we were anywhere else but here today, I'd urge Abby to rest until quite recovered from the ordeal of birth but as it is, both she and Mr. Glennie are insistent on traveling immediately. At least she has the buggy and the mules."

"Aye," Choctaw Joe agreed. His face was serious. "Anything rather than risk being marooned here for the winter. Old Greenwood told me a long yarn about the three lads from that company that he led up this way, two seasons ago. They thought they could winter over here, guarding the wagons and goods that they had to leave behind. They could hunt for their supper and last through the winter, but the critters all went down to the lower mountains, the lake done froze over, and the snow got to twenty feet deep... I know, seems like something too bad to believe ... but I know mountains, mountains jus' like these. Winter comes early, stays late and freezes the ba ..." Choctaw Joe suddenly appeared to recollect Ma's presence, and mine. "... freezes hard. I b'lieve that we are just in the nick of time here, Cap'n Kettering."

"Why we aren't wasting any time today," Pa nodded. "We'll be up and over the top of the pass by sundown tonight or know the reason why. Herlihy says the pass is wicked steep. We should double or triple-team the critters, he says. Put half the teams up on the top where they can pull on level ground and drop chains down to the other half. Sort of like we did, crossing the Green – only fighting the angle of the slope rather than the current. He's going up first thing, with a load of chains, to set up our rig." Pa squinted at the eastern sky, now somewhat lighter with the sun coming up behind the clouds. "I reckon we'll start with young Henry's cart, first. Then Deacon's wagon. Miz Glennie's buggy – they're the lightest. Then ours."

There was urgency in our breaking camp that morning. Everyone felt it. Winter was about to catch us on the wrong side of the final divide, and we had make tracks as soon and fast as we could. Pa and the others had dreaded this during the last months of travel as the year waned. Before Pa had struck our tent and Ma packed away the rest of our cooking things, and hers and Pa's bedding, Mr. Herlihy and his brothers were already climbing the pass with the strongest of all our ox teams, laying out a pair of chains as they went. The top of the pass was veiled by soft drifts of cloud, and persistent snow, snow that came drifting down like fat feathers. When it was quiet for a moment, I could hear the snowflakes rustling as they settled on everything.

Ma commanded, briskly, "Don't stand around staring, Sally! Run put these blankets in the wagon. I need to go help Abby Glennie and the baby get ready!"

As Pa said would happen, Henry Steitler's light cart went up the pass first, with his yoke hitched to it, along with our own trusty Brandy and Star. We watched from below, as the cart wobbled upwards, slewing from side to side as the poor oxen struggled to keep their footing in the snow and the layer of ice underneath. The chains pulled taut, as the other teams on top pulled. As I saw later that day, when Ma and Jon and I reached the top, Mr. Herlihy had run them over a felled tree trunk, braced between a pair of standing trees just past the top of the pass. If it had not been for those oxen pulling with all their might and their hooves on level ground, I doubt that Henry's cart and those critters hitched to it would have been able to make any headway. The angle of the trail was just too steep. It would have been even harder for the bigger wagons, like ours and Mr. Glennie's.

Deacon Zollicoffer's mule wagon went next, with Deacon Zollicoffer and Choctaw Joe in it. I felt so sorry for their poor mules, slipping and sliding everywhere, as that wagon inched upwards, drawn up by the chains and the laboring teams at the top of the pass. I was standing next to Pa, and he was talking to Mr. Martindale, as they watched.

"A mortal lot of work," Mr. Martindale observed, and Pa agreed.

"Still less work than building a hoist and lifting our wagons up a sheer cliff-face."

"Leastwise," Mr. Martindale agreed, "This way, you don't have worry about what happens if someone loses their grip and the damned wagon falls."

That was the first two of our party's three light conveyances. The Glennie's buggy was next. I followed Ma, who went at Mr. Glennie's elbow, as he carried his wife from where they had camped to the buggy. Ma had the bundled baby in her arms. She handed the baby to Mrs. Glennie after she was settled in the buggy.

Mrs. Glennie looked very pale, tired and gray-faced, with huge dark shadows under her eyes. Ma didn't look all that rested herself, but she sounded bright and cheerful enough

"We'll be along, in three shakes of a lamb's tail," Ma promised. "My husband says we'll bring our wagon up next, to show that it's perfectly safe. Don't you dare exert yourself, in your condition, Abby."

"I won't, I promise," Mrs. Glennie replied, with a wan smile, just as Hansel, one of the German boys, came slipping and sliding down the pathway already scoured through the snow by wagon-tracks and ox hooves. I believe the snow was already turning to slush as the day warmed, the ice underneath melting into the mud. Hansel dragged the ends of the chains down from above, from where they went over the tree-trunk. Hansel, Mr. Glennie and Mr. Martindale made the ends of two chains fast to the tongue of the buggy.

"Here we go," Mr. Glennie said to his wife, and waved to Mr. Herlihy at the top of the pass. The buggy lurched off, as Ma and I watched with Hansel.

This passage up the mountainside did not go as readily as the first two. The lightweight buggy, unburdened by nothing much besides Glennies and their baby, slewed from side to side as the mules fought to keep their footing, and the chains pulled them inexorably forward, until they were about a quarter of the way. I began to fear that the buggy might tip over entirely before it got very much farther up the pass. It seemed that Mrs. Glennie feared the same, for she began to scream.

"No – let me down! Get us out! I won't go another foot!"

Ma went running after the buggy, stumbling as she waded through the snow and mud. Mrs. Glennie, with the bundled baby in her arms, fighting off the arm of her husband, had already scrambled down from the buggy. She crouched in the snow, and I saw that her eyes were white all around, like the eyes of a panicking horse.

"It'll be the death of you!" Ma pleaded for Mrs. Glennie to get back into the buggy and be carried in it to the top of the pass, but Mrs. Glennie was adamant against Ma and Mr. Glennie both.

"I don't care!" Mrs. Glennie answered. "I don't care – I won't ride, not to the top of this pass! I won't, I won't!"

She was insistent that she wouldn't get back into the buggy, and stood against all pleading from Ma, and her husband to see reason. I really didn't blame her for that, for the slope was so very steep and narrow, hemmed on either side with trees, and the buggy and mules were lurching all over the trail.

"We'll walk up together then," Ma finally relented. "We'll go so very slow and careful. Sally, you carry the baby, will you? We'll stop and rest every few steps."

Mrs. Herlihy and Shivaun appeared at Ma's side, with Jon and the Herlihy boys all trailing after, like ducklings following their mother. Mrs. Herlihy took one side, and Ma the other, and between them they led Mrs. Glennie up the mountain, step after cautious step. About every twenty steps, she was so faint as to nearly collapse in their arms. She would sit in the snow, gasping for breath and as pale as if she were close to death. I could tell that Ma wanted to argue her into good sense, sense to ride in the buggy, even if the buggy were bucketing all over the trail, but Mrs. Glennie wouldn't hear a single word. The buggy got hauled all the way to the top of that pass, followed by our wagon, the first of Herlihy's, then one of the Glennie wagons in a painfully slow manner, all during the time that we plodded up to the top.

I carried the bundle of the sleeping baby; all to be seen of her was a tiny pink face, with shawls and blankets bundled tightly around her. She was prettier, but much heavier than my china-headed doll, Priscilla. I carried her in both arms, not wanting to risk dropping such a precious little thing, although my wet moccasins offered no purchase in the slush, and I slipped and slid to my knees fairly often in that climb. These moccasins were the ones which Ma had traded for at Fort Laramie, and I wore because I had grown out of my shoes sometime around that we passed over the continental divide.

At mid-morning, clouds lifted, and the sun finally emerged from behind them, blinding white snow and blue in the shadows behind the trees. It didn't honestly make things better for us; just muddy as the snow softened and melted. My moccasins and woolen stockings soaked through from the meltwater and mud; so was the skirt of my dress and petticoat was. My feet felt like lumps of ice. Ma and Mrs. Herlihy kept up a constant murmur of encouragement to Mrs. Glennie. She was deathly pale – even her lips went gray and bloodless. I knew Ma was worried sick, even as Mrs. Glennie tottered the last few steps to the top of that high pass.

A little beyond was a level place, which the oxen had tramped into bare mud, through passing over and over the place again, in hauling the wagons up to the brink of that pass. But further beyond that, out of the way of the fouled trail which had been trodden into the snow, someone had set up our tent and made up a pallet bed within. A huge bonfire burned before the open front of the tent, and it was warm, blessedly warm and mostly dry. I think Mr. Glennie and the other men had seen to it, in between the hard labor of drawing the wagons up that steep pass, and the urgency of getting there, against snow which might fall again after sundown. Mrs. Glennie fell onto the bed which had been laid within the tent and piled with blankets and our two buffalo robes. I think she was either in a dead faint or fallen into an exhausted asleep from the exertion of climbing the trail.

Ma covered her with some blankets and turned to me. "How is the baby? There hasn't been a peep out of the child since ..."

"I think the poor ween must be hungry," Mrs. Herlihy observed, for the baby began to stir, pursing that tiny rosebud of a mouth. "Ought we to wake Abby to nurse..."

Ma shook her head. "She's exhausted nearly to death – I dare not. I know! Go find Jemima Shaw! Her little one isn't weaned. She'll be able to wetnurse this poor little mite."

"Does she not have a name, yet?" Mrs. Herlihy was all righteous concern. "Aye, she ought to be baptized as soon as possible, for the good of her innocent soul!"

"I'll mention it to Abby, as soon as she rests," Ma replied, all distracted she was as the sight of my soaked feet. "Sally! Oh, my land – take off those wet things at once!!" Ma took the baby from me, handing her to Mrs. Herlihy, as Shivaun went in search of Mrs. Shaw.

Ma tut-tutted over my feet, which were numb and ice-cold to touch, but fortunately not frost-bitten. She made me strip off my soaked stockings and soggy moccasins, wrapped my feet in a blanket and left me in the tent with the sleeping Mrs. Glennie and Mrs. Herlihy, while she went to our wagon to search out a pair of clean, dry stockings from her own trunk. I was glad of that chance to rest, where it was warm from the fire, after the exhausting climb up to the top of the pass. But then the baby began to cry; a thin, discontented fussing, and nothing which Mrs. Herlihy could do to soothe her had any effect.

"She's hungry, the poor little mite!" Mrs. Herlihy exclaimed. Mrs. Glennie slept, or was deep in a faint, I couldn't tell. Ma hadn't returned, nor had Shivaun with Mrs. Shaw. I was afraid that the baby crying would wake Mrs. Glennie, who was ill and badly needed to rest, but that thin wailing also set my nerves on edge.

I could tell that the baby wailing so also frustrated Mrs. Herlihy. Rocking her and singing something in the old Irish language didn't work the expected magic. That is until Deacon Zollicoffer appeared at the tent opening, with his rusty old top hat in his hands, saying,

"Beg pardon, ladies – I just wanted to see if there is anything you require ... oh, dear, is the little angel unhappy?"

"She is, indade!" Mrs. Herlihy replied. "And nothing will sooth her until her mother is waking to herself again, or until she nurses..."

"Here, let me try," Deacon Zollicoffer offered, almost shyly. "My dear wife always said that I had a good hand in soothing babies – so do my sons' wives. It's a gift, they said..."

"And a blessed one, too!" Mrs. Herlihy handed over the little wailing bundle, and to all our surprise, she stopped crying as soon as the Deacon held her.

Mrs. Herlihy crossed herself. "Truly, you are blessed with a gift, your reverence! A fine gift!"

"To comfort the afflicted, and soothe the grieving," Deacon Zollicoffer replied. He looked so pleased and happy, with the little baby in his arms, a baby who seemed instantly to forget that she was hungry, and bewildered, and possibly a bit cold, that her mother was so very unwell and tired, and here we were all marooned on a snow-covered mountain in the wilderness ... it was a blessed gift, as Mrs. Herlihy said.

Presently, Shivaun returned, quite out of breath and puffing, with Mrs. Shaw, whose own baby boy was not above eight months old, having been born just before the Shaws and the Piersons and all departed from Independence. She took the baby from Deacon Zollicoffer, who fled hastily as soon as Mrs. Shaw unbuttoned the front of her dress. He nearly collided with Ma, as he hurried away. Ma had her arms full; another blanket, two pair of knitted woolen stockings, one of our kettles and her medical box.

"Sage tea!" she announced to me, as I put on the stockings gratefully. My feet were still cold.

"Shivaun explained everything," Mrs. Shaw said. "There, my sweetie, as much as you like!" She crooned to the baby, as she held the tiny infant to her bared breast. "Oh, dear

– I have forgotten how tiny babies can be at the start! Little Jimmy has grown so, in the last half a year!"

"They do so, indade!" Mrs. Herlihy agreed, looking fondly at what little could be seen of the baby's tiny pink face, cushioned against Mrs. Shaw's breast and sucking greedily at it. "Here my three little imps were once as small as this wee darling, and now they are great galumping lads, nearly as large as Himself."

"that's the thing with children," Ma gave me a fond look. "An infant one minute, and then the next, it seems like they are grown enough to have one foot almost out of the door. Now, I'm going to brew up some sage tea for everyone ... the greatest sovereign remedy there is, inside and out, for practically every ill that there is."

"But it does bring on curious dreams," Mrs. Herlihy pointed out. She and Ma discussed this, while Mrs. Glennie slept, and her baby nursed at Mrs. Shaw's breast. Meanwhile the water boiled, and our shoes and moccasins steamed gently in the warmth of that lovely fire, as they dried out.

I was glad for the tea, and the rest, after that miserable toil, climbing the pass. This was the final obstacle for us ... well, perhaps not the last of the hardest part. We still had a ways to go ... but it seemed like the worst was over. For us, anyway.

Chapter 17 – Golden California

Miraculously, Mrs. Glennie awakened on the following morning, insisting that she was perfectly fit and fine. She walked to the buggy with the baby in her arms, perfectly steady and firm. Her husband helped her up into the seat and passed the baby to her. Once in the buggy, the baby lay in a basket at her feet, asleep and content, her little rosebud of a mouth pursed closed, as Mrs. Glennie took up the reins for the mule team.

"The wonder of the age!" Ma confessed to Pa, over nooning later that day. The sky remained clear, although it was bitter cold, and no more snow fell – well, it fell indeed, in the high mountains, but not on us, to Pa's relief. And the relief of practically everyone else. I recollected what Pa had said, after talking to Mr. Stanton, with his train of supply mules – that the folk at Sutter's Fort told him that the high mountain pass would be open for another month, at least.

I didn't believe that Ginny and her family were more than about a week behind us. They would be safely over the pass, and traveling down the mountain before winter fell for certain. So, I didn't worry about them so much, after that.

I was considerable disappointed, over the next few days, as we journeyed on. There were places where the trail sloped so steeply downhill that the men were forced to unhitch the oxen, lest they be overrun by the wagon, and lower the wagon down the hillside to level ground by means of ropes tied to the back axle. Here I had been thinking that once we conquered the high pass and beaten the snows of winter by a short head – that we had finished our long journey. We were tired and worn, our everyday clothes faded and worn to shreds, our oxen were slab-sided and skinny, hardly able to pull the wagon with any energy at all. Boomer too was tired – his footpads worn nearly raw.

We still had flour, bacon, sugar and coffee among our supplies, but the German boys had almost nothing left of theirs, save half a box of hard-tack. Henry Steitler would have been in the same condition save for that he shared our campfire and meals. The German boys would have gone hungry save for Choctaw Joe helping them hunt for deer. The deer at least, were plentiful once we reached the lower ranges. Once, Hansel managed to shoot a bear, a very fat one, and we all shared in the meat. Mr. Glennie had plenty remaining of his supplies, and might have had more, but he was generous about sharing.

On the first Sunday after we crossed the highest range, we took our rest. Deacon Zollicoffer held a worship service and conducted a baptism of the Glennie's baby daughter. Everyone attended, even the Papist Herlihy family.

It was a day which has long remained in my own memory, for we were camped in an open meadow, I think it was about halfway down the mountains, almost into the foothills. There were pines about, tall and dark, but the grass of the meadow was amazingly green – such a green that I had not seen since the early days on the trail. But behind us, the mountains sketched a harsh white outline against the sky. The day was mild, a bit cool, with a fresh breeze.

"'tis a curious place, this California!" Shivaun McCarty observed. "As green in the autumn of the year as other places are in spring!"

"It does feel like a spring day," Ma whispered, as she stood next to us. "California is everything that I had hoped that it would be," she added, and then we were quiet, for Mr. McNabb played the first few bars of the hymn *Guide Me, Oh Thou Great Jehovah.* We sang with gratitude, especially the bit about being guided through a barren land, and the flowing crystal springs. I reckon that we all knew about crystal springs, barren lands, and following pillars of fire and cloud. Deacon Zollicoffer looked as happy as I had ever seen him, as he gave thanks for the Almighty's guidance – guidance through the wilderness, as he put it.

Then he took the Glennie's baby daughter from her mother – all dressed in a long white infant's gown, she was – and dribbled a bit of water on her head, from a silver dish shaped like a shell. Deacon Zollicoffer looked so happy, pleased and proud. The baby whimpered a bit, and then Mrs. Glennie took her back, and she promptly went to sleep.

Her name was to be Amelia Deborah Susannah Glennie – the Susannah part was for Ma because Mrs. Glennie was so grateful for the help that Ma provided at the birthing, and the Deborah for the woman in the Judges chapter of the Bible. If it were me being christened that first Sunday on the far side of the mountain wall, I'd have fussed ever so much more about being lumbered with four names! *Imagine having to embroider all those initials on every single handkerchief and pillowcase!* Then we all sang another hymn... and that was it. Sundays for us were only partially a day of rest, in that we didn't need to travel.

"We're nearly there, aren't we, Ma?" I asked, and Ma smiled at me.

"We are, Sugar-plum!"

"Is it everything that you and Pa hoped for?" I asked, wistful-like. Ma smiled at me; she looked so happy, so young, as pretty as Shivaun McCarty at that moment.

"It is," She answered, and I thought about it some more as we set about cooking supper. Ma asked me to make us a dried-apple cobbler, with the last of the apples that we had in our supplies, so I about cutting up the last leathery scraps, and soaking them in a bit of water, while Ma slivered up onions and carrots for a stew made with beef jerky that we had dried from an ox that had to be dispatched and carved up after being crippled by Paiutes along the Humboldt.

We could have had fresh venison, I suppose. The Piersons and the Taylors did, but Ma was very much against wasting food. Just because we had gotten to that land of plenty, Ma said it would be unfitting to waste the jerky, which was starting to soften a bit and would have to be eaten soon before it spoiled entirely.

Tomorrow, we might have venison. But tonight, we would eat the last of what he had brought with us with such care.

We were so happy to be almost-nearly-all-but-there in California. The golden promised land, which Grandpa Reverend claimed would be flowing with milk and honey. It wasn't any of that I could see, for which I was kind of grateful. *If it was anywhere close to literal, a river of milk and honey would be awfully sticky, and what about when the milk went bad and turned disgusting?*

It also meant that soon our company would break apart. Everyone that we had traveled with for so many months – would all go their own separate ways. Perhaps we would see them, now and again – but never as comrades of the long trail.

Would that include Henry Steitler? I confess to feeling a mite sad about that. Jon loved Henry, looked up to him, almost as an older brother already. That thought made my heart hurt, just a little bit. I recollected what Pa had said about Henry wanting to find his own fortune and strike out on his own. He was of that proper age, after all. I recollected how Pa had told me that Henry might feel obliged against his own inclination, if Pa asked him about being part of our family. Henry might say yes, counter to his true desires, on account of the respect which everyone had for Pa. Then I thought – maybe I could bring the matter up to Henry. If it only were me, suggesting that Henry be Jon's big brother – well, Henry could say yes or no to me, according to his real feelings. The more I thought about it, as Ma and I hovered over the cookfire, the better I liked the thought.

Now, the only concern was picking the right time and place to speak to Henry. I had best do it soon. Almost at once, I had that better time. Ma gave me the best reason in the world to go look for Henry.

"Sugar-plum, you want to go find your brother and Henry? Tell them supper will be ready soon and they should wash up and straighten themselves like well-mannered young gentlemen. I think I saw them down by the river, after church," Ma added. "If I know how boys divert themselves, they will be soaked to the skin and covered with mud. And by chance, if you should happen to see Deacon Zollicoffer, tell him from me that he would be welcome to supper with us tonight."

"I will, Ma!" I was happy and nervous all at once, now that I had that perfect chance.

The little river that we were following was a small and icy stream, tumbling over rocks in a froth of white, and then in calm ripples where it was deeper. It was shallow in the main, but I could tell from the way that it curved around old dead tree trunks and water-tumbled boulders that it would run high and fast in the spring, when fed from rain or snow-melt. Where the last of the days' sun fell on the water, it seemed to shimmer, as if there were tiny gold and silver sequins stirred into the sand and gravel.

I followed the sound of excited boy-voices: Jon and the Herlihy boys squelching around in the shallow water, trying to build a dam, with rocks and a couple of water-sodden logs. Henry perched on a ledge, a little removed from where the boys splashed back forth in the shallows at the river edge. I saw that he was whittling, but also keeping watchful eye on the little boys. So was Boomer, settled at his feet.

I hiked up my skirt so that I wouldn't catch my toe in the hems and fall ungracefully as I scrambled up to where he sat.

He looked sideways at me and smiled. "Sally-Sarah, are you here to tell me that supper is nearly ready?"

"I am," I replied. "But that is not the only thing. You know that we are only a few days away from the Johnson place ... Mr. Bayless says that is a settlement which marks the end of the trail, although most folk say that Sutter's Fort is truly the end ... but everyone will be going their own way, in another few days." I stopped to gather my own thoughts, and to put what I wanted to say into the right words.

"This I know," Henry confessed. "And I am sad ... will be so sad, to say farewell to so many good friends ... friends who stood by me when..." he suddenly sounded as if he were choked by grief, remembering. That gave me an opening, a way to say the words.

"You don't have to say goodbye to us," I said. "You see that ... well, Jon and I really like you. So do Pa and Ma. If you like and if you choose... you could stay with us. The Ketterings."

"Truly, Sally-Sarah?" He looked at me sideways again, with a wondering expression – as if he could hardly believe it to be true. "Did Herr-Capitan Kettering say so to you?"

"Pa did," I assured him. "I asked him, some weeks ago. And he told me ...that he would very much like to ask you to be a son to him, but that he was afraid that you would feel obligated, against your own heart's desire. That he thought you really would want to go out in the world and seek your fortune and agree, only because you felt grateful ..."

I stopped then, because Henry was folding up his pocketknife, and putting it in his pocket. He was looking out on the river, over my brother and the Herlihy boys frolicking in the shallow water, and I could see that he was moved beyond having easy words to reply.

Finally, he said, "There was only me. Vati and Mutti and me. After we came to America. And then there was only Vati and I. I would have liked brothers and sisters. But there was only us two. Vati had twelve brothers and sisters when he was a boy. He told me stories of how it was ... so many! His brothers and his cousins, his sisters and aunts. They had such fun. Family. Christmas. Skating on the river when it was frozen. A family! I suppose that I will want to go and seek my fortune someday, when I am older ... but not just now. A family. I would prefer that for now. Very much. If you would tell Herr-Captain Kettering ... I would be most honored."

"I will!" I promised, but I was singing in my heart. We wouldn't have to say farewell to Henry, now. He would remain with us, be a loving responsible brother to Jon and a sturdy help to Pa. I stood up, so light in heart that I felt like I could fly. "Jon!" I called to my brother. "Ma says to leave off playing and wash up for supper!" Jon came happily splashing towards us, and Boomer instantly rose to his paws. "Honestly, I can't see why you and your friends want to play in such cold water," I added. Jon grinned at me.

"It's not that cold, Sally!" he replied. We were walking back towards the wagons, while Henry remained on the riverbank, watching over the Herlihy boys. I think he felt kind of responsible to see that Liam didn't fall in the water and near drown himself again.

Honestly, boys!

"Be that as it may, it's nearly suppertime," I told him, firmly. "Did you happen to see where the Deacon went? Ma said if we saw him, we were to ask him to supper."

Jon squinched up his face in thought. "I think he went down that way, to the edge of that meadow. He said that he could almost see California from there."

"We'll go and find him," I said, and whispered into his ear. "I told Henry about how we wanted him to be a Kettering, now that we're in California – and he said that he would like it. Like it very much. I'm going to tell Pa now, since he thought Henry would prefer going out and making his fortune, rather than stay with us."

"Truly?" Jon beamed and gave me an impulsive hug. "Wait until I tell Donal – that I have a brother now! Do you want to tell Deacon, too?"

"We may as well," I replied. I was so happy with this day, so happy that I thought I could fly like a bird, like an angel. We were safe over the mountains, and it wasn't bitter cold during the daytime, Jon's leg was all better and Henry was agreeable to being part of our family. I thought that I might share such joyful tidings with the Deacon and see if perhaps he knew some special prayers to say over Henry on joining our family.

We could see Deacon, sitting at the edge of the meadow, with his back against a tall tree – a kind of natural seat, with a view of the meadows and the blue-shadowed folds of hills beyond. The late afternoon sun painted long shadows over those hills and the meadow. I held my breath, for there were three deer, moving half-seen in the shadows, not far from where Deacon Zollicoffer sat with his head back, and his opened Bible across lap. A little breeze fluttered the pages back and forth. He seemed to sit very still, as the deer wandered closer. There was a quality of unreality about that stillness, and the Deacon's serene expression, and I then felt a prickle of unease. Something was wrong.

"Jon," I said, very calmly. "Run ahead and find Pa and Mr. Bayless."

It was as I thought, with Deacon Zollicoffer so still and pale, his eyes unseeing. The deer vanished into the woods as Jon went running towards our camp, and Deacon never moved.

"It's so sad," I said later, much later on that day. "He never got around to preaching to the Indians, as he wanted to do when he set out. He wanted that more than anything else in the world. God had tasked him to do that, just like the prophets in the Old Testament."

"There was a saying," Ma remarked, in thoughtful consolation, "About folk who unknowingly entertain angels and saints – Mayve Herlihy tells many such tales. Perhaps we did ... or we simply traveled with a very good man. I will write to his family in St. Louis, when we reach Sutter's, and tell them that he was among good friends and at peace when he passed away. He was such a welcome presence in our party! I suppose that in the spring, there will be travelers returning to the States who will carry a letter to his sons in St. Louis. I will also mention that you took very good care of their father, Mr. Bayless."

"Crazy old coot," Choctaw Joe looked meditatively into the fire. "Wasn't near the trouble that I thought he would be, as a traveling companion. I might take that letter of yours, Miz Kettering – and tell them myself."

"He will be missed," Pa said, then. He lit his pipe with the end of a twig thrust into the coals of our campfire. "It strikes me that perhaps, our Lord Savior really intended the

Deacon for another mission – to minister to us, as we wandered in the wilderness. He only <u>thought</u> he was to preach the Word to the heathen Indians, but perhaps he was really meant to shepherd and tend to us, in our long journey."

Postscript – 5 Months Later

We had been living near Sutter's fort for some time, while Pa did work as a carpenter and he and Henry searched around for land to purchase. They came home for supper one afternoon and told us that another settler was telling everyone at Sutters' that Ginny Reed and her mother and the rest of their family were safely brought down from the mountain camp where they had been snowed in and stranded since early winter. It turned out that the Reeds and their friends, along with the others of their wagon company had left crossing the mountains too late. They all were caught by winter storms and snow as deep as ever had been seen when they tried the high pass above the lake. I was afire to see Ginny; we had all been afraid that we would never hear of any of them again. I was so glad to know she was alive and her family had survived, although it was rumored to have been a terrible close thing.

Pa gave permission to Henry the very next day to take me to the house where Pa said Ginny and her family were staying. I was so glad to know that she was alive – that everyone in their family were alive, or as close to living as it was. I didn't know what to expect, since it had been near onto a year since we had last seen each other. I had a sudden fear, as I knocked on the door, that she had never gotten any of my letters and had completely forgotten our friendship.

I needn't have worried; Ginny opened the door and upon crying out my name, she fell into my arms. We hugged, right there in the doorway. I think she was crying a bit, and we couldn't talk coherently at first. She took my hand and led me into the parlor.

"I was so worried!" I exclaimed. "Did you get my letters? I wrote to you three times! Where is Patty ... is she still in the mountains? We saw your father and Mr. Herron when they passed us on the trail! What about your Granny Keyes – is she all right?"

Ginny stood back from me, still sniffing and wiping tears from her face. Then she hugged again. "She is here, now too – she and Dolly! I only got two of your letters. The one that Mr. Clyman carried for you, and the one that you left by the Sink, out in the desert. Oh, I was so happy to see that one, since I thought that everyone had forgotten about our sad plight!

Sad, indeed; her family had encountered the most dreadful, ghastly hardships, passing through the desert, and then marooned in the high mountain pass! The hardship went on for months and months, while all that long while we in our company passed safely into California. Ginny was so thin when I hugged her that she felt as if she were made of nothing but twigs, and her calico dress hung on her limbs as if she were a scarecrow. Her eyes were huge in her face, and the dark curls which I had so envied previously were scraped back from that face, like straw – stick straight and lifeless.

"Granny died early on," she replied. "Even before we were a month or so out on the trail. She was easy in her passing. We made a nice grave for her. She shouldn't even have ventured with us," Ginny added. "But that she wanted to go with Mama and us and wouldn't even hear my uncles arguing against it. She wanted to be with us, and didn't care two pins that she was near to dying. It may have been a mercy, anyway ... that she passed away so early in the journey." Ginny shuddered, and her expression was one of such desolation that I guessed at what a horror had taken place in the mountains. "It was so awful, Sally. Just horrible. We had nothing to eat for weeks and weeks and weeks, but pieces cut from ox-hides and boiled and boiled and boiled. Nasty, but that's all that we had. Ma saved out a few bits of food for us for Christmas day, and it made us all so very happy – Patty and Jimmy and Tom. But when they came for Ma and I and Jimmy to take us down the mountains and away from there ... Patty and Tom had to stay behind. They were too weak to walk, and too heavy for the men to carry. They had to wait for Papa to come for them." Ginny managed to force a smile. "Patty kept Dolly close by her, all through those awful months, until Papa brought her and Jimmy safely out of the mountains."

'It's whispered about," I ventured, "Among the folk at Sutters ... that eventually, there was nothing but dead bodies to eat."

Ginny shook her head, vigorously and swallowed as if she were trying not to be sick. "Some did – it was awful to see. We didn't, though. Although we cooked and ate little Cash – the dog. His paws and everything. I don't like to think about it, Sally! But we were so dreadfully hungry!"

I swallowed, too – slightly sickened. I thought about Boomer and ventured very carefully. "No, I wouldn't like to think about it either ... but if it is a dog that loves you and wants to save your life. It's not so awful, then, if you think about it that way."

Ginny shook her head. "I'd rather <u>not</u> think about it anymore. Tell me what happened with you and your father's company! You wrote to me in your first letter that there was to be a wedding! Miss Pierson and the Scotsman with the blue-painted wagon? Did they really get married?"

"They did! They weren't the only ones! Shivaun McCarty and Mr. Taylor of our company got married right here at Sutter's, two days after we got here. There was nothing but talk of how very few American girls there were in California, and all young men lining up to propose to those few girls that there are ... so Mr. Taylor spoke up for her before she got proposals from anyone else, and she said yes, because she knows him well from the trail, and he has a good trade. But her brother-in-law only gave permission after Mr. Taylor promised that he would be a Catholic, because she is, being Irish and all."

I paused, as Ginny had a momentarily distant expression on her face, as if she had just thought of something else. But she giggled, and replied, "Oh, I had a proposal of marriage, too! Can you believe it? From one of the young men who brought us down from the mountain! Me in rags, and near to starving! Who would have thought of marriage at a time like that?"

I giggled, too. "I've had three proposals – from complete strangers, just in the time that we have been here! Pa and Ma wouldn't permit me to accept any of them, even if I wanted. Just wait! You'll have more proposals of marriage than you will count! Let's see ... of things that happened to us. My brother Jon fell from our wagon, and we thought that he may have broken his leg where the wagon wheel passed over it, but he didn't ... and then Liam Herlihy fell in the river, and everyone but Ma thought that he was drowned and dead. Deacon Zollicoffer – he was a missionary who wanted to preach to the wild Indians – he did die, just as we got to California, but then he was terribly old. Henry's father, Mr. Steitler, was killed when his wagon rolled over on him. You remember Henry, now? Well, he's staying with us, and is going to our brother..."

"Silly Sally," Ginny giggled again. "I would think that he would be the one that you should marry – even if he is your brother?"

And we laughed some more about that, and I thought how fine it was that all our families now were safe in California, at the end of the trail which led west toward the sunset.

Historical Notes – West Toward the Sunset

This is a work of fiction; the Kettering family and their companions on the emigrant trail to California in 1946-47 are all creations from my imagination, although based on real people and historical accounts written by and about them, who made that epic journey. The character of Choctaw Joe Bayless is very loosely based on the mountain man James Beckwourth – who was of mixed race, raised and educated by his white father. As a young man, he went west as a wrangler and fur trapper. He related his memoirs of a wide-ranging and adventurous life in the far west to a perhaps rather credulous biographer in the 1850s. However, the other frontiersmen who appear in this story, James Clyman and "Old Man" Caleb Greenwood were real people, and were journeying from California to the East as I have described. The party which "Old Man" Greenwood mentions as having led up the Truckee River two years previously, was the Stephens-Townsend-Murphy party, which was the subject of my 2007 novel, *To Truckee's Trail*. Lansford Hastings, the author of the *Emigrant's Guide* was also a real person, as was his guide to the California/Oregon trail.

The Reed family are, of course, also real people. The sufferings of the scattered company bearing their name and that of their friends, the Donners became a cautionary tale down to this present day. James Reed was exiled from the scattered company, as described here, and later led efforts to rescue his family and friends. Charles Stanton – who had been sent ahead to bring supplies back to a company who had nearly run out of them – returned, just in time to die along with almost half the party stranded in the high mountains.

The shortcut which Hastings proposed in his guidebook was one which led more or less straight west from a point on the regular trail two hundred miles east of Fort Hall, which skirted around the south of the Great Salt Lake and rejoined the conventional trail to California near present-day Elko, Nevada. The established trail described an arc to the north, before coming down into Nevada, following the Humboldt and Truckee Rivers before crossing the Sierra Nevada. Theoretically, the shortcut appeared promising, as a more direct route. But it was a trail which Hastings had never actually traveled until the spring after his guidebook was published – and that from west to east without wagons. He did meet up with a large party of wagon emigrants that season as he had promised, and successfully guided them over his new route, but it meant brutally hard labor of making a trail through the mountains in order to bring those emigrant wagons across Utah's Wasatch mountains, followed by a nearly hundred-mile-long waterless trek through the desert. The trail which they blazed through the Wasatch was later enlarged and traveled by Mormon settlers, establishing their settlements in the Salt Lake Valley.

While the Hastings-led party arrived in California safely, the Donner-Reed company, which had not been able to catch up to Hastings' group, had fallen behind and fallen apart. They gambled on Hastings' shortcut to make up time they had lost. The unexpected difficulty of the new trail and the trek through a waterless desert worked against them. By the time they reached the high pass in the Sierra Nevada, they were out of food, draft animals and time. Patty Reed's cherished little wooden Dolly is one of the most touching relics preserved of that awful time. One can only think of how much comfort that doll provided for a small child throughout that horrific experience, stranded in the mountains with death all around.

The details of the wagon-train emigrants are all based on historical accounts. The various incidents on the trail are all based on contemporary accounts; the encounter with the immense herd of buffalo, fording the various rivers, trading at Fort Laramie with the Sioux, the ascent of the Roller Pass in the High Sierras, among others.

Contrary to what is usually depicted in Western movies and TV shows, the most common draft animals were indeed oxen – with mules as perhaps a secondary. Mules were expensive, and liable to be stolen by those Indians who viewed stock theft as an enjoyable open-air sport and test of skills and cunning. Also, as historian George R. Stewart pointed out, in a dire food emergency, the oxen could be butchered and eaten. So could mules, but not without overcoming some cultural prejudices. Most emigrant wagons did not serve as a kind of RV, with all the comforts of a home on wheels; the Reed "family wagon" being an exception to this. Emigrant wagons were most usually packed tightly and all the way up to the canvas covers with food supplies and gear necessary for a journey which would take most of a year, with few or no resupply points along the way. Most families traveled with tents and lengths of canvas to set up nightly camps. It's also commonly depicted that wagons circled with the nightly camps and cooking fires set up on the inside of the circle, which is inaccurate. Most usually, the wagon tongues were chained to the wheels of the wagon ahead in the circle to create a stock corral for the valued animals such as mules and horses, while families and individuals set up their camp for the night along the outside of the wagon circle.

I should also note that as the costs of outfitting a wagon, team animals and supplies for a year of travel were considerable, those emigrants setting out on the trail west before the 1849 Gold Rush were almost always fairly prosperous, solid and hardworking citizens to begin with. The group of young German immigrants, who pooled their resources to afford stock, wagon and supplies is based on a real group of wagon train emigrants of that year.

It is a matter of fact that an astonishing number of fatalities on the trail were drownings – it was not common then for Americans to know how to swim.

I have tried to duplicate the society of middle America at this time; reflecting the opinions and prejudices felt by ordinary people, rather than dressing up my characters in conventional and modern attitudes. There was a lively mistrust of Catholics left over from the long wars following the Protestant Reformation and carried over to the new world. As an aside, I note that Sally Kettering is a twelve-year-old girl who hears the names of Mayve Herlihy and Shivaun McCarty and spells them accordingly – it would actually correctly be Maeve and Siobhan, but Sally would likely never have seen Irish names spelled out in print.

Generally, Protestant Americans entertained mild to moderate suspicions and doubts of Catholic newcomers to the United States like the Herlihy family. There was also suspicion of Mormons as religious non-conformists. Suspicions which frequently boiled over into violence. This eventually led to the majority of Mormon believers establishing a separate colony on the shores of the great Salt Lake, in present-day Utah.